Ellen Olney Kirk

**Dorothy Deane : a children's story**

Ellen Olney Kirk

**Dorothy Deane : a children's story**

ISBN/EAN: 9783337214975

Printed in Europe, USA, Canada, Australia, Japan

Cover: Foto ©Andreas Hilbeck / pixelio.de

More available books at **www.hansebooks.com**

# Dorothy Deane

## A Children's Story

BY

## ELLEN OLNEY KIRK

WITH ILLUSTRATIONS

BOSTON AND NEW YORK
HOUGHTON, MIFFLIN AND COMPANY
The Riverside Press, Cambridge
1898

JULIA, MARION, and HERBERT LIONEL INGHAM

of "Mangroville," Paget, Bermuda

this little chronicle of the doings of old-time

New England children is lovingly

inscribed by their

Aunt ELLEN

# CONTENTS

# LIST OF ILLUSTRATIONS

# DOROTHY DEANE

## CHAPTER I

Mrs. Bickerdyke always knitted twenty face-
cloths for Christmas presents. On this 23d of
December she was hard at work on the sixteenth
of the number, and her little great-granddaugh-
ter, Dorothy Deane, was sitting beside her doing
up the fifteen already completed, into packages.
Each knitted face-cloth was folded round a cake
of Ivory soap; both were inclosed in a square
of white tissue paper and then neatly tied with
narrow blue ribbon.

When Mrs. Bickerdyke bestowed one of these
souvenirs upon one of her poorer friends, it was
her habit to say, with her commanding glance, —
" Now, there can be no excuse."

And it must be confessed that even when rich
and well-to-do people received these tokens, —
people to whom cakes of soap and wash-cloths
could offer no unusual opportunity, — even they

had the feeling that Mrs. Bickerdyke was ex-
horting them to wash and be clean. For everybody knew that both Mrs. Bickerdyke and her
daughter Hester lived only to do good to who-
soever came within their reach.

Mrs. Bickerdyke was a handsome old lady, in
spite of her rather eagle-like nose and glance.
She was always well dressed, wearing in the
morning a black stuff gown, with a fine lawn
handkerchief folded over her shoulders; and
black silk in the evening, with a fichu of bob-
binet lace. Her head was set off at all times by
a widow's cap of the sheerest white material. In
front of the spotless frills of the cap, and resting
on the old lady's tranquil forehead, were four
puffs of white hair. When Dorothy first came
to Swallowfield to live, she used to sit looking
at Mrs. Bickerdyke, wondering whether those
four puffs of hair belonged to the cap or to
her grandmamma's head. Nowadays Dorothy
knew, but I shall let her keep the secret. I
will only say that after the little girl found it
out she wondered almost more than she did
before.

At this present moment Dorothy was trying
to keep all her thoughts upon the knitted face-
cloths and cakes of soap. She knew that although Mrs. Bickerdyke was knitting vigorously,

there was a vigilant eye upon her own doings, and that at the least deviation from the prescribed rule she would hear, —

" Not that way, Dorothy. Undo it all and begin again."

This feeling of being overlooked made the little fingers stiff and awkward. The pieces of soap slipped, the paper tore, the ribbons tangled themselves up into knots. Oh, how tired she was ! It seemed to Dorothy as if all her life long, indeed from the very beginning of the world, she had been tying up face-cloths. Time was always long, oh, so long, in Mrs. Bickerdyke's sitting-room. Nowhere else in the world did clocks tick so slowly or so loudly as here. But now all at once something unexpected happened.

" Why, grandmamma," Dorothy burst forth in surprise, " that 's the end of the ribbon."

" You must have used it too freely," said Mrs. Bickerdyke sternly.

" No, really and truly, grandmamma, I have measured off every one and cut it by the piece of tape you gave me."

" Go upstairs and ask your aunt Hester if she has any more ribbon."

As Dorothy left the room she drew a long breath of relief.

"Oh," she said to herself, "I do hope that aunt Hester has n't got the least bit more."

She saw as she went into the hall that the street door stood open, and that her aunt stood talking to a person outside, as if giving directions to some one about to take a journey. "Tell your mother the best connection is by the 10.15 train," she was saying. "I hope you will have a pleasant Christmas. Good-by."

She was about to close the door when a voice cried out, —

"Oh, Miss Hester, there is Dorothy! May n't I come in and speak a few words to Dorothy?"

It was Marcia Dundas, and Dorothy loved Marcia Dundas almost more than anybody except her own mother.

"Dorothy is helping her grandmother to-day," replied Miss Hester.

"Oh, aunt Hester," cried Dorothy eagerly, "grandmamma sent me to ask you if you had any more ribbon. I have used up every bit."

"Come in, Marcia," Miss Bickerdyke now said, yielding rather ungraciously. "You and Dorothy may sit down on that divan and talk for fifteen minutes by the clock."

The two children looked at each other, each with a little smile of satisfaction as they took their places side by side in absolute silence.

Miss Hester, who was a tall, slender woman, with a fine, quiet, earnest face, went slowly up the stairs.

"We're going to spend Christmas at aunt Mary's," Marcia said. "We're going to-morrow, for four days."

"Oh dear," cried Dorothy, and the corners of her mouth went down.

"I shan't like it," said Marcia, as if her mind were quite made up. "I shall keep thinking about you and Lucy and Gay."

The two exchanged a smile. Dorothy was eight years old and Marcia eleven. Dorothy was perhaps no smaller than others of her age, but she had a way of looking younger and smaller; while Marcia was overgrown, with long legs and arms, so that her frocks seemed always too short for her. Dorothy had a nice little round face, with large, meditative brown eyes, and a pair of sweet, smiling lips that everybody liked to kiss. Her hair, bright gold in color, was cut short and curled in large, loose rings all over her head. Marcia's hair was very long and dark and thick and rough and shaggy, like a pony's mane. She wore it braided in two great untidy plaits, which, always in the way, were always being flopped first on one shoulder and then on the other. The braids, however, being

a part of Marcia, each flop was full of character
and significance. Dorothy thought Marcia's face
quite the most beautiful face in the world. Her
skin was like ivory. Usually she was pale; but
when she became excited, her cheeks grew as
red as roses. Her eyes were black, laughing,
rather saucy. Her well-cut mouth could easily
express a great many meanings. She could look
proud, she could look disdainful; but the moment her lips parted, and her small, even teeth
showed, — why, then, the sun came out!

"I shall want to hear about everything you
do for Christmas," Marcia went on. "Do you
expect any presents, Dorothy?"

"Oh, I should hope so; don't you?" Dorothy
exclaimed.

"Oh, it's our Christmas present going to
aunt Mary's," said Marcia. "She has sent the
money for our journey. That's why I hate it
so."

"Oh, you'll have something else," said Dorothy, encouragingly.

"Nothing I want," returned Marcia. "Oh,
how I wish one had only to walk into shops at
Christmas time and pick out just what one
liked without having anything to pay! Oh,
would n't I just enjoy picking out things!"

"Go into shops and take whatever you

wanted!" said Dorothy, drawing a deeper breath. " Why, they would n't let you."

" At Christmas, you know. I think that would be the nicest possible sort of Christmas!"

" I should think it would," murmured Dorothy. " What should you pick out?"

" Chocolates," said Marcia, with instant decision. " Lots of chocolates and oranges and bananas and everything good to eat, you know. Then all sorts of things to wear: frocks and hats and muffs and tippets, besides books! oh, the greatest quantity of nice books about pirates and soldiers and kings and queens."

" Would n't it be splendid?" said Dorothy, kindling at the magnificence of the idea. " It would be almost better than having Santa Claus come down the chimney."

" A great deal better. I never did care about Santa Claus. I never believed in him, hardly even when I was a baby."

" Oh, Marcia!"

" Are you such a goose as to believe in Santa Claus?"

" I want to," said Dorothy earnestly. " I 'll believe in him all my life long, if he only brings me what I have asked him to bring me."

" What have you asked him for?" Marcia inquired with a little shrug of her shoulders.

" I don't dare tell."

" Oh, tell me," Marcia insisted. " I 'm going away, so there 's no harm in telling me."

" I want two dolls," Dorothy piped in her soft, clear little voice ; " one big and one little. Then I want a large, nice paint-box and a writ-ing-desk."

" Well, you do know what you want, don't you ? " returned Marcia, laughing. " I know what would happen to me if I asked for two dolls, one big and one little, a paint-box, and writing-desk."

" What ? " demanded Dorothy.

" Why, I should n't get them," Marcia re-plied. " But then you 're lucky, and I 'm un-lucky " —

" Oh, I 'm not lucky, am I ? " said Dorothy, with little, happy dimples coming in her cheeks. She did not know the world very well yet, and so could not be sure. It was pleasant, nevertheless, to be called lucky by Marcia, who knew all sorts of things better than Dorothy.

" Everybody is lucky except me," Marcia pur-sued. " I should n't mind so much if it was n't for mamma, but nothing goes right with us. Papa has been ill again, so no money has come from him. Mamma had surely expected some, but I don't know that I did. I 've got used to having things go wrong. Rosalie went away yesterday."

" Oh, did she go, too?" inquired Dorothy. " I hoped she would like to stay."

" Oh, no; everybody goes, — nobody stays with us. I made mamma's coffee this morning and poached her an egg. I don't mind."

Dorothy listened with a critical air, her head a little on one side like a wise bird's.

" Mamma tells me," she now observed, " that when I cannot have what I like I must try to like what I have."

" Well, do you?" inquired Marcia with high disdain.

" I try to make believe sometimes," said Dorothy with a half sigh.

" I don't," returned Marcia with a decisive little nod ; " if I 've got nothing to eat but dry bread, I just say it 's dry bread. I don't tell people it 's plum pudding."

" Oh, I don't mean telling what is n't true," expostulated Dorothy.

" I know what you mean. But I don't like dry bread, and I will not tell anybody I like dry bread and think it 's good and wholesome. That 's what you would do. I want my bread fresh, spread thick with butter, then a layer of jam on that and cream on top! "

The fifteen minutes were up. Miss Hester's
foot was on the lowest stair. She held in her
hand a roll of blue ribbon. Almost before
Dorothy knew what was happening, Marcia had
departed and she herself was again sitting beside
her grandmother, tying up cakes of soap in
knitted face-cloths. All the happy hopes that
had been bubbling up within her while she was
talking with Marcia seemed to have vanished.
It was dreadful to think that for five whole days
she could not see Marcia. She no longer believed that Santa Claus would bring her the
two dolls, the paint-box, and writing-desk, that
she had begged for. All at once the dreadful
thought occurred to her that perhaps she would
have to accept one of these face-cloths and
cakes of soap from her grandmamma. Oh, how
could she bear it ? When she had sat hour after
hour tying them up with blue ribbon, to be
obliged to have one for her own ! Oh, how
angry she was going to be if it happened so, —
how raging, — how furious ! All the blood in
her body seemed to rush to her cheeks.

"It must be too warm here," exclaimed Mrs.
Bickerdyke. "Your whole face is crimson,
Dorothy. Look at the thermometer."

It was a rule of the house that the rooms
must never be warmer than seventy-four degrees

Fahrenheit. When Jerusha, the maid-of-all-work, had first come, it had been explained to her that she must never let the thermometer go above seventy-four degrees. Miss Hester next morning missed the thermometer, and on making inquiries learned that Jerusha, seeing that it was in danger of going too high, had hung it on the porch.

Jerusha by this time understood all the ways of the house. Dorothy understood some of them, and was pleased to make the discovery that the mercury pointed to seventy-seven degrees. Doors had to be opened on the instant; a distant window raised. Dorothy ran round like a little cyclone, delighted at the excuse for movement.

Her aunt looked down from the upper landing and called, —

" Dorothy, if grandmamma does not need you, come to my room a minute ! "

Mrs. Bickerdyke had just cast on the stitches for her seventeenth face-cloth, and decided to lie down and take a little nap. Dorothy went slowly up the stairs, her heart feeling as if it had jumped into her throat. Miss Hester always seemed to see into her heart and to know just what was passing in her mind, and Dorothy's conscience was not clear at this moment.

She was not quite sure but that it was her rage
at the thought of having to accept one of her
grandmamma's face-cloths that had sent the
thermometer up to seventy-seven degrees.

Miss Hester was sitting at her desk writing
down a list of things in her note-book, and Dorothy, entering, stood looking at her, not ventur-
ing to interrupt. Aunt Hester was not at all
old like grandmamma, but still she was not at all
young. Dorothy, as we have seen, had many
speculations in her mind, and one was whether
Miss Hester might not early in life have been
exposed to the freezing cold and never quite
thawed out afterwards. Her face was so pale,
so regular, so quiet. Her dark hair, just touched
with silver threads, was always so immaculately
smooth. Her eyebrows were very dark and very
straight; her eyes, too, were dark, yet had a
clear light in them. Between the brows were two
little up and down wrinkles; then there were
deep lines on each side of the thin, straight
lips.

Dorothy thought to herself, —

"Oh, I could n't love aunt Hester, I really
could n't. She makes me feel cold somehow."

At this moment Miss Hester, turning, looked
at Dorothy all over and through and through,
as if she read as on a printed page her every

thought, feeling, and wish. Just as Dorothy
expected to be consumed by her aunt's righteous
indignation, Miss Hester inquired, —

" Should you like to go to town with me to-
morrow, Dorothy, to buy a few Christmas presents ? "

" Oh, aunt Hester ! " Dorothy burst out. Then
she paused and drew a deep breath. " Do you
really mean it ? " she faltered.

" I inquired whether you would like to go to
town with me to-morrow to buy Christmas presents," Miss Hester repeated, with the look and
tone of one who has no time to waste on unmean-
ing questions.

" Yes, please, aunt Hester," gasped Dorothy.
She suddenly regarded her aunt from a quite
different point of view, wondering if she might
really thank her, kiss her, hug her, cling to her ;
but no, she did not venture.

At 9.55 next morning Miss Hester and Dorothy took the train for town. At 4.02 they
returned. It had been a bewildering experience
for Dorothy, but any one looking at the little
girl as she sat beside the rather severe looking
lady in a sealskin pelisse would have known
that the day had been a happy one.

" You can put the parcels on the rack, Dorothy," Miss Hester had said to her.

" Oh, please, aunty, may n't I go on holding them ? " Dorothy pleaded. " I do so love to hold them."

So she sat straining her little arms round three great packages. Her heart beat lovingly against them. Once, when she was sure her aunt was not looking, she kissed the brown papers which wrapped them up, one after the other. She knew so well what was inside : in the long slender parcel two dolls, one big and one little ; in the oblong thin one a box of paints ; in the square thick one a writing-desk.

Everybody in the long train of cars was loaded down with brown-paper parcels, but probably none of all those Christmas presents was to give the same amount of pleasure that Dorothy experienced in clasping her aunt's purchases to her heart.

When Mrs. Deane (Elizabeth Deane was Dorothy's own mother, to whom I must now give a passing introduction to the reader) arrived at the house at six o'clock that Christmas eve, she knew the moment she met her little girl's eyes that something very pleasant had happened. Dorothy could look intensely serious, but when anything made her smile it was hard for her to leave off smiling. Usually she was pale, so when a spot of color began to burn on each cheek, one might safely guess that she was excited. Dorothy's eyes, too, had a way, when she was fairly waked up, of getting on fire, as it were. When she ran to throw her arms round her mother, she was smiling, her eyes were aglow, and her cheeks were just the color of a pink shell.

"Don't ask me anything yet, mamma," she whispered. "I'll tell you when you put me to bed. But oh, it's perfectly beautiful!"

When I have told how Dorothy looked, I have also described her mother, except that Mrs. Deane was twenty years older than her little daughter, and that while Dorothy's hair was bright gold and in close little curls all over her head, Mrs. Deane's was bright brown, and so long that it could be coiled up in a knot. Twenty-eight is not such a very great age when one has reached it. Mrs. Deane was not so old that she could not have enjoyed pleasant times quite as much as Dorothy, if they had come in her way. Elizabeth had had a pretty hard tussle with life since her husband died, six months after their wedding day, and five months before Dorothy was born. He had been Mrs. Bickerdyke's grandson and Miss Hester's nephew. It took Mrs. Bickerdyke and Miss Hester almost six years to forgive Elizabeth for having married Frank Deane. Finally, however, they had come to see their duty clearly, and they had offered a home to Dorothy and an occasional place of refuge to Elizabeth.

"Of course you must pay for the child's board, and for your own when you are with us," Miss Hester had said in her quiet, earnest way. "We could not afford to take you in on other terms. But you will have the comfort of feeling that Dorothy is well looked after, that she will never be neglected, that she will have the training her father had before her."

Elizabeth Deane was grateful. It was what she had longed for. She had a position in a large school for girls; she taught elementary French, and music, and English; she corrected exercises and compositions; she prepared and looked over examination papers; she tutored; she coached; she drilled; she was, in fact, a low-priced teacher-of-all-work, never having had diplomas or degrees. Her bag was always full to overflowing with exercises, examinations, and essays. Her pocket bristled with blue, red, and black pencils. She almost never had a real honest holiday. She was always taking extra work; always trying to earn a little more money; always working towards a possible future when Dorothy would need a generous outlay for her education. Now she was to have just Christmas, for on the morning after Christmas she was to go back to school to look after the pupils who stayed on through the vacation.

If Elizabeth had not really understood Mrs. Bickerdyke and Miss Hester, she would not have been willing to give up Dorothy to their care. She knew that they were conscientious, that they were always looking beyond the pleasure of the moment, but that their hearts were kind, even if they did feel it to be wrong that any erring human being should have too smooth and easy a road. For example: when Dorothy had first come to Swallowfield her hair was long and floated over her shoulders. Elizabeth had loved to brush these "goldilocks," and she had done it so gently, Dorothy could have slept during the operation. Not so when this duty became Miss Hester's; if she pulled and twisted the tangled curls, she would say, —

"You must learn to bear pain. You will have a great deal of pain to bear before you die, and you must remember that pain is good for you."

This was sound, bracing doctrine. Elizabeth saw the truth of it, yet she acted on a different theory. Just because there is so much inevitable pain to bear in life, it seemed to her a pity to inflict unnecessary tortures. Accordingly, one morning Dorothy woke up to find that her pretty, fluffy, baby curls had all been clipped off in her sleep.

That was two years ago, — a long past event. Let us get on with our story.

When Mrs. Deane took Dorothy upstairs that Christmas eve, Dorothy whispered to her, —

" Oh, mamma, I am going to have such beautiful presents ! "

Mrs. Deane heaved a soft little sigh.

" I am afraid, dear, — that Santa Claus " —

" But, mamma, aunt Hester bought me four splendid Christmas presents to-day, — just exactly what I asked Santa Claus for."

" Why, my dear child, you must not think that " —

" Yes, mamma, she did ! Two dolls, one big and one little," insisted Dorothy. " A paint-box, — oh, the most lovely paint-box, with four saucers and four brushes, and then the sweetest little writing-desk ! "

" Dorothy, dearest, your aunt would never have bought you such presents, — never in the world," said Mrs. Deane earnestly. " Put the idea quite out of your mind. If she bought them, they were for somebody else, — not for you."

" Oh yes, she did buy them for me ! " Dorothy maintained, smiling and dimpling, her eyes alight, her cheeks rosy. "Aunt Hester said, when we came to the doll-counter, 'Now, Dorothy, if you were to have the choice of two dolls, one large and one small, which of them should you pick out?' Then it was just the same with the paint-box and writing-desk."

Mrs. Deane shook her head. It had not been her experience to gather grapes from thorns, nor figs from thistles. The principle upon which Miss Hester acted was not to try to make Dorothy happy, but to make her good. Still, who could tell? It is the unexpected that happens. Dorothy might as well have the present comfort of hoping and believing. Accordingly the little girl went to bed that Christmas eve hugging in anticipation the two dolls, the box of paints, and the writing-desk, which she was to receive on the morrow.

# CHAPTER II

## MERRY CHRISTMAS

WHEN one wakes up on a Christmas morning, it does not at first seem anything in particular. One generally wakes up three hundred and sixty-five times a year ; one thinks to one's self, "Oh, if I could only have one more nap!" One turns to find the right spot on the pillow, then comes from some corner of the brain a flash of illumination, Why, it's Christmas! The idea of wanting another nap on Christmas morning!

Dorothy actually could not keep her head down on her pillow. She sat up in her little white bed and looked across at her mother, who seemed to be fast asleep. Some faint light was struggling in through the shutters. It was certainly daylight, not lamplight or gaslight, and everybody knows that at Christmas - time when the sun is up it is time for everybody to get up.

At any rate it could do no harm to look and see what time it was. One little foot stole out

of the warm bed, then the other; the little body
and head followed. It was just light enough to
see by the clock which stood on the table by
Mrs. Deane's bedside that it was six minutes
past seven. Oh dear! Dorothy knew that on
Christmas, as on Sunday mornings, breakfast
did not come until a quarter past eight. How
could any one, whose eyes were so wide, wide
open, and whose heart was beating so that it
seemed to jump into one's mouth, be expected
to wait more than a whole hour? Dorothy
decided that where she was concerned such patience was quite out of the question. She crossed
the room without making as much noise as a
mouse. She turned the knob of the door, oh, so
gently! but it ungratefully opened with a sharp
click. No matter. She was on the top of the
landing, her hand on the balustrade.

"Dorothy," a voice came from Miss Hester's
room, "go back to bed this minute."

"Oh, aunt Hester," Dorothy murmured piti-
fully. "I was n't going to touch anything! I
just wanted one peep."

"Go back to bed, and do not get up till the
bell rings," said Miss Hester inflexibly. "I
will not have you exposing yourself to the
cold."

Dorothy, with a huge sigh, turned back. She

was trembling and shivering, and when her mother, who was now awake, held out her arms,
Dorothy nestled into them gladly enough, for it
was a very cold morning. When Mrs. Deane
found that all Dorothy's ideas were still running
on presents, — that is, on the two dolls, little and
big, the paint-box, and writing-desk, — she tried
to direct her to some higher Christmas thought
and suggestion by repeating, —

"When shepherds watched their flocks by night,"
and

"It was the winter wild, while the heaven-born child."

But then Dorothy's turn came, and she capped
these verses by repeating, —

"'T was the night before Christmas."

It was all of no use. The little girl was hankering after fresh sight and touch of those beloved
packages. Even after she was washed and
dressed, there still was an interval before the at-
tainment of her heart's desire. Miss Hester read
prayers; then breakfast must be eaten, — a more
elaborate breakfast than usual, with beautiful
buttered waffles. Buttered waffles, according to
Dorothy's way of thinking, were quite thrown
away on a Christmas morning. They ought,
instead, to be reserved to fill up the vacuum of
those empty days in the year when one was not

longing in every nerve and vein and muscle and
bone and throb and beat of one's body to get at
one's presents. But,

"Time and the hour runs through the roughest day."

When Miss Hester finally said, "Now, mother, I will call Jerusha and John Pearson, and
we will distribute our little Christmas offer-
ings," Dorothy was as much startled as if she
had not been expecting it ; there came a knot
in her throat, and tears started to her eyes.

Mrs. Bickerdyke led the way into the parlor ;
Miss Hester followed; and Mrs. Deane and
Dorothy, then Jerusha and John Pearson, filed
after. A long, slim black stocking hung against
the chimney-piece. On a table beside it were
packages of different shapes and sizes, and un-
derneath the others the three that Dorothy had
brought home in her arms the day before.

"Oh, good - morning, you dear, beautiful
things," the little girl said to herself as her eyes
fell on these. She smiled and nodded and felt
very happy, yet could not help crying just a
little.

Mrs. Bickerdyke sat down in the armchair,
and Miss Hester laid in her lap five little packages done up in white tissue paper and tied with
blue ribbon.

"You shall begin, mother," Miss Hester said.

"Elizabeth," called Mrs. Bickerdyke in her fine, stately way, "here is a little present I have made for you. It is a trifling thing, but it possesses at least the merit of being useful, — I may say indispensable."

As she said "indispensable" she looked at her daughter-in-law in a way which no one with any sins of omission of soap and wash-cloths on her conscience could have borne.

"I am sure I thank you very much, dear grandmother," said Elizabeth Deane. "It was very, very good of you."

"Here, Dorothy, here is one for you as well," Mrs. Bickerdyke proceeded. "I myself wrapped this up for you. Now let me see a bright, happy, clean face for a whole year to come."

"Thank you so much, dear grandmamma," Dorothy answered cheerfully, for the sight of the three precious packages and of her stocking full to overflowing made her feel she could easily endure what only two days before had seemed so unendurable.

"Come here, Jerusha," said Mrs. Bickerdyke, addressing the tall, angular, mottled-faced, middle-aged New England woman, who now advanced a few steps. "Take this little present," Mrs. Bickerdyke went on. "You will find it useful, and you will at the same time value it because I knitted the wash-cloth with my own hands."

Jerusha took the package with a slight nod, but vouchsafed no other thanks.

" Here, John," Mrs. Bickerdyke now called to the man who took care of the garden and did odd jobs about the house ; " here is a nice wash-cloth and a cake of soap for you. Henceforth, there can be no excuse."

" Thank ye kindly, ma'am," said John Pearson, instantly dropping the parcel into his pocket. " I should n't presume to use it, ma'am, but will keep it as a keepsake."

Miss Hester now advanced with her own presents ; she gave a small volume to Elizabeth and to Dorothy, to Jerusha and to John Pearson.

" It is a handy edition of Pilgrim's Progress," she explained to each in turn. " Please to accept it with my best wishes."

Elizabeth Deane then brought forth a fine handkerchief for grandmamma and for Miss Hester, a calico dress pattern for Jerusha, and some warm gloves for John.

" And here, Dorothy, is what Santa Claus brought for you," Elizabeth said to her little girl, taking down the stocking.

Even while Dorothy joyfully grasped the

stocking, she still stood regarding the three packages which lay together on the table, her eyes wide open with eager expectation.

" Were you counting on anything more, my dear? " inquired Miss Hester, with a searching glance.

"Oh, no indeed, dear aunt Hester," Mrs. Deane made haste to say. " Dorothy is delighted with what she has received, and is most grateful."

Miss Hester lifted the little table with its three packages and put it away in the corner.

" These things shall wait until after we have had dinner," she now remarked.

Dorothy, hearing this explanation, smiled into the stocking she was holding. It was better perhaps to wait. To have everything at once would have been almost too much. The stocking bulged into so many queer shapes, she could not begin to guess what it contained. She looked up at her mother, met her look and smiled, then sat down on the floor and began to explore.

There was sure to be a wonderful "find " in the stocking Elizabeth Deane packed for her little girl. At the very top were two oranges ; then came two round flat boxes of bonbons, a knitted Tam O'Shanter cap, a pair of silk mittens, a pair of worsted mittens, and three nice

little hemstitched and embroidered handkerchiefs. Cap, mittens, and handkerchiefs were
the work of Mrs. Deane's "leisure moments."
All these, together with a dozen lady-apples,
were crammed into the leg of the stocking,
while in the foot were the drollest little odds
and ends, — a tiny doll, nuts, barley-sugar birds
and animals, a cat in bronze, a little knife, and,
— oh, it would be no easy matter to catalogue
everything the long, slim stocking contained.

Mrs. Deane had just one thought in life when
she saw, heard, or enjoyed anything. "Oh, if
Dorothy could have this! If Dorothy might
hear, see, or feel this!" She had so hoped that
these trifles, gathered together by a loving hand,
would make Dorothy happy, it troubled her now
to see the longing, lingering look cast behind her
at the brown paper parcels on the table when she
was called to go upstairs to dress for church.

"I think, dear," Mrs. Deane said as she kissed
the little upturned face, "that you had a very
nice Christmas."

Dorothy laughed roguishly as she whispered,—
"It hasn't all come yet."

Mrs. Deane shook her head.

Dorothy went to church with Miss Hester;
Mrs. Deane staying at home to read the service
to Mrs. Bickerdyke. Lucy and Gaynor Lee sat

in a pew near Dorothy, and the three children
looked at each other whenever they had a chance
all through service. When Lucy held up her
hand with thumb and fingers outstretched three
times, of course Dorothy at once guessed that it
meant she had so many presents. How delightful it would have been to stop and exchange
confidences after church, but Miss Hester was
holding Dorothy's little hand inside her own as
they came down the aisle, and that meant that
there must be no loiterings or whisperings. Indeed, when she was walking with Miss Hester,
Dorothy's entire strength was sure to be ex-
pended in the effort to keep up with her aunt's
long, rapid strides. Miss Hester liked, when
she and Dorothy were together, to ask questions
which should stimulate the child's thinking
powers, thus reaching some solid, good result.
So now, while they raced home, Miss Hester
said, —

" Tell me, Dorothy, when was the first Christmas ? "

" The first Christmas ? " gasped Dorothy,
repeating the words just to gain time.

" When was the first Christmas ? That was
what I asked you."

Dorothy's head was spinning round. It was
so hard to have to think when it was not too

easy a matter to breathe. The first Christmas!
When could it have been?

" Of course you know, Dorothy, you know
perfectly well," said Miss Hester in her earnest,
severe way.

" With Noah in the ark," suggested Dorothy,
in a soft, fearful little voice.

" With Noah in the ark!" repeated Miss Hester in a voice that made Dorothy tremble.
" Tell me what Christmas means."

" It means," faltered Dorothy, — " it means
presents."

" Presents!" said Miss Hester sternly. " Is
that all?"

" Turkey for dinner," Dorothy murmured,
wholly confused and upset.

Now what Miss Hester had been afraid of was
that the real deep down and sacred meanings of
Christmas were lost on Dorothy; that she had
a covetous little heart thirsting after selfish
pleasures and selfish possessions, wholly taken
up with the idea of presents and feasting.

At this moment, however, there was no chance
for Miss Hester to correct those false impressions. They were in sight of their own house,
and Mr. and Mrs. Fuller were descending from
their carriage at the gate, and Mr. Samuel Bickerdyke was walking up from the station towards

them all.   Mrs. Fuller was Miss Hester's sister,
and she and her husband lived at North Swallowfield; Mr. Samuel Bickerdyke, the only
brother, was a childless widower, who practiced
law in the city.   They had come as usual to
eat Christmas dinner with their mother, and
now, after exchanging greetings and Merry
Christmases, they all went in together and found
Mrs. Bickerdyke and Elizabeth Deane sitting
before the fire.

Of course each one of the newcomers received
one of the three packages which lay on Mrs.
Bickerdyke's black silk lap.

" A face-cloth ! " exclaimed Mrs. Fuller, as if
she had never in her whole life been so surprised
or so delighted.   " And a cake of soap !   Why,
my dear mother, how pleased I am ! "

Mr. Fuller, too, who had a round, rosy face
with blue eyes, beamed his thanks.   " What
a thing it was to have just that sort of useful
present ! "

Mr. Bickerdyke was of sterner stuff, and never
pretended to be pleased out of mere compliance
with other people's wishes.   He simply gave a
sort of grunt.

" Never make presents myself," he said as he
sat down.   However, he bestowed on Dorothy a
brand-new ten-cent piece after she had kissed

him; and he was, we may as well explain, the best sort of son and brother, giving Mrs. Bickerdyke and Miss Hester half their income. Mr. and Mrs. Fuller had sent a turkey and six chickens, so they could accept the face-cloths and cakes of soap, even a copy of Pilgrim's Progress, with a clear conscience.

Dinner was to be served at two o'clock, and it was a relief to Dorothy to help Jerusha prepare the celery and the cranberry jam, and arrange the pieces of bread under a fold of the napkins. Jerusha was a little cross, but as she always said, with a turkey on one's mind, how could one take things lightly? Dorothy was used to Jerusha's ways, and to-day was so happy, she could laugh when Jerusha found fault with her. It was delightful to reflect that dinner was getting ready all the time; that dinner would soon come; and, more delightful still, to think that dinner would be over, and *then!*

At one minute past two Mrs. Bickerdyke sat down in great spirits at the head of the table, with her son and son-in-law on either hand. Miss Hester was at the other end, with Mrs. Fuller on her right and Elizabeth Deane on her left. Dorothy was squeezed in between her mother and Mr. Fuller, and Mr. Fuller's elbow constantly made itself felt as he used his knife and

fork and spoon. Conversation went on for a
time quite briskly while they ate their oyster
soup, for each person had some remark to con-
tribute about the weather or their minister's
family. Along with the turkey came a pause,
which Mrs. Bickerdyke broke by asking if there
was much sickness over in North Swallowfield.
This subject was most useful and lasted through
two helpings apiece of turkey, to say nothing of
vegetables and cranberry jam ; for there had
been an epidemic of influenza, besides two cases
of typhoid fever, among the Fullers' neighbors.
Dinner was progressing cheerfully. Dorothy
was gazing at the splendid chicken-pie which
Jerusha had just set before Miss Hester, thinking how nice it was, when, all at once, Mr. Samuel Bickerdyke uttered a sort of groan, sat
back in his chair, and looked most unhappy.

" Oh, Hester," cried Mrs. Bickerdyke in great
distress of mind, " something must have dis-
agreed with Samuel."

" What is wrong, brother Samuel ? " inquired
Miss Hester.

Mr. Bickerdyke's face certainly suggested keen
physical discomfort, or else unhappiness. At
this question he shook his head mournfully.

" Why did n't you tell me," he returned,
" that there was a chicken-pie coming ? "

And he looked at the huge crusty pasty, into which Miss Hester was thrusting a silver knife, as if the sight pained him.

" Why, brother Samuel," Miss Hester said in her quiet, even way, " don't you know that we always have chicken-pie for Christmas ? "

" Perhaps he forgot, for it used to be mother's way to have everything on the table at once," suggested Mrs. Fuller.

" Now, for my part," Mr. Fuller observed cheerfully, " I like Hester's new-fashioned way. A man has a chance, as it were, with a fresh course to take a fresh start, and goes at it with a fresh appetite."

These reflections, however, failed to console Mr. Bickerdyke.

" If you had just simply told me it was coming," he said disconsolately.

" I 'm an old woman," Mrs. Bickerdyke now remarked, " and for my part I never did see any good in new-fangled notions. Now I have always felt that what was good enough for my father and mother was good enough for me. People used in those old times to be governed by reason and common-sense."

Mrs. Bickerdyke had of late fallen almost completely under the severe but righteous yoke of Miss Hester's ways, but there were times when,

as it were, she chafed slightly, and this was one
of them.

"I recollect," she now proceeded, "when I
was a little girl like Dorothy there, eating the
best Thanksgiving dinner I ever ate in my life.
There were two turkeys, two pair of geese, two
pair of ducks, and three great chicken-pies, besides six mince, apple, cranberry, and pumpkin
pies, all on the table at once."

"Oh, grandma!" exclaimed Dorothy, "how
did you know what to eat first?"

It was quite against all rule for Dorothy to
speak at table, unless spoken to. At this moment, however, everybody was so much concerned with Mr. Bickerdyke's troubles that
nobody noticed Dorothy's breach of etiquette
except her mother, who smiled and clasped the
little hand nearest her.

"I don't so much insist on everything being
on the table at once," Mr. Bickerdyke explained,
"if I am only prepared for what is coming."

Miss Hester, no matter what regrets she might
feel at having taken away her brother's enjoyment of the dinner, was helping the chicken-pie
as if nothing had gone wrong.

"Will you have some, brother Samuel?"
she inquired when his turn came.

"Oh, do take a little, Samuel," pleaded Mrs.

Bickerdyke almost tearfully. " It seems to me I could n't rightly go on eating my dinner unless you did."

This consideration, perhaps, had its weight with Mr. Bickerdyke. At least he accepted a plateful of the beautiful flaky crust, with the breast of one chicken, the wing of another, and the leg of a third, all well covered with rich gravy. It quite cheered up Dorothy to see him eat it. Then how surprised she was when he took a second helping equal to the first!

" If I had only known," he still murmured complainingly, — " if I had only known it was coming, I might have been better prepared for it."

Mr. Fuller's eye twinkled, but he had learned never to make jokes at his mother-in-law's. Mrs. Bickerdyke, with the keenest satisfaction, watched the rapid diminution of chicken-pie on her son's plate.

" I do think," she observed, with a sigh of relief when he had finished his second supply, " that Jerusha makes good pies."

" If I had only known it was coming," said Mr. Bickerdyke; " and I do feel, mother, that you or Hester ought to have warned me."

He was looking at the pie, and Dorothy was very much interested to see whether he would

have a third helping.   He had no chance.   Jerusha all at once whisked off the dish, then set
herself to clearing the table of vestiges of dinner, preparatory to offering the sweets.

Mrs. Bickerdyke also felt a little disappointed.

" Could n't you have taken a little piece more,
Samuel? " she asked tremulously.

" No, no; plenty, plenty.   Enough is as good
as a feast," Mr. Bickerdyke answered, but with
such an evident attempt to make the best of circumstances that Dorothy was certain in her own
mind he had some slight hankering after that
possible third piece.   It is true he partook of
mince-pie, pumpkin-pie, and ice-cream, but each
time he accepted anything he went back to his
grievance about not being prepared for that
chicken-pie.

# CHAPTER III

IT was well past three o'clock when they rose from the dinner-table, and that was the signal for the breaking up of the family party. The Fullers' carriage was waiting to take them to their daughter's house to spend the remainder of Christmas day. Mr. Bickerdyke wished to make the 3.45 train to town. He sadly put on his great-coat and muffler, and bade good-by to his mother and sister, saying that he had been glad to see them, — that, although he should have felt more like enjoying his dinner had he known about the chicken-pie, it had still been his wish not to rob other people of their satisfaction in their Christmas meal. Then, after shaking hands all round, he drew on his warm gloves, took his umbrella, and went out the door, down the steps, and up the street.

Dorothy stood at the window watching the Fullers get into their carriage and uncle Samuel vanish round the corner, but what she was thinking of was that *now* the time had come! She

had waited so long; she had tried to be patient;
but there is an end to everything. She wanted
those dolls, and that paint-box and writing-desk,
to see, to touch, to handle!

"Dorothy," called Miss Hester.

Dorothy knew that her aunt was standing beside the little table which held the three brown
paper parcels. Yet something seemed to hold
her back from answering the call. She could not
help trembling all over at the thought of how
happy she was going to be.

"Dorothy!" Miss Hester called again.

Dorothy turned a little flushed, quivering face,
with eyes running over with glad tears. She
could not speak a word. She half smiled as she
went towards Miss Hester.

"I do not need to tell you, Dorothy," Miss
Hester now said, "what is in these bundles, for
you helped me choose the things yesterday. Now
I am about to give you a great privilege. I am
going to let you take these things to children
who have very few presents, and very little to
give them comfort and pleasure. If your mother has no objection, I should like to have you
put on your hat and jacket, and carry the dolls
to Jane Smillie, the paint-box to Robbie Todd,
and the writing-desk to Emily Brown."

Miss Hester was looking down into the little

expectant, upturned face, which had a look as
if the child did not quite comprehend, but was
waiting to hear more.

"Do you quite understand, Dorothy?" demanded Miss Hester, taking in the whole meaning of the dazed, helpless expression gathering
in the little face.

It was Elizabeth Deane who answered for
Dorothy.

"She quite understands, aunt Hester. She
will take the presents; I will go with her, if you
do not object."

"I want to have Dorothy repeat the names,
so that I may be sure that the presents go as I
direct," Miss Hester said. "The dolls are to go
to Jane Smillie."

Miss Hester paused and waited. Dorothy's
lips opened and then shut tighter than ever. Her
mother put her hand on her shoulder and said,

"The dolls are to go to Jane Smillie, aunt
Hester." Elizabeth's wide, quiet gaze met Miss
Hester's, and Miss Hester decided not to force
Dorothy to repeat the formula.

"The paint-box to Robbie Todd," she said
briskly, "and the writing-desk to Emily Brown,
with Miss Bickerdyke's and Dorothy Deane's
wishes for a happy New Year." Then holding
out her hand to Mrs. Bickerdyke, she added,

"Come, dear mother, it is time for you to lie down," and the two went away arm in arm, leaving Dorothy alone with her mother.

The moment the door was closed, Dorothy seemed to wake up. She dashed at the sofa, gathered all the cushions, and flung them on the floor. Then she put her hand on a chair as if she were about to upset it. But Elizabeth Deane said quietly, —

"Dear, you are behaving very naughtily."

"I know I'm naughty," Dorothy returned fiercely. "I want to be naughty. I'm going to be just as naughty as I know how to be."

Elizabeth knelt down on the floor and held out her arms wide. Dorothy stood at a little distance, with red cheeks and bright, sparkling eyes, her lips set close, gazing back at her mother, not yielding to the proffered clasp. But Dorothy could not look long unmoved into her mother's sweet, sad, tender face. Her mood changed. Her breast began to heave. The corners of her mouth curved down.

"She — knew — I — wanted — those — things," she faltered, one word coming slowly after the other. "She — heard — me — tell — Marcia — I wanted them. Then she took me to town and told me to look and choose — to tell her those I liked best " —

" My darling," began Elizabeth, as the voice
died away for a moment. It was only for a
moment.

" I hate aunt Hester," Dorothy cried out at
the top of her voice. " I just do hate her, and
I hate grandma — I do, I do, I do." She finished by throwing herself on the floor, face
downwards. The flood of her sorrow, her disappointment, and her rage broke over her. She
sobbed, she moaned, her breath came in angry
pants. Her hands caught and pulled at everything within reach, her feet as well. In fact,
at this moment Dorothy was such a naughty,
rebellious, wicked girl, I quite blush at the idea
of offering her as my heroine. But then she
had rather a hot temper, and having been very
happy, very hopeful, her disappointment was in
proportion to the happiness and hope she was
compelled to give up.

" Dorothy," said Mrs. Deane after waiting a
little. Then, when there was no answer, she
said again, " Dorothy, my own dear little girl, I
want to tell you what Christmas means."

" It means nasty, horrid things," declared
Dorothy, lifting her head and showing a stormy
face. " It means just having a face-cloth and a
cake of soap and a mean little book. I 'll never
read that book; I 'll never wash my face with

grandmamma's face-cloth, *never, never, never!*
I just hate Christmas."

" No, you don't hate Christmas," said Elizabeth ; " you hate your own disappointment, and
I, too, feel very unhappy about your disappointment. But then your aunt Hester knows, just
as I know, that it is a very poor sort of Christmas that makes us think only about getting our
own comfort and satisfaction out of it. What
Christmas means, Dorothy, is that every year
we do the most we can to have Christ born again
into the world. And how do we do that ? "

" I don't know," Dorothy replied hesitatingly,
her bright, impatient gaze fixed on her mother.

" Before Christ was born at all, the world was
so hard and cruel," said Elizabeth. " Everybody
thought only about what he or she wanted for
himself or herself ; some people even liked to
make others suffer pain in order that they themselves might have a keener sense of enjoyment.
What Christ did was to show men and women
and little children that the best sort of happiness came in thinking first about making other
people happy. He taught us that if we give
up looking after and expecting pleasures and
rewards for ourselves, — why then, we are free
of a burden and can have wide, loving, generous thoughts for others. Christmas means that

love and charity must be born afresh into the world."

Her persevering look and tone made itself felt at last. Dorothy was thinking; that was clear.

"Now," continued Elizabeth, "have you denied yourself anything this Christmas? Have you said to yourself, ' I wish I could make somebody very happy ' ? "

" I want to be happy myself," Dorothy declared stoutly.

" Yes, and think how much you will enjoy giving the dolls to Jane Smillie. Poor little Jane; she does n't live in a bright, sunny, warm house with flowers all about; she has no good dinners to eat. I don't suppose she ever in her life had anything better than a rag doll to play with. How happy she will be with these ! "

Dorothy had gradually lifted herself from the floor and sat looking at her mother; but at this suggestion she gave a little cry, quivered from head to foot, and gasped, —

" Oh, I want them myself, I do want them myself ! "

" Not so much as Jane wants them. Jane is only five years old, — just old enough to know how to play with dolls. You are beginning to enjoy books."

" I wanted two more dolls. I wanted them to put to bed at night with Gill and the Countess."

" But just think what good times Jane will have. Every night you can say to yourself, ' I can guess what Jane is doing.' "

Dorothy was again sitting up. She heaved a little sigh.

" I don't so very much mind Jane's having them."

" No, indeed ; you will find that it will be a real pleasure to think of her having them. And perhaps you can tell her what to call them, and tell her how to play with them, — all about Gill and the Countess."

" I did n't feel quite sure," Dorothy murmured, with a queer little sort of smile at her mother, " how Gill would like my having two new dolls. She fell down and smashed her face, she was so jealous, when I had the Countess."

" I think both Gill's and the Countess's feelings would have been dreadfully hurt," said Mrs. Deane, " if you had brought in two fine, brand-new dolls."

Dorothy had jumped up on her feet.

" I shall tell Jane what she must call them," she now said, running towards the table; " I know what their names are."

Then when she put her hands on the packages the feeling of loss and pain came over her again.

"Oh, mamma," she murmured piteously, "I do want the paint-box."

"But not so much as Robbie Todd. He is getting better of that trouble with his knee, but he will not be able to walk about for months to come. Think what fun he will have sitting up and painting pictures."

However, Dorothy's tears were streaming.

"I want to paint pictures, too."

"You have your old paint-box, dear."

"But there are only four colors left, and not one single pretty one; just an ugly green and purple and yellow and black."

"You can think that Robbie has beautiful colors."

Five minutes later, Miss Hester, glancing out of the window, saw Mrs. Deane and Dorothy set off in the highest spirits, Dorothy holding both arms clasped tightly about the three brown paper parcels, just as she had held them yesterday. The low sun was lighting up the west with crimson and gold and flame. In the east a great moon, almost at its full, loomed large in rosy and violet mists.

The house was lighted up and the table was

spread for tea when the two came back, entering
flushed and eager and full of smiles.

"Oh, aunt Hester!" Dorothy cried, dashing
into the room, "it was just beautiful. I never
did have such a good time before. Oh, I do
thank you so much for letting me give those
presents!"

Dorothy was so full to overflowing with high
spirits that she even ventured to throw her arms
round Miss Hester. Miss Hester had felt it to
be a duty to disappoint Dorothy; to set her to
thinking of others instead of herself. She was
not cruel, and now, with the little arms round
her neck, an odd sort of softness came over her.
She had to make an effort to say calmly,—

"Well, did the children like the presents?"

"Oh yes, indeed they did! Jane just danced
up and down," said Dorothy. "I told her she
must call the dolls Elsie and Poppy, for that
was what I was going to call them if they had
been mine, but she said she wanted to call them
both Dorothy. One, 'big Dorothy;' and the
other, 'little Dorothy.'"

Dorothy's own clear laugh rang out.

"So I let her," she added.

"And Robbie Todd?"

"Robbie Todd couldn't say anything he was
so pleased, but his mother did. She said it was

just what she had tried to save up money to buy for him, but there were so many things that had to be bought, — oh, it's beautiful that he has got the paint-box, aunt Hester!"

"How about Emily Brown?"

"Emily Brown is going to write you a note. She said she never knew before what Christmas was," Dorothy replied, beaming. "She can write to her sister now while she lies on the lounge, and never trouble anybody to bring her ink and pen and paper, for she has them all in the desk."

"Now it is time to get ready for tea," said Miss Hester.

Elizabeth Deane gave one little glance at Dorothy, who understood, and now faltered in a soft, breathless, shamefaced sort of way, —

"Oh, aunt Hester!"

"Well?"

"I was naughty this afternoon, — dreadfully naughty."

"I am very sorry to hear it."

"You see," Dorothy explained, "I did want those dolls and the paint-box and the writing-desk dreadfully, — yes, dreadfully. But now I'm glad, — I'm really and truly glad, aunt Hester. I do like this sort of Christmas best."

Miss Hester kissed the cool little lips.

Two hours later, when Dorothy went to bed, she took her two dolls, — Gill with a smashed nose and two painfully dislocated arms, and the Countess, a most superfine creature in blue silk and silver spangles, — and put them on top of her pillow, and looked at them with a serious, critical, penetrating gaze.

" They would n't have liked it, mamma," Dorothy then whispered to her mother, after she had read the secrets of the two dolls, who, propped against each other, stared steadily, each in an opposite direction, — " they would n't have liked it at all if I had kept big Dorothy and little Dorothy."

When she had undressed and knelt at her mother's knee, she repeated her usual prayers, then asked if she could make up another out of her own head.

This was the prayer out of her own head : —

"O Lord, I thank thee for having such a beautiful birthday. I hope it will have many happy returns. For Jesus Christ's sake. Amen."

# CHAPTER IV

MARCIA DUNDAS came back from her Christmas visit just before New Year's. There was a window on the landing halfway up the staircase at Mrs. Bickerdyke's, out of which Dorothy always paused to look in her journeys up and down. Just before noon on the Thursday she saw the white flag flying out of the oriel window of Dundas House.

Marcia had long since established a code of signals, so that Dorothy and Lucy and Gaynor Lee always knew what she was doing and wishing and contriving.

A white flag meant: All come over; I've got something to tell you.

A blue flag: All come over; I'm going to make something perfectly delicious to eat.

A red flag: All come over; I'm going to walk.

A black flag: I'm awfully lonely; do come.

To see these signals, to feel the very heart and soul drawn out of one by Marcia's imperi-

ous summons, yet not to be able to answer it, —
to be kept at home by sickness, weather, or
other circumstances beyond their control, was
considered a very serious trouble by all these
children.

Lucy and Gaynor Lee were twins, and were
almost two years older than Dorothy. They
were the youngest of a family of ten children,
and were so quiet, so docile, that as long as they
made their appearance regularly at meal-times
with smooth hair and clean hands and faces, it
was taken for granted they were in no mischief.
Four hours a day they spent at school, where
they received the best marks. Miss Hester, too,
besides their teachers, held the twins in high
esteem. Some joking person has said that one
ought to be very particular in the choice of one's
parents. It might also be wisely observed that
one ought to be very particular in the choice of
one's neighbors; and, indeed, one's neighborhood
does seem to be a circumstance under one's control. The fact is, however, that there are a
great many things in life that we have to accept
as we find them, not to say, be happy that we
get them. Miss Hester was rejoiced that Dorothy had such nice little neighbors as Lucy and
Gaynor. When they came to see Dorothy, the
two little girls seemed perfectly happy in cutting

paper dolls and dressing them in tissue paper, while Gay, lying face downwards on a rug, his chin propped up with his two hands, buried himself in a book. The twins were so pretty, with their smooth, fair hair, their blue eyes, their straight little noses, and mouths with a short, curled upper lip showing their teeth when they smiled ; they were always so neatly dressed ; they had such good manners, it did seem a very excellent arrangement that Dorothy could get to their house, and they to hers, by slipping through a wicket in a corner of the yard where Jerusha dried her clothes. What seemed to the three children the delightful fact which altered all their lives was that, by stealing through a gap in the arbor-vitæ hedge just beyond the play-room at the foot of the Lees' lawn, they were on the grounds of Dundas House, and, except themselves, nobody in the world the wiser. For Miss Hester knew nothing about that gap in the hedge. Now and then when, with her aunt's permission, Dorothy went to spend the afternoon with Marcia, Jerusha would take her round the long way by the street, and ring the bell at the great door. Nor did Miss Hester know about the code of signals. She had not seen the white flag flying that day, and when Lucy and Gay came in to ask if Dor-

othy could play with them, she would never
have thought of guessing that, three minutes
after she saw Dorothy's red hood and jacket
vanishing through the wicket which led to the
Lees', the three children and the two dogs, Carlo
and Flossy, were arriving breathless, — where
do you suppose? Why, in the great kitchen of
Dundas House.

"Oh, I'm so glad you've come," called Marcia, who was at the big fireplace engaged in
cleverly raking out a new bed of glowing embers from under the blazing logs; "I was just
going to put out the blue flag. I'm making
some chocolate for mamma."

Dorothy and Lucy and Gay had lately risen
from a bountiful meal, but anything Marcia
could offer in the way of refreshments was sure
to be acceptable.

"When did you get home?" Lucy inquired
sedately, as soon as all three were established
on the settle before the fire.

"Last night at seven o'clock," returned Marcia. "Oh, but wasn't the house cold! I put
mamma to bed, and she is only just getting up.
Gay, do you mind just stirring that chocolate?
I want to drop these eggs."

One reason that Dundas House seemed to the
children so superior to other people's houses was

that everything was so different,—so little formal
and cut-and-dried. Mrs. Dundas, being something of an invalid, rarely left her room. A
great part of the time there was no servant, except old Chloe, who came for a day or two every
week ; and thus Marcia was left to run the
establishment. Marcia's housekeeping was not
a science nor an art, but a dodge. She liked to
cook, and could make an exquisite cup of coffee,
tea, or chocolate. Now, after setting Dorothy to
toasting two slices of bread, she arranged on a
tray a graceful little meal, consisting of a small
pot of the chocolate, the poached eggs, bread,
and a pat of butter. This was to go up to Mrs.
Dundas.

"Now, Gay," Marcia said, pausing at the
door, salver in hand, "keep stirring the chocolate, and somebody toast all the rest of the
bread, and I'll be down again in a few minutes."

Gay and Dorothy were very proud when
Marcia permitted them to help her. Gay had
become quite expert in turning pancakes, and
Dorothy's toasted bread was sometimes just the
right shade of golden brown. They hoped that
finally they might arrive at the point of helping
Marcia make a welsh rabbit; but so far they had
only looked on first and eaten it afterwards.

Carlo and Flossy knew Dundas House, and the
ways and manners of the kitchen, as well as did
Gay and Lucy and Dorothy. In fact, the two
dogs went everywhere with the children.

"Just like Mary and her little lamb, only
more so," as Marcia said. But then they were
such knowing, loving, sympathetic creatures! If
Gay and Lucy ever did contrive to go anywhere
without them, they were always sure to say,
"Oh, how Flossy and Carlo would have enjoyed
this!"

Flossy was snow-white, with hair like spun
silk and a tail like an ostrich plume. Carlo had
somehow contrived to get the most beautiful
black setter head on his black-and-tan body, — a
sleek head, with long silky ears; a wise, mag-
nanimous face, with eyes that one could look
into and never get to the depths of, they were
so full of dumb, loving expression, that is when
they were not full of mischief. At this moment
both dogs were squeezed in between Dorothy
and Lucy and the fire, enjoying the warmth,
smelling the toast and chocolate, and thinking
to themselves something good was coming presently.

The kitchen was a great pleasant room with
two windows opening on the south, with wide,
old-fashioned window-seats, and another to the

east. There were two chimneys, one taken up
by a long unused and rusty range; but the other
had this wide open fireplace, where one could in
a moment kindle any sort of a fire, from a handful of twigs to one of great logs that would
make a blaze that roared up chimney.

No house in Swallowfield could compare with
Dundas House, and until this generation the
Dundases had represented to Swallowfield people all that was most splendid and aristocratic.
They had been great people in colonial times;
they had figured in the Revolutionary days, and
had done no little towards the building of the
nation. But spending, never harvesting, has its
results sooner or later, and, alas, the Dundases
had grown poor. The death of old Madam
Dundas, twenty years before, had ended the magnificence of the family. Her grandson, Paul,
the only Dundas that was left, went away to
make a start in life. The house was closed,
shuttered, barred. Grass had grown on the
drives. The beautiful old garden, with its borders of box and its hedges of privet, had become
a wilderness. This state of things had gone on
for seventeen years; then, three years before the
opening of our little chronicle, Mrs. Paul Dundas and her daughter, Marcia, had come to stay
in the empty old house, which still remained poor

unlucky Paul's sole possession. Paul had now
gone out to South Africa to see if he could not
make the fortune which he had not been able
to make in his own country. Just as soon as he
saw his way clear, he was to send for his wife
and child. Almost any day the summons
might come; thus although in some of the
rooms the ceilings were ready to fall, although
the glass was broken in many of the windows,
although the range and water-pipes were rusty,
what did it matter? They were only staying
there, not living. So Mrs. Dundas and Marcia
adjusted themselves to this casual existence, just
as one accepts the miseries of a sea voyage, trying to sleep through the gales.

Mrs. Dundas had been much admired and
sympathized with on her first coming to Swallowfield. She was a tall, slender, graceful
woman, with much charm of manner, if she
chose to exercise it. But she grew listless and
melancholy; hope deferred maketh the heart
sick, and she knew nothing else but hopes constantly disappointed and constantly rising out
of their own ashes. Swallowfield people soon
found out that she cared for nothing except re-
joining her husband. She had perhaps a melancholy pleasure in going about the rooms where
her husband had grown up to the age of seven-

teen. He had told her about the garlands above
the doors ; the flutings in the mantelpieces with
cherub faces in the corners. There were some
fireplaces with tiles set about the brickwork, and
Mrs. Dundas, as she studied out the pictures and
the stories, could remember little stories and
incidents that her husband had told her. The
chairs, the couches, the bookcases, all were a
part of the story of Paul ; even the way the sun
came into the house at morning and evening.

Miss Roxy Burt was the only woman in Swallowfield who had established any sort of in-
timacy with Mrs. Dundas. Miss Roxy had
had a nephew who had died at the age of sixteen, and he and Paul Dundas had been play-
mates. Miss Roxy in her pony-phaeton was
often seen driving up the grass-grown avenue to
Dundas House, but nobody else. What Swallowfield people felt was that Mrs. Dundas's ways
were different from theirs. She had no thought
of keeping up the place ; lived contentedly at
sixes and sevens ; allowed Marcia to outgrow her
clothes ; had herself no thrift, no faculty, yet
could not contrive to keep a servant in the
house. The difference was not, however, because she could not keep her servants. Everybody in Swallowfield had such troubles except
the Bickerdykes, who possessed Jerusha. It was

more of a grievance to Swallowfield people that when Mrs. Dundas had a servant, her habit was to breakfast in bed, at least in her own room, and to give out directions for her dinner without ever going down to the kitchen. Then, too, such directions for her dinner! She liked dishes out of the usual way, all beautifully served. Mrs. Dundas seemed unable to understand that a knowledge of how to make croquettes and prepare sweetbreads does not come by nature. She was also exquisitely dainty about all that she wore; as Swallowfield said, " bathed four times a day and changed her clothes every half hour." This made no end of washing and ironing, so that the bewildered maid-of-all-work, who was expected to be an expert cook, laundress, and parlor-maid, if she stayed more than a week was certain to depart at the end of a month.

Marcia was bright by nature, and experience had sharpened her. She took the ups and downs of life philosophically, generally declaring that she preferred the downs, for then she knew where she was. To have a servant meant complaints. She hated hearing complaints. It also meant the need of ready money. They never had ready money. Twice a year, there came a few dividends; not quite enough to settle the outstanding bills fully, but sufficient to tide them

over the brief interval until, as Mrs. Dundas
said in her easy, graceful way, — " until I hear
from Mr. Dundas."

Marcia, poor child, was used to bills. All
her life long she had seen and heard of bills.
To Marcia's consciousness, bills grew on even the
most innocent experience, just as thorns grow
on roses. Of course a new hat or a frock or a
pair of shoes meant a bill. One could understand that. What seemed odd to Marcia was
that necessary things, — things that one absolutely could n't get along without, like eggs,
chops, beefsteaks, loaves of bread, milk, and
cream, — things, in fact, that ought to rain
down, meant bills. It was odder yet that things
one hated to do, like going to the dentist's, having doctors, and taking medicine, — things that
really one ought, in justice, to be paid for doing,
— meant bills, just as if one had done it all
with a view to selfish enjoyment. But to return
to our story.

Dorothy had toasted four slices of bread.

" Is that enough ? " she asked Lucy, who sat
on the settle, and Gay, who was faithfully stirring the chocolate.

" I don't think it is, quite," replied Lucy.

" I — I — I — " Gay began, for poor Gay
stammered slightly.

"Count three, Gay," said Lucy.

This counting three was the bane of Gay's existence. The doctors had ordered him always to count three before he spoke, as his stammering was not yet a confirmed habit, and might easily be cured by coolness and resolution.

"One, two, three," Gay now said. "I feel pretty hungry myself."

The dogs, too, scenting the coming feast, watched all the preparations with a look of personal interest and expectation.

At this juncture Marcia descended, seized two slices of toast, with a saucy, laughing face, and ran off with them to her mother.

"I'll be down in another minute," she said. "Lucy, you can be setting the table."

Lucy obeyed. They all obeyed Marcia, who knew not only how to keep her foot on their necks, but to make them all love, admire, and worship her. She also made them work. At least once a week Marcia was sure to set her visitors to polishing her two copper saucepans, her tea-kettle, and biggin. A workman is known by his tools and a cook by his saucepans. The great fire in the great fireplace had to be fed, and they were all used to carrying logs and collecting bundles of fagots. Everything that Marcia told them to do became interesting:

scouring saucepans, beating eggs, or foraging
for water-cresses, berries, and nuts. Without
Marcia, everything was safe, tame, dull. She
expanded possibilities for them, and added im-
mensely to their enjoyment.

Even the chocolate and toast would have been
nothing unless she could share it with them, and
now here she was ready to sit down, and the
feast began.

" Oh, children," was her exclamation, as soon
as she had poured out the chocolate, " I 've got so
much to tell you. Then when we are through
eating and drinking, I 'll show you the things
I 've brought you."

As Marcia uttered these words, she gave a
comprehensive little nod all round the table.
That she had brought them presents was the
most delightful surprise.

" Oh, Marcia ! " exclaimed Dorothy fervently.

" Oh, Marcia ! " said Lucy.

" M—M—M— " Gay was beginning, when
Lucy put in admonishingly, —

" Count three, Gay."

Gay had no time to count three. Marcia was
talking on and on. He had to look his thanks.

" I 've had a perfectly splendid time, children," she proceeded, sitting at the head of the
small, square deal table, drinking her chocolate

out of a great gilt cup with a broken handle, which necessitated her holding it up to her lips with both hands. Her black eyes were dancing ; her cheeks were bright red ; her long braids, tied with a scarlet ribbon, were thrown forward over her left shoulder. " I have learned all sorts of things. I know a great deal more than I did before I went away."

This sounded incredible, for the children had long believed that what Marcia did not know was not worth knowing. They all looked at her with expectant eyes. She nodded back at them.

" First," she began, " I 'll tell you about my journey. When we took the train the day before Christmas, it was so full of people mamma had to sit down on one side of the aisle with an old lady, and I went in with a nice-looking gentleman, — not so very old. It was warm in the cars, so I took off my jacket and laid it across the back of the seat in front of me, behind a woman with four children. When we came to the junction, she had to get out in a terrible hurry. Besides all the four children, she had a basket with a puppy in it, and too many bags and parcels to count. The gentleman I was sitting with helped her with the children and the puppy and the bags and the bundles, carrying them down the aisle to the door of the car. Then when he

THE FEAST BEGAN

came back, there she was on the platform outside making signals.  He threw up the window.
' I 've left my shawl and Robby's jacket in the
rack,' she called.  The train was just beginning
to move off.  He reached up, found the shawl and
Robby's jacket in the rack; then what did he
do but take my jacket, too, and throw all three
out of the window."

" Out of the window ? "

" Out of the window."

" Your jacket, too ? "

" He — threw — your — jacket — out — of
— the — window ? "

" That is just what he did.  ' Oh, sir,' I cried,
' you have been and gone and thrown away my
jacket ! '  ' Your jacket ! ' said he ;  ' what do
you mean ?  It was Robby's jacket ! '  ' Robby's jacket was in the rack.  My jacket was
here in front of me.'  ' Why did n't you say
so ? '  said he.  I told him I had no time.
' Bless my soul ! ' said he.  ' What business had
you to put your jacket there at all ? '  He began to scold.  He said that was always the way
with women.  They could n't sit down neat,
snug, compact ; they were always slopping over.
' What did your jacket cost ? '  he went on.
' More than I can spend to buy another,' I
answered.  ' What was it made of ? '  he asked.

'Sealskin?' I told him not exactly sealskin.
'Well,' he said, 'I'm thankful if it is n't sealskin. I have bought one sealskin jacket this
winter; another would ruin me. But why on
earth'— Then he went at me again. He said
that once when he was young he went a journey
on a stage-coach, and one of the passengers was
a young woman with four parcels, who kept saying, 'Great box, little box, bandbox, and bundle,'
putting her hand on one after another article
of her luggage as she spoke. 'That's the sort
of woman a man might have some pleasure in
traveling with,' he said. 'I should be proud to
have a woman belong to me who could keep her
mind on her belongings.' Just then the conductor came along, and the gentleman told him
what had happened to my jacket. 'We shall
stop at Smithtown for five minutes, and I will
wire back to the junction and have the jacket
sent on,' answered the conductor, as if everybody
every day threw jackets out of the window. 'I
don't suppose he'll find it,' the gentleman said
to me very fiercely. 'I dare say I shall have
to take you and fit you out with a new jacket
when we get to town!' Then he asked if I were
traveling alone. I pointed out mamma to him.
He made up a face. 'I suppose I must go and
ask her pardon,' said he. Up he jumped.

'Madam!' he shouted at the top of his voice,
'I've thrown your daughter's jacket out of the
window. It's just like me. The other night I
was coming up in the Elevated, when I saw a
little boy sitting all alone and crying. I took
him up in my lap and asked what was the matter. He told me he wanted his mother. She
had set him down there and had n't come back.
" Heavens and earth! this child has been deserted by its own mother!" I cried. I rushed
out to the guard and informed him what had
happened. " I 'll hand him over to the policeman
at the next station," said he ; " these mothers
have n't any heart." We exclaimed over the in-
fernal barbarity of the action until the train
slackened up; then I seized the little blubbering
chap and was about to pitch him to the guard to
hand over to the policeman, when a woman I
had n't seen before gave a yell and rushed towards me, crying, " Put my child down, you vil-
lain!" The boy, madam, was hers. She had
simply gone to the end of the car to speak to an
acquaintance. I give you my word of honor,
madam, that I thought there was n't a passenger
in the car except the child and myself. The
conductor as well thought the car was empty.' "

" What did your mamma say ? " inquired Dorothy.

"She said," returned Marcia, drawing herself up to an elegant height, — "she said, 'You seem, sir, to be rather an impulsive man.'"

"What did he say?" inquired Lucy.

"He said," answered Marcia, "'Madam, I am an impulsive man, and I'm proud of being an impulsive man. Hang it, madam, I would rather run away with children and throw jackets out of the window every day of my life, than to be one of your self-satisfied, cut-and-dried mummies who sit and look on and see their fellow-beings in distress and never lift a hand to do them any good.'"

The children laughed, but not with the same ringing note that Marcia put into her mirth. Gay, in particular, had something on his mind; it was clear that he was struggling with some question. His lips moved, he made an explosive sound, but nothing articulate came.

"Count three, Gay," said Lucy.

"One, two, three," said Gay heroically. "D— did you get your jacket, Marcia?"

"*I* hope he had to buy you a beautiful new one," Lucy suggested.

"No," said Marcia. "After we had stopped at another place the conductor told us the jacket was coming by the 11.55 way train, and would reach the city thirty-five minutes after we got there. In any case we had to wait almost an hour. We sat down in the waiting-room, and the gentleman kept bobbing in and out. 'Why does n't that train get in?' he would roar. 'There 's been some smash-up, I 'm sure of it.' But when the time was up he appeared with my jacket all right. I put it on, and he said, 'Remember next time not to let your things lie around loose, but keep your eye on them!' Then he handed me a box. 'What is this?' I asked. 'Never mind,' said he. 'It 's for a Merry Christmas and a Happy New Year,' and off he went."

"And what was in the box?" inquired Dorothy.

"I 'll show you," said Marcia triumphantly.

Indeed, as the chocolate was finished to the last drop and the toast to the final crumb, and as at least the first chapter of Marcia's surprising adventures was told, the next thing in the programme was to show the children what she had brought them. She had left the box in the hall just outside and now produced it.

"It was just the most wonderful box of candies you ever saw in your lives," she said. "To begin with, see what a beautiful box it is. Mamma says I can use it all my life as a workbox. Then inside there were six layers of choco-

lates, each with a different flavor.   See, I've
saved one of each for each of you."

" Oh, Marcia ! "

" Oh, Marcia ! "

" Oh, M— "

" Count three, Gay."

It was certainly an act of self-denial on Marcia's part to have saved three out of each layer
of bonbons, but she had ample reward in seeing
what pleasure she was giving.

" But you have n't got any yourself," cried
Dorothy in distress.

Marcia observed with a proud and pleased air
that she had already eaten so many nothing
could possibly induce her to touch another.
Nevertheless her lips closed presently over one,
and finally over two more of Dorothy's share ;
which proceeding gave Dorothy quite as much
satisfaction as it gave Marcia.   Lucy and Gay
ate theirs ; not that they were greedy, but what
was theirs was theirs, and there was the end
of it.

This was but the beginning.

"You see," she now explained, "at aunt
Mary's there is so much to eat; then if she
took us anywhere there was generally more to
eat ; and one afternoon I went to a sort of four-
o'clock tea with Bel and Lil, and they kept pass-

ing round cakes and bonbons and ices. Well, of course I had to eat the ices. I could n't bring them; but I 've got all the cakes and all the bonbons."

"Oh, Marcia!" went all round again.

The cakes were a trifle crumbled, but oh, how delicious! The bonbons were wrapped in paper. To think of Marcia's having remembered them all the time she was away!

"I used to carry off an orange from table every chance I had," continued Marcia. "They all laughed at me. They said it was the way somebody did in 'Cranford,' wherever that was. They had an idea I sucked them in my room. But I did n't. I saved them all for mamma. I 've got thirteen. Mamma loves to eat an orange when she first wakes up in the morning."

Altogether the children felt with increased admiration that Marcia had made a substantial gain out of her visit.

# CHAPTER V

## DOROTHY AT HOME

A GREAT deal that went on in the way of chocolate-making in the kitchen fireplace, and other doings at Dundas House, was only guessed at outside. Still, Swallowfield people were in the habit of saying that old Madam Dundas would turn in her grave were she to suspect how things were ordered nowadays in the stately old mansion where she had lived so long.

Miss Hester Bickerdyke, in particular, was not without an uneasy feeling that Marcia was not just the sort of playmate for Dorothy. Miss Hester admired Marcia, and pitied her even more than she admired her; but did Marcia offer a good example for Dorothy to follow? That was the question. There was a little couplet the children were fond of repeating when together, —

> "If I'm I, and you's you,
> What do we care, who's who?"

which came from Marcia, and which displeased Miss Hester. Marcia, poor girl, was somehow

so different from regularly well-brought-up children. Mrs. Dundas was too languid and indifferent to look after her daughter properly.
Marcia's hair was so untidy ; her feet so ill-shod.
Then, too, she grew so fast that she was constantly getting beyond her clothes. Miss Hester
would give a glance at the skirt of her frock and
say in a freezing tone, —

" Your dress is too short, Marcia."

However Marcia might suffer under the
*douche* of Miss Hester's disapproval, she never
showed it, but would reply, —

" I 'm going up like Alice in Wonderland
after she drank out of the bottle. 'Good-by,
feet,' " and Marcia would look down at her
shabby shoes and laugh ruefully.

To Miss Hester, as well as to other Swallowfield people, not to have a regular meal set
out three times a day ; not to have washing on
Monday, ironing on Tuesday, clearing up generally on Wednesday, doing the bedrooms
Thursday, the living - rooms Friday, and the
altogether, including baking, on Saturday, was
flat heresy and schism. Perhaps Mrs. Dundas
was equally of that way of thinking, and might
herself have liked to have things decently and
in order : obsequious servants, tradespeople calling regularly and taking orders respectfully,

knowing that there was always a big balance at
the banker's to settle all accounts. The poor
lady's dream was probably of just what Swallowfield people demanded of the Dundases. All
that and more was to come to pass as soon as
Paul Dundas made the fortune he was working
for. Then Marcia would enjoy the advantages
she had so far missed.

Marcia, meantime, could not, like her mother,
live in the past and in the future, but tried to
make the most of the present. Life was full of
disappointments, troubles, and humiliations for
her, but she was too much interested in what
she had to do to think of any personal vexation
beyond the moment. She was never contented
to be still ; she must always be doing something.
She was scornful of Lucy's and Dorothy's playing with paper dolls.

" Such mean things," she declared ; " you can't
even hug 'em ! " Yet, taking the scissors out of
the little girls' hands, she would fashion the
most wonderful dolls and dresses out of tissue
paper. If she saw Gay reading, down went
Marcia on the floor beside him and devoured the
page with him. To read was for Marcia instantly to long to put into action all she had
read. Whatever other people had done, she
believed she could dare and do. Why not? Had

anybody that ever lived had more than eyes,
ears, and a brain behind the eyes and ears;
hands and feet, and a will to govern hands and
feet?

Marcia's attendance at school was rather irreg-
ular. She was one of the older pupils at Miss
Pratt's, where Gay and Lucy went. She was
no prodigy of learning, and, bright as she was in
practical matters, in certain of her studies she
found no little difficulty. But Marcia's theory
was that if one needed to do a thing, why, one
did it. When she was obliged to grasp some
intricate bit of knowledge, as, for example, that
seven times nine made sixty-three, she grasped it
with both her hands, as it were. Then when she
correspondingly made out that nine times seven
also made sixty-three, she put up the white flag;
and when Dorothy, who was on the watch, crept
through the gap in the hedge, Marcia ran towards her with sparkling eyes, threw her arms
about her, and cried, —

"Oh, Dorothy! I wanted to tell you."

"Well, what?"

Dorothy was not so far advanced in mathe-
matics, hence she was very proud indeed at
being initiated into the wonderful mystery of
seven times nine making sixty-three, and nine
times seven also making sixty-three. Marcia

found Dorothy most sympathetic in receiving impressions. Dorothy, indeed, picked up a great many bits of information, and was herself inclined benevolently to pass them on. Once she said to Miss Hester, —

"Aunt Hester, did you know that a thousand is just ten hundred?"

"Yes," Miss Hester replied, "I know so much."

"I thought perhaps you had n't happened to hear it," said Dorothy, a little disappointed. Accordingly it was John Pearson whom she asked if he were aware of the fact that anything you could see or hear or taste or touch or smell was a noun.

"A noun?" said John. "What's a noun?"

"That is what I am telling you," Dorothy answered. "Anything you can see or hear or taste or touch or smell is a noun."

"How did you happen to hear that?" inquired John skeptically.

"Marcia told me."

"Marcia's smart," John conceded. "Do you mean that this here snow-shovel I'm making paths with is a noun?"

"Yes," said Dorothy. "And your pipe, too, that's a noun."

John took his pipe out of his mouth.

"I can see it an' taste it an' " —

"Smell it," suggested Dorothy.

"Curious now, I never thought of my pipe's being a noun," John observed, gazing at the piece of clay affectionately. "It does seem to make things clearer, don't it now?"

"Yes, everything almost is a noun," Dorothy pursued. "The shed there, that's a noun, and the window and the trees and the snow" —

"That is, the snow is a noun till it melts, I suppose?" observed John. He was clearing away the last night's snowfall, and Dorothy was helping him.

This query about the snow quite staggered Dorothy. She said she would ask Marcia. Here was the snow now, — they could see it, taste it, touch it; but suppose a thaw were to set in, — what then? Could a noun melt and absolutely vanish out of sight?

"I tell you," said John Pearson, rather proud of having upset a theory, "people, that is some people, know a good deal, but they don't know everything."

"Marcia does," insisted Dorothy; "that is, almost everything."

"I tell you, Dorothy," said John impressively, "it's hard work to know everything. Marcia may know a thing or two more than most people, but she can't know everything."

"Oh yes she can," retorted Dorothy.

Mrs. Deane's Christmas holiday had ended the day after Christmas. Dorothy was more used to having her mother away from her than with her; still it was always the same dreadful, dreary settling down to things when Mrs. Deane went away. Now Dorothy began to look forward to Easter, when there would be one or two happy days again.

Dorothy's life went on in this wise : breakfast at a quarter before eight ; then at nine o'clock a bell rang and Dorothy sat down at her desk in Miss Hester's room and studied her lessons until a quarter to ten, when she was called to read and spell. Next came a recess of an hour, which in pleasant weather she spent with John Pearson out of doors, and in bad weather playing in her own room or talking to Jerusha in the kitchen. An hour and a half of lessons followed, and that brought the day almost up to dinner-time. After dinner Dorothy sat for three quarters of an hour with Mrs. Bickerdyke, and learned to sew or darn or knit, — "something really useful," as the old lady said. According to Mrs. Bickerdyke, all the evils of the last quarter of the nineteenth century might safely be laid to the fact that instead of spending all their time at their needle, women nowadays go gadding about from morning till night. Not even snowstorms, blizzards, or deluges of rain can keep them at home, for every one of them has rubber-shoes, waterproofs, mackintoshes, and umbrellas. Mrs. Bickerdyke's wish was to bring Dorothy up in the good old-fashioned way, and it would be no fault of hers if the little girl did not know how to stitch, hem, fell, over-and-over, gather, whip, make button-holes, embroider, quilt, and darn.

Dorothy used to like to hear grandmamma Bickerdyke's stories about what was done, and how it was done, when she was a girl. When the task at her needle was accomplished, she sometimes was taken by Miss Hester to visit sick and poor people. Miss Hester, as we have seen, liked to stir the spirit of self-sacrifice. More than once, after she had asked Dorothy to choose the kind of pudding for Jerusha to make for dinner, she would say when it was put on the table, —

"I think we will eat rice and sugar and milk for our dessert, and take this tapioca cream to Johnnie Long."

Constant habits of disappointments like this developed gradually in Dorothy's mind a feeling of suspense as to whether anything dangled temptingly before her eyes was really to be hers.

But she soon learned philosophically to console herself for the loss of her favorite pudding by thinking of Johnnie Long's enjoyment of it.

In going to see poor people, Dorothy liked best to have a nice pudding or a doll or a paint-box to take along. For when Miss Hester gave nothing but good advice, the poor people did not seem to appreciate their visits so much. Everybody knows that it is more blessed to give than to receive good advice. The point Miss Hester particularly insisted on was that everybody should be clean. She did not believe that godliness was even possible until people were clean. After they had scrubbed and scoured their beds, their tables, their floors, their clothes, and themselves, then there was some chance of physical and spiritual improvement. There were not a great many destitute people in Swallowfield. Mrs. Vance and the shiftless Porters with their ten children were the worst off, and it was for their benefit that Miss Hester preached her sermons on the efficacy of soap and water.

Dorothy and Mrs. Bickerdyke had been making some clothes for Mrs. Vance, and when they were all finished Dorothy went with Miss Hester to give them to the poor woman. They found her sitting over her stove, in her dingy little room, drinking tea.

Miss Hester explained that they had brought her two whole suits of nice fresh underclothing.

" Now, Mrs. Vance," she proceeded, " I want you to take a bath and put these on."

" Take what?" questioned Mrs. Vance grimly.

" A bath, — a good all-over bath," said Miss Hester.

" Me take a bath?" returned Mrs. Vance scornfully. " Me wet myself all over? I never did such a thing in all my life."

" It is high time you did," insisted Miss Hester. " I wash myself from head to foot the first thing every morning when I get out of bed."

Mrs. Vance glanced at her visitor, then looked away, and said with an air of offended propriety, —

" Well, if I did, I guess I would n't tell of it."

The Porters' ten children were never clean, but Miss Hester hoped that, by beginning early with them, she might enforce ideas of personal cleanliness. Mrs. Bickerdyke's knitted washcloths and cakes of soap were quite thrown away on this family. Once, Miss Hester, in despair, told two or three of the elder girls, whom she was trying to civilize, that she would give them each a penny if they would go home and wash their faces. This powerful argument prevailed over natural instinct, and for months afterwards three or four Porters at a time would ring at Mrs. Bickerdyke's door-bell, send in word that they had washed their faces, and demand payment according to promise.

What Dorothy particularly enjoyed in her home life was having a good talk with Jerusha in the kitchen.

Jerusha had lived with Mrs. Bickerdyke for more than twenty years. She was young and untrained when she entered the house. To Mrs. Bickerdyke, and to Miss Hester as well, there was but one right way in the world and that was their way, and for Jerusha to be initiated into their way was no light experience. John Pearson came into the kitchen one day and said, —

" Here, Jerusha, I want them seeds well soaked, an' I want it done my way."

To John's surprise, Jerusha burst into tears.

" What in goodness is the matter, Jerusha ? " demanded John. " Don't cry."

" I must cry," said Jerusha. " First there 's Mis' Bickerdyke says I must bile water fresh from the well for every cup of tea and coffee I make, — an' make it when it 's just on the bile, — and make it just her way ; then there 's

Miss Hester says I must sweep a room just so,
put my broom down bottom upwards, and then
dust it first with a dry cloth, then with a damp
cloth, besides settin' a table an' waitin' on it her
way, and now here 's you with your ways."

That was twenty years ago. By this time Jerusha had her ways. They governed the house-
hold. Not even Miss Hester ventured to go
against them. The strict rule in the house had
developed in Jerusha's mind an awful conscien-
tiousness. On certain days her general wrath
against moth and dust became a holy crusade.
Before Jerusha's reign, Mrs. Bickerdyke used
to lie in bed and trouble her soul because she
was afraid the maid would not get up in good
season. Nowadays, she lay and wished that
Jerusha would be content to lie in bed a little
later. There were mornings, indeed, when the
old lady trembled at the sound of that step on
the stair. When it gave forth a certain martial
tread, she knew that Jerusha would turn her
out of her warm, comfortable room that day
and sweep it and wash it and polish it and
garnish it.

Dorothy knew all Jerusha's ways; all the
signs of the weather. She had only to peep
into the kitchen to know whether it promised a
happy haven, or whether the domestic ship was,

as it were, scudding under bare poles, with no friendly beacon in sight. When the washing and ironing were over; when the house was clean from top to bottom; when the silver was rubbed, the glass polished; when there were six loaves of bread, three of brown and three of white, in the box; three kinds of cakes and as many of pies in the store-room, and shelves on shelves of preserves, jams, and jellies, then Jerusha was a peaceful person to live with. There was a low, wooden rocking-chair, painted black with gilt markings, in which several generations of Bickerdyke children had sat, that used to be placed on a certain round braided rug for Dorothy when all things suited. Dorothy had great comfort in that chair, gently swaying to and fro, watching Jerusha, who was always doing something; listening to the comfortable noises of the kitchen, the burning of the fire, the sissing of the tea-kettle, the ticking of the clock, the purring of Rory O'More, the cat. Jerusha was no talker, but she could listen. Everything that passed in Dorothy's mind, everything she had said and done, and what Marcia, Lucy, and Gay had said and done, was translated into speech for Jerusha's benefit. Mrs. Bickerdyke used to complain sometimes, and with good reason, that Dorothy did not tell her everything; but with

her grandmamma, somehow, there seemed to be
so little that was worth telling, whereas with
Jerusha each thought and fancy and hope and
memory seemed to have a life of its own, —
wings, feet, and a voice, — and would make its
way out.

Really that sense of repose, of intimate com-
panionship, which Dorothy felt in the kitchen
with Jerusha, was as pleasant as a down pillow.
Jerusha was not, to Dorothy's thinking, exactly
handsome, but she had the nicest face in the
world. It was full of little knobs, as it were,
and each one took on a high polish. Her eyes
were small, but they were wonderfully bright.
They seemed to have no brows nor lashes, —
really they were very odd little eyes, but they
could twinkle and snap with fun. Her cheeks
shone like a streaked red apple which has been
rubbed hard. Her hair was black and of the
glossy sort, and it was Jerusha's way to pack it
all in one small knot on top of her head, giving the effect of a big button. Her lips always
looked as if her mind were quite made up, but
a queer, grim smile for Dorothy was generally
lurking somewhere about the mouth.

Jerusha was proud of her laundry work; she
was proud of her sweeping and cleaning; she
was proud of the rugs she braided; but the one

thing she excelled most people in she had no
pride about. She was a capital cook, but, to her
thinking, cooking came by nature. She helped
a little, as John Pearson helped the flowers.
" But, laws! they grow and they blow of their-
selves," she would have said.

Marcia had learned more than one trick of
cooking from Jerusha. Marcia, too, was a born
cook. Jerusha liked to roast a good piece of
meat, to cook vegetables, bake bread, and the
like; but what she loved to do was to make cake.
At the sight of butter, eggs, flour, sugar, clean
bowls, a stirring-dish, spoons of different sizes,
and buttered tins, life became to Jerusha sheer
satisfaction and pleasure. She used to think
out the kinds of cake she was to make days
beforehand. It was her joy to make angel cake;
perhaps on account of the associations. She did
not actually believe that angels in heaven ate
that particular variety of cake, but, as she and
Dorothy agreed, they might have done so with
satisfaction. Dorothy sincerely hoped they did.
Angel cake was for occasions, — like fruit cake,
raised loaf cake, pound cake, cake made in layers
with fillings of chocolate, cocoanut, whipped
cream, nuts, bananas, and oranges. These choice
confections were for company times. For other
times there was sponge cake, ginger cake, and a

Dutch cake, that is, a particularly delicate bread sweetened slightly and with a few raisins. Of course, there was always a loaf of rich cake in the closet to offer to casual guests.

But what most nearly appealed to Dorothy was Jerusha's little round cakes. In the dark pantry stood two huge stone jars, which every Saturday afternoon were filled to the brim, one with crisp and the other with soft cakes. Few of these ever went to the table, yet by the following Friday the contents of these jars had grown so

"Small by degrees and beautifully less"

one had really to go down to the very depths to find a cake. Who the "forty thieves" were that got into these jars may be guessed at. Even Carlo and Flossy knew where the cakes they loved came from, and, if they could find their way into Jerusha's kitchen, would stand and gaze at the door of that pantry as if they expected it to open of its own accord.

The children were always trying to decide which variety of Jerusha's "cookies" was the best. There was one crisp kind, cut in heart-shapes, full of currants and sprinkled on top with sugar, of which they never tired. Another, thicker, softer kind, with scallops, contained caraway seeds; Lucy decided that this was her favorite. Gay liked a soft, thick, cinnamon cake, sweetened with molasses; there was such a richness and depth of flavor to it. Dorothy had a fancy for what Jerusha called " Fairy Drops," — delicate, delicious, wafery things, with a dab of frosting on top; but there was another sort, with jam, which was even more delicious. The trouble about the richer ones, with jam or frosting, was that one could not eat so many. The little plain ones with caraway seeds one could go on munching endlessly. Marcia liked all kinds of Jerusha's cakes, some for one thing, others for another. Even Herbert Lee, Lucy's and Gay's brother, a boy of thirteen years, and, to their thinking, almost, if not quite, grown up, who hardly ever confessed that he approved of anything, did not disdain Jerusha's cakes.

" Halloo," he would say, " what 's this? " when he came upon the children having afternoon tea with milk and water and cakes. And, taking two or three of the cakes abstractedly, as if he did not know what he was doing, he would walk away, eating them with an air of contempt rather than relish, then come back, and absent-mindedly gather up another handful. The children were pleased to observe that Bert was not too proud to eat the cakes, but his condescension

seriously scrimped their own measure. With
only Marcia, Gay, Lucy, Dorothy, and the two
dogs, the stone jars were easily emptied. Bert's
appetite, added to theirs, soon created a famine.

Once, when eggs seemed plentiful, Jerusha
made an angel cake, and told Dorothy she could
take it over to Marcia's mother. Dorothy had
rarely seen Mrs. Dundas, but now, finding no
one in the kitchen or in the hall, she had no
other resource than to make her way up the
stairs and tap at the door of the great south
room where Mrs. Dundas spent her solitary life.

"Come in," said a voice.

Dorothy, holding the cake in one hand, with
the other tried to turn the knob of the door, but
in vain. In another minute the door opened
from inside, and a tall, pale lady, with dark
hair and eyes, stood looking down at her.

"Who is this?" she asked.

"Dorothy Deane," replied Dorothy. "I've
brought you an angel cake."

Mrs. Dundas took the cake from Dorothy and
set it on the table. Then she leaned down and
kissed Dorothy.

"Come in," she said. "Marcia will be back
presently." Dorothy entered the great room
with a sort of awe. Mrs. Dundas had gathered
about her much of what the great house offered

in the way of comfort or of luxury. There were
pictures on the walls, pictures propped up
against the wainscot, pictures in chairs; books
innumerable in the cases and lying about in
piles. There was an open fireplace with a few
logs burning, and in front of it two armchairs.
In the corner was a large divan covered with
rugs and piled with cushions. It seemed to Dorothy as if this tall, stately, languid lady had
been reclining there.

Mrs. Dundas sat down in one of the armchairs and motioned to her visitor to take the
other, but Dorothy preferred the footstool. The
two looked at each other for a moment in silence,
then Mrs. Dundas said, —

" You are all so good to Marcia."

" Oh, no ! " exclaimed Dorothy in surprise.
" It 's Marcia that 's good to us."

Mrs. Dundas smiled; a peculiar, melancholy
smile.

" One of these days," she said, " I hope that
Marcia will be in a position to do something for
her young friends who give her so much pleasure. Just now we are only living from day to
day, waiting to hear some good news from
Mr. Dundas."

" Yes, ma'am," said Dorothy softly.

Her eyes traveled round the room.

"Do you like it here?" inquired Mrs. Dundas.

"It's the most beautiful room I ever saw," answered Dorothy.

"Is it?" said Mrs. Dundas. She smiled again. "It's my prison, you know," she added, "and when one is in prison one longs to escape from it."

Dorothy gazed at her in surprise. She had such very different ideas of a prison.

"Let me see," Mrs. Dundas now observed; "your mamma is away."

"Yes, ma'am," said Dorothy. "She is a teacher in a school."

"She must miss you very much," said Mrs. Dundas. "At any rate, I have my Marcia, if I have nothing else."

She looked at Dorothy with such a deep, steady gaze, Dorothy felt as if something oppressed her.

"I had better go now," she said, rising.

"Very well. Thank you for the cake. Good-by, dear."

Mrs. Dundas put her arms round the little girl and folded her in a close embrace.

"I pity your mother," she said; "she must miss you."

When Dorothy told Jerusha about her visit,

Jerusha was at first inclined to feel aggrieved
that her angel cake had not been received with
more enthusiasm. But John Pearson, who happened to be sitting by the stove, said, —

"It comes hard to Dundas pride to receive.
They used to give."

Dorothy had almost as much comfort in John
Pearson as in Jerusha. She could always de-
pend on John. He had no ups and downs. He
lived on the hill, in a neat little place of his
own. He had lost his wife about a year before
the beginning of our story, an excellent, hard-
working woman, who had helped him in every
way for almost thirty years, and had brought up
a family of four children, of whom three, two
daughters and a son, were living at home at the
time of her death.

Miss Hester had taken Dorothy with her
when she went to condole with the family on the
death of Mrs. Pearson.

"It is a very great loss," said Miss Hester.
"It is a terrible thing to lose a good mother."

"Yes, an' she were the very best o' mothers,"
answered Jemima Pearson. "You may well
say, Miss Bickerdyke, it is a turrible thing to
lose her. Then, you see, Miss Bickerdyke, we
be so taken aback, as it were. It's such a surprise! For we always planned, Miss Bickerdyke, that father should go first."

John Pearson was not present when this conversation took place, but he had, perhaps, gathered the idea from other discourses that his daughter felt as if the lot had fallen to the wrong person. He was for a time considerably dazed; liked to sit in the sunshine and muse, to the neglect of his work. Miss Hester waited, then saw that John had regathered his forces, and was displaying almost more than his old energy as he went at his hoeing and weeding.

"I am glad to see, John," Miss Hester then observed, "that you are taking your trouble in the right way."

"Why, yes, ma'am," said John. "I did n't at first rightly understand it."

"Now you have made up your mind to submit cheerfully."

"Why, yes, ma'am," John replied. "You see, Miss Hester, she wor always the best kind of a care-taking wife; always on the lookout to make things comfortable for me like. An' this is just a fulfillin' o' Scripter."

"How so?"

"What her feelin' was," said John, "was to go like the dove out of the ark and find me a dry place."

In bad weather John had a safe retreat in the loft of the old unused stables at Mrs. Bickerdyke's. Dorothy and indeed all the children liked to join him there, especially in fruit time, for pears, apples, and even bunches of grapes were apt to be forthcoming.

Sometimes on spring days a shower would overtake John while he was planting the garden, with Dorothy helping, and at such times they would both run to this shelter. John would mend and polish his tools, look after his seeds started in boxes, while Dorothy, perched on the high window-ledge, would watch the sunshine and clouds chase each other across the fields, and listen to the drip, drip, drip on the roof.

John was not a great reader, but he knew one book by heart, "Masterman Ready;" and at such times he liked to repeat a chapter out of it.

"Oh, John," Dorothy would cry, "should n't you like to be cast away on an island?"

"I hain't never had no such chances," John would reply.

It might happen, Dorothy argued. Almost everybody sooner or later went to sea, and why might they not be shipwrecked? Thus the subject of their being castaways was always open to discussion.

"I suppose we should all have to go," said Dorothy.

"I should say," suggested John, "not speak-

ing in a disrespectful manner to no person, that
they ought to be all hale and hearty, and
rather young."

"You feel as if, perhaps, grandmamma
would n't do?" said Dorothy.

"And I don't feel as if Miss Hester would
rightly like it," John pursued.

"We should have to have Jerusha to cook,"
pleaded Dorothy; "but how could we take her
away from aunt Hester and grandmamma?"

John would not commit himself on this point,
but Dorothy had a feeling that what he really
wanted was the party of castaways she herself
wanted; namely, herself, John Pearson, Lucy
and Gay, and Marcia. Yet how could they get
on without Jerusha?

# CHAPTER VI

It takes a great many different kinds of snowstorms to make a New England winter. There had been flurries which blew the snow into the ditches and hedges and so amounted to nothing; there had been soft, wet, slushy snows that melted almost as soon as they came; there had been a white, blinding, drifting cloud out of doors which nobody could see through, but which piled itself in the wrong places and left the right spots bare. But on the twenty-fifth of January came a wonderful sort of snow-storm, — the sort which promises sleighing and sledding and coasting for weeks to come. First it rained and snowed together, then hailed and froze the whole mass solid. But that was only the beginning. Next it snowed steadily for twenty-four hours, without a breath of wind to disturb it, and afterwards it rained a little while it was clearing off. Finally came a cold wind out of the northwest, and oh, how cold it was, and what a beautiful crust it made on the deep, deep snow!

Marcia had kept the black flag flying all through this snowstorm, and Dorothy and Lucy and Gay had felt a little remorseful for their own joy in the snow. Marcia did not like snow. In fact, the rigors of winter tried her soul in a variety of ways, bringing home to her a sense of the deprivations at which she could snap her fingers in pleasant weather. It was a point of honor with Dorothy, Lucy, and Gay to believe all Marcia said; but when she said she did not like to slide down hill, it did occur to them that she was merely trying to make the best of it, and that, if she only had a sled —

So when on that bright, crisp, clear afternoon, Dorothy with her sled, and Lucy with her sled, and Gay with his sled were all going down the slope in the Lee orchard, then climbing up again, in spite of the joy of it, there was still a little wistful feeling which pulled at their hearts. Not even the black flag had been seen flying from the oriel window to-day. Marcia, almost for the first time they could remember, had given them no sort of an invitation to " come over." What could she be doing ? What could she be feeling ?

They had been coasting for more than an hour; first Lucy, then Gay, then Dorothy ; then Gay took the lead, and finally Dorothy. The hill

was not steep; their sleds did not go at light-
ning speed; but still it was all pleasant and
would have been delightful if the thought of
Marcia — sitting at home without any sled —
had not disturbed their hearts and consciences.

The sun was by this time near the horizon in
the centre of a bright flare of red and gold in
the southwest sky. All round the horizon was
a belt of rose color shading into violet, and in
the east hung a great yellow moon about full.

" I suppose it's almost time to go in," observed Lucy, as, when they reached the foot of
the hill, they all gathered the strings of their
sleds into their hands and prepared to mount
again.

" Th—th—th— " began Gay.

" Count three, Gay," said Lucy.

Gay could n't stop to count three, he was so
excited. He pointed to the top of the hill.

" Oh, Marcia," cried Dorothy, " I 'm so glad
you 've come."

" So am I," said Lucy.

" I, too," faltered Gay.

The three toiled up the slippery slope, tum-
bling over each other in their effort to reach
Marcia. She was not looking unhappy in the
least; on the contrary, her eyes were sparkling,
her cheeks were glowing, and her lips smiling.

It began to dawn on the children that there was something unusual, something almost magnificent about her appearance, for she was dressed in red from top to toe, — red bordered with gray fur. Her frock was red, her jacket was red, and so was her cap. If they had not been afraid it might not be polite, they would have said, " How grand you are, Marcia ! "

As it was, they only stared, until Marcia, understanding their dumb admiration, called, —

" Did you ever see anything so splendid ? "

As she asked this she laughed, but still it was clear that she had pride and joy in her new clothes.

" Beautiful," said Dorothy. " I never did see you look so beautiful, Marcia."

" Where did they come from ? " inquired Lucy.

" Out of the camphor chests up in the garret," said Marcia. " Mamma was shivering, don't you see ; I said, ' I 'm going to find something warm to wrap you in.' I took a bunch of keys and went upstairs. Almost the first one I tried turned the lock of the chest, and there on top, wrapped in paper, was a great fur cloak, beaver outside and squirrel inside. I ran downstairs and said, ' Here 's a rabbit-skin to wrap my baby up in ! ' Mamma stared and asked,

'Whose is that?' I told her it was mine.
Whose else could it be? Except papa, I'm the
only Dundas there is left in the world. Mamma
laughed, put it on, and said she was delightfully
comfortable. So I went rummaging for myself
and I found this." She turned herself round for
their inspection. "We had to rip it and clip it
and sew it up again," she explained. "Then
mamma made me the cap out of the odds and
ends."

She was in such high spirits that she needed
something on which to spend them.

"Now, if I had a sled," she exclaimed.
"Sometimes I think coasting is poor fun, but
this is such a splendid, deep snow."

"Oh, Marcia," cried Dorothy, "take mine."

"Take mine," said Lucy.

"T—t—take mine," stammered Gay.

Marcia looked at the offering of their sleds
with a half-disdainful shrug.

"They're so little," she returned. "I'm too
long-legged for them. What I want is a great
long sled with steel runners."

"Like Bert's," suggested Gay on the instant.

"Yes, Bert's is something like a sled," confessed Marcia.

"And Bert isn't using his," Dorothy burst
out; "he has gone over to Rosemaryport."

" Bert never likes anybody to touch his things," observed Lucy in a cautious tone, for she saw the sudden gleam that came into Gay's face.

" I don't care," said Gay, and was off like a flash. Marcia seemed not to know what Gay had gone for, but Dorothy knew and was pleased ; Lucy also knew, and was awestruck, not to say a little frightened. Marcia, never at a loss, began to tell the girls what she had been doing all through the snowstorm, but long before she had come to the end of her story, Gay appeared dragging a toboggan-sled.

" Is that Bert's ? " Marcia inquired, taking possession of it on the instant. " I 'll do something for you one of these days, Gay."

They all felt that if Bert had seen Marcia at this moment with her red, fur-trimmed dress and jacket and cap, even he would not have been displeased, for, with the colors of the sunset lighting her up in her red frock, Marcia was really a dazzling spectacle.

" Let me go," cried Marcia, and off she went, the sled flying as if it were alive, and carrying her far across the orchard, even up a little on the opposite bank.

The others gazed at her with admiration. They had been contented with their own modest

doings, taking the descent gently, with little
shoves to encourage their progress.   But who
could expect Marcia to be so easily satisfied?

"Oh, this is n't high enough; it is n't steep
enough!" she cried.  "Let 's go over to Bishop's
Hill."

Gay, being a boy, liked the idea of going to
slide down Bishop's Hill.   But being a "twin,"
and the other half of him, as it were, being a
girl, he had to repress a great many of his
yearnings.   Now, what Lucy said was, —

"Oh, Marcia, it 's so late!  It 's time to go
home."

"Home?   It won't be tea-time for an hour
and a half or more," Marcia declared.   "There
is time enough to do anything."

And at this moment the church clock struck
five.

The sun was down, but the afterglow lighted
up the sky in the west, and in the east the great
round moon was growing brighter each moment.

"Leave your sleds here," said Marcia; "we
will take them on the way back.  Now, Dorothy,
you and Lucy jump on the big one, and Gay
and I will drag you."

Marcia's quiet decision settled the matter, not
only satisfactorily to her own mind, but to Dor-

othy's and the twins'. She could not only put spirit into them, but a feeling of emulation and a desire to act up to her requirements of them. Not to like to do what Marcia wished to do was to be poor, tame, paltry. Accordingly, Dorothy and Lucy, each with a demure, smiling look, seated themselves on the sled. It frightened them both a little to think of the big sled and the long hill.

"I hope," whispered Lucy, — "I hope I shan't be much afraid."

"I don't mean to be afraid if I can help it," Dorothy replied.

Marcia and Gay, taking hold of the rope, dashed along the orchard, the sled swinging this way and that behind them, more than once almost running against the trunk of an apple-tree. They thought it was such fun that Lucy and Dorothy, who had at first held on with all their might, feeling as if they might be thrown off, also began to pluck up a spirit. Presently the orchard was left behind; they crossed the quiet road and reached the foot of the hill, which on its north side had a long, gradual incline. Marcia and Gay were now forced to stop for want of breath, so Dorothy and Lucy said they would drag the sled up the hill, and off they set, Marcia and Gay lagging behind.

The village boys and girls had been sliding here all day, so that the way was well worn. But at this moment everybody had gone home, and it was as if there were nobody in the whole wide world except these four, under the great dome of sky which every minute filled more and more with the broad white light of the moon. It really seemed to Dorothy that they had entered a new world altogether. Of course that was the same moon that looked into her window at home, yet somehow it had not a home-like look. If Marcia had not been there, she would have been afraid. As it was, even while she trembled a little, she liked the wonderful whiteness that covered the river, the bridge, the far-off hills. In the southwest was still an arc of rosy and golden light, but everything else was spotlessly white. Even the branches of the trees were laden with snow. Dorothy could not feel quite comfortable. The greatness and far-offness of the sky touched her with a sense of awe. The utter silence (for their voices did not seem to break the silence) weighed upon her. She felt as if they were intruding upon this world of snow and ice and sunset and moon-light, yet, all the same, there was a little intoxication in the idea that whether or no she ought to be here she was here; and that hereafter, when she saw the moon shining in at her window, she would know what it was doing in these wide, lonely places.

" Is n't this perfectly splendid ? " exclaimed Marcia, when they had all reached the top of the hill and stood taking a long, deep breath of satisfaction. " Does n't it seem as if the whole world belonged to us ? "

Marcia did not, however, stop long to muse over the silent stretches of untrodden snow. She had taken possession of Bert's toboggan and established herself in front.

" Now, Dorothy," she said, " you sit next to me, and then comes Lucy. Gay will push off, and then jump on behind."

Everything went beautifully. Gay put his hands on the toboggan, ran with it a few steps, gave one violent shove, then sprang to the end of the seat, clasping Lucy, who in turn put her arms about Dorothy, who had hold of Marcia. Marcia steered, and the sled, not once swerving, ran with a not too swift but pleasant motion down the long inclined plane, stopping at the base in a sensible, moderate way. Then all together they pulled it up, and took the same slide once more.

" Now, Gay," said Marcia, " you steer and I 'll push it off."

Marcia gave the sled a powerful start, and off they went at twice their former pace. Dorothy and even Lucy had by this time quite warmed to the sport; and now, as the keen wind cut in their faces as they made this headlong rush, they tasted the joy of doing something wild and adventurous. The feeling of success, besides the sense of quickened vitality, put Marcia a little beside herself. She danced, she frisked up the hill, and they all danced and frisked.

"Don't you wish," she cried, "that the whole world did belong to us; that we were just by ourselves, and could go on always doing just as we wanted to?"

"How should we get anything to eat?" inquired Lucy.

"Oh, we'd kill bears and things, just as the men do when they go to the north pole," Marcia answered. "I'll be a bear." She went down on her hands and knees and began coming towards them with loud roars. Gay immediately followed suit, and went down on all fours. Dorothy and Lucy had to endure this double attack, and drag the sled up-hill at the same time that, on their two legs, they ran away from the bears, who, after waddling about a little longer and spending their breath in strange noises, came after them.

"I'll tell you what we will do," said Marcia, always eager to do a little more.   "We'll have one slide down the west side."

Now the angle on the west side was very steep.

"See how splendidly it goes," Marcia cried, picking up a little block of ice and snow and sending it spinning.   The east side of the hill also dropped away suddenly, and was, besides, broken by groups of cedar-trees; a fence, too, ran across it.   Here on the west, however, was no visible break or impediment, and after the first ridge was passed there came a long series of easy slopes, over which, so Marcia explained, the sled, after gaining its first powerful impetus, would bound like a bird.

"I shouldn't wonder," she added, "if we went on clear across the meadow."

Dorothy, Lucy, and Gay felt their spirits rise to Marcia's demands.   It did look steep at first, but they kept their eyes fixed on the farther spaces, where any inequality of surface was lost in the general whiteness.

Marcia now took the front place, put out her feet firmly, and told Dorothy to come close behind her.   Lucy sat next, and Gay was to start them as at first.

"Now, then," cried Marcia, "we're ready, Gay."

Gay was just about to put his hands on the
sled, when — where was it? What had happened? The sled had started off as if it had
life of its own, and went plunging down the
steep grade, leaving Gay behind.

What Marcia thought to herself was that Gay
had overdone the thing. How they did fly!
There — what was that? Had they run against
a rock? For a moment everything seemed to be
in air. The sled had swung halfway round and
for a while went on sidewise. Then came another bounce. Marcia had to hold on with both
hands; but there, it had righted itself!

" Now we 're all right," said Marcia.

She was all right, for the sled was now career-
ing on at a high rate of speed, taking the billows
of snow smoothly as a ship rides the waves.
The runners glided on with a soft, hissing sound,
pleasant to hear.

" Here we go ! " Marcia said again, laughing;
for by this time the sled was almost half across
the wide meadow.

" Here we come ! " she said again, and here
she came, indeed, hard up against the fence.
Had it not been for the fence, she was ready to
believe the sled would have gone on over the
railroad, down the lane, and across the river.

Marcia had longed to accomplish this wonderful feat, and now gathered herself up and turned with pride to say to the others, " Did n't I tell you so ? "

She had been so busy holding on with feet and hands, and trying to keep the course of the sled straight, that she had not found out until this moment that she was the only passenger. Nothing but the white moon and the faint, far-off stars was looking at her. She gazed stupe-fied over the great shining plain of snow behind her, on which she could not see one single moving object.

" Where are you all ? " she ejaculated, trying to make her voice heard ; but only a faint sound came, which returned to her ears with a derisive echo.

She began the walk back, but to pull the sled across that slippery, shining waste of ice and snow was a dreary affair. Where could the children be ? Were they hiding ? There was nowhere to hide. There was no shadow any-where ; all was open before her like the face of a clock.

" Where are you ? " she shouted.

Was that the echo, or did she hear a faint whoop ?

Far above her rose the summit of the hill, white and symmetrical, the sky-line sweeping

sharply against the sky, here and there taking on
a halo of misty gold where some point caught
the light.

Was something moving there? On she
toiled, slipping, sometimes falling, again sliding; occasionally helping herself across a level
place by throwing herself across the sled, giving
it a push, and thus covering a good bit of the
distance. She was obliged to round the hill to
the base of the long incline, for to climb up
the steep side down which she had come looked
like climbing up the side of a house; and presently she saw two little figures coming down
to meet her.

"Well!" said Marcia, pausing. "Well!"

She expected that the two, whom she gradually
identified as Gay and Lucy, would account for
themselves. What they said, however, was,
"Where's Dorothy?"

"Where's Dorothy," repeated Marcia blankly.
"Don't you know?"

"I supposed she stayed with you," said Lucy.

Each began to explain to the others what had
happened. Nobody quite understood, but all
three wished to exonerate themselves from any
share of blame. The sled had started off of its
own accord and on its own account, Gay said.
He had no chance to get on. Then Lucy, miss-

ing him, had turned round, and, in doing so, had
fallen off, and, being only a little way down the
hill, had gone back to Gay. When she looked
again at the sled, it was far away in the distance,
— a mere speck on the snow. They had supposed that Dorothy was with Marcia.

"She was n't with me," declared Marcia.
"Where can she be?"

"Let's call," said Lucy.

They all called, "Dorothy, Dorothy, Dorothy!"

How awful the silence was! How terrible the
face of the moon! How cold it had grown!
They all trembled and shivered as they stood
listening. There was something in the dead
quiet of the world under the skies which frightened them all.

"Oh, here's John Pearson," Marcia exclaimed suddenly. "Oh, John, we 've lost Dorothy!"

Now what had happened to Dorothy was that
when the sled struck the side of a rock halfway
down the hill, it careened for a moment, and
Dorothy, whose hold upon Marcia had not had
time to tighten itself, had bounded off and
slipped smoothly the whole length of the hill,
finally settling down in a hollow between two
snowbanks. She was slightly stunned, and lay

there for some minutes without any clear consciousness. Then she had a sensation of cold,
and thought to herself that the bed-clothes had
fallen off her, for she supposed she was in her
little bed at home. She reached out her hand
to draw up the blanket, but did not find it. No
matter; she felt rather comfortable. She would
go to sleep again.

Who was that calling? She half started up.
Was it aunt Hester? Then that odd, drowsy
feeling quite overpowered her. Again she heard
voices, and this time they did call " Dorothy."
Every faculty and sense were now on the instant
sharply awake, and for the first time she opened
her eyes. Where was she? What was it?
The great shining sky and the white snow surprised her.

" I wonder if it 's heaven ? " Dorothy said to
herself. She turned over and the moon shone
full in her face. She sat up and tried to think ;
then, feeling very queer, sank back.

" Oh, here she be," said a familiar voice.
" I 've found her," the same voice called loudly
to somebody farther off.

A figure not only bent over her, but gathered
her to itself. Something clasped her.

" Are you hurt, Dorothy ? " somebody inquired.

"Oh, no, not at all, thank you," she tried to reply, but could n't quite be sure whether she really said it. It was pleasant to feel warmer, and she had no difficulty in going off to sleep. It was rather disagreeable to feel that the light was shining brightly on her face. She was surrounded by little figures pressing up to her. Somebody kissed her.

"Why, Lucy," Dorothy said now, with a feeble little laugh, "you are crying." She laughed again. "Why, Marcia's crying too," she added, surprised. "I did n't know Marcia ever cried."

Dorothy must again have dropped asleep, for something roused her.

"Let her be," said John Pearson. "Of course I 'd ought to tell. I tell you, Miss Marcia Dundas, you 're old enough to know better. She 's a tender little critter to be led into mischief."

"Now, John Pearson," argued Marcia, "you say Dorothy is n't hurt, and if she is n't hurt, why, there 's no harm done."

"But you had n't ought to "—

"I tell you, John Pearson, the children wanted to do it just as much as I did. Did n't you, children ? "

"Yes," Dorothy observed unexpectedly.

"Well," said John, "you had n't ought, —

but laws! I've been young, myself, once. An'
bein' young, a young thing is still old enough
to know it's alive and wants to do things, and
there's no great harm done if it's nothin' actually wrong. We've got to buy our expe'unce,
an' buy it dear, somehow. Suppose you does
somethin' foolish at the time, if it's not wrong,
it finally grows to be a comfort. If it ain't a
comfort, it's an awful misery. For what we do
when we're little, we do for life, — we don't forget. When I was a boy, up to home, I used to
weed flower-beds for Mis' Brown. One day she
had been making cherry bounce, and she called
me and giv' me the cherries she had used to
throw to the pigs. Eatin' was eatin' in those
days, an' I thought wild cherries was pretty
good, — too good to give pigs until I'd had all I
wanted. So I just sat down surruptiously, as
it were, an' ate them cherries until I was satisfied. Then I tried to get up to go and give the
rest to the pigs, but it were actually astonishin'
how quick I set down again. Everythin' seemed
to be whirling round and round, — the sun an'
the sky an' the trees an' the grass an' the
flower-beds. It didn't seem safe to sit on the
bench any more, so I jest fell down on the grass
an' laid hold of it by the roots, for the whole
world was a-whirlin' an' a-turnin' upside down,

and I knew I should fall off if I did n't hold on
tight."

" Why, what was the matter, John Pearson ? "
inquired Marcia.

" I 'm ashamed to say, Miss Marcia, the rum
that them cherries had been soakin' in had gone
to my head.   Now, of course, 't ain't right to be
tipsy, an' 't ain't right to steal wild cherries surruptiously, as it were, but all the same I had
bought my expe'unce.   A man must hev his
expe'unce.   Hevin' hed my expe'unce, I left off.
Ben a teetotaler ever since.   I 'd ben there, and
know'd what 't was like not to be a teetotaler."

Dorothy had partly heard this, and now, when
something began to buzz in her head, she said,
or tried to say, —

" I guess I 've had some cherry bounce."

She opened her eyes, and was surprised to find
herself at home in the kitchen with her head
against Jerusha's shoulder.

" No real harm done," Jerusha was saying.
" She 'll sleep it off.   She was out too long in
the cold.   I 'm glad I sent you after her."

" It 's that Marcia Dundas," John said.

" Children have to learn," observed Jerusha.

" Expe'unce," murmured Dorothy sleepily.
Her feet were warm, now, and she felt wonderfully comfortable.   She kept smiling to herself,

and when Jerusha carried her into the dining-
room and put her in her chair at the table, she
felt very happy at the sight of the hot bread
and milk in her bowl.

"Why, the child's asleep," she heard Mrs.
Bickerdyke say.

"Oh, no," murmured Dorothy, smiling more
than ever. "I'm not asleep."

"Why don't you open your eyes, then, and
eat your supper?"

"I guess I've had some cherry bounce," murmured Dorothy.

"Cherry bounce!" said Mrs. Bickerdyke.
"Cherry bounce! Jerusha, have you been giving
Dorothy cherry bounce?"

"Hain't got none to give," Jerusha replied.
"She's dazed like with the cold. That's what
ails her."

Dorothy tried to sit up. She wanted to eat
the hot bread and milk, but, curiously enough,
her eyelids seemed glued together, still she could
see Mrs. Bickerdyke's white cap and gray puffs
between her closed lids; they looked so far off.

"I c'n see you, grandmamma," Dorothy now
remarked reassuringly.

"She's jest dead with sleepiness," Jerusha
observed. "I'll feed her."

Nothing more was clear to Dorothy's mind

that night.   She had such odd dreams.   Mrs.
Bickerdyke was talking about cherry bounce and
asking if John Pearson could have given it to
Dorothy, when somebody — was it Dorothy? —
replied that John was a teetotaler and had been
ever since he was thirteen years old.   Then presently she was in a warm bath and it felt very
nice.   Somebody was hugging her and kissing
her.   " This must be mamma," Dorothy tried
to say, but oddly enough it was her aunt Hester.

" It must be the cherry bounce," Dorothy said,
for certainly everything seemed so oddly turned
round.   It was n't even her own bed she was in.
It was her aunt Hester's.

# CHAPTER VII

DOROTHY was not quite well the next day, or at least Mrs. Bickerdyke and Miss Hester were afraid she was not well, and accordingly they kept her on the lounge and fed her upon gruel. Miss Hester said she had taken cold. Mrs. Bickerdyke could not free herself from the thought that cherry bounce had something to do with Dorothy's condition. She questioned the little girl on the subject, but, odd to relate, Dorothy could not to-day remember anything about cherry bounce. Everything that had happened yesterday had become very much mixed up in her mind. She slept a great deal, but finally towards evening woke up, feeling quite refreshed and like her usual self.

"Should you like to see Gay and Lucy?" Miss Hester asked her then.

"Oh, yes, please," Dorothy replied.

"And Marcia?"

"Is she here? Oh, please, aunt Hester, I should like so much to see Marcia!"

Marcia and the twins came up and stood in the doorway, at first a little awed, not only by the sight of Dorothy lying bolstered up on the divan by cushions, but at the sight of Miss Hester's beautiful, stately, spotless room, with its white hangings.

"Oh, Dorothy!" said Marcia, bounding forward after that one moment's pause and clasping her arms round the little girl; "you aren't really ill, are you?"

"Oh, no; I'm all well now," Dorothy replied. "I wasn't anything except oh, so sleepy! Somehow I couldn't keep awake."

They all drew a breath of relief, but they all smiled half furtively as they looked at each other. And that smile and that glance meant that they remembered pulling the big sled up the hill; that they remembered how the keen wind had caught their breath as they went down; the white moonlight, too, and the strange quiet under the great pale sky, and the sunset colors dying away. They remembered all that had happened, some of which Dorothy knew nothing about.

"Did Bert mind?" inquired Dorothy in a soft voice.

"N—n—not much," Gay answered.

What had happened when Bert came home

in the morning was that, after one single look
at his sled, he said to Gay, —

"Somebody has had my toboggan."

Gay had tried to carry off the matter with
an air of indifference, when Bert went on to
observe, —

"I would n't be a sneak."

"I 'm not a s—s—s—sneak," answered Gay.

"A gentleman does n't do those things," Bert
had then remarked. Lucy and Gay had trembled for a time, but Bert had had his say on the
subject. Nobody really knew about the coasting
by moonlight except the four children and John
Pearson.

"I cannot let Dorothy talk much," Miss Hester
now observed; "but if you children like to stay
with her quietly for an hour, and talk to her" —

"Could we tell her stories, Miss Bickerdyke?" asked Marcia.

Telling stories was the very thing. Marcia
and the twins sat down on the rug between Dorothy's divan and the grate. A little daylight
streamed in for a while at the window, but
gradually it died away, and there was only the
light of the coal-fire, which grew brighter and
brighter.

"You begin, Gay," said Marcia; "then I 'll
tell one."

Gay liked to tell stories. The only trouble was that Gay's stories somehow always sounded familiar. Dorothy said she liked best to hear stories that she knew, but Marcia insisted that Gay should tell them something they had never heard before.

"Yes, do tell us something new, Gay," Lucy also pleaded.

"Well, I'll try," said Gay. He shut his eyes and leaned his head back against the chimney-piece. When he shut his eyes and gave all his mind to his story, his stammering ceased. It was only in conversation that the words would not come.

"Once," he began, — "once upon a time there was a boy whose father and mother had died before he was born."

"Died before he was born!" broke in Marcia incredulously. "How could they die before he was born?"

"Anything may happen in a story," said Gay. "This little boy's parents died before he was born, and he had to grow up by himself."

"What was his name, anyhow?"

"His name was Ferdinand, and they called him Ferdy for short, and his sister" —

"Oh, so he had a sister! What was her name?"

"Isabella, and they called her Bel."

"Was she older or younger?"

"Just a little tiny bit younger."

"Well," said Marcia with a hopeless air, "I confess I can't for the life of me understand how, when a boy's father and mother died before he was born, he could have a sister younger than himself."

"He c—c—could," returned Gay indignantly. "That's the point of the story; but if you keep interrupting "—

"I only could n't exactly see how two children could be born and brought up without any relations."

"Oh, they had an uncle! He brought them up," Gay now explained. "This uncle was an awfully cruel man. You see the kingdom really belonged to Ferdy and Bel, but "—

"Do you mean they were a prince and princess?"

"Of course Ferdy was a prince and Bel was a princess. You don't suppose I should think it worth while to tell a story about common people. The kingdom really belonged to them, but this uncle, who was now king, had killed their father and mother before they were born."

"How did he kill them?" demanded Marcia greedily.

" He poisoned them."

" What did he poison them with ? "

" He made up a poison out of all sorts of things, and they died right off. The strange thing was that when he tried to poison Ferdy and Bel, the same stuff did them good; they kept growing bigger and bigger and fatter and fatter."

" That was curious, was n't it ? " mused Dorothy.

" Well, as they would n't die of the poison," Gay proceeded, " the cruel uncle wanted to get rid of the children in some other way. So he told them to put on their hats and jackets, and he would take them on a picnic ; but what he did was to carry them to a great big black forest, and then ride off and leave them."

" Oh, I know that story by heart ! " said Marcia with disgust.

" So do I," added Lucy. " It's ' Babes in the Wood.' "

" Now I like to hear stories over and over again," murmured Dorothy.

" You just wait," Gay protested. " I tell you this is a new story."

" Very well. Ferdy and Bel are left in the woods, and the cruel uncle rides off," said Marcia, with an air of knowing all about it. " Go on and let's see what happened next."

"Ferdy and Bel liked it first-rate," Gay re-
sumed; "that is, at first. There were lots of
berries and fruits and nuts, and they had a jolly
good time. They would have liked to live there
always, except that it got cold sleeping on the
moss at night, and there were bears came an'
looked at 'em."

"Why did n't the bears eat them?" inquired
Marcia.

"'Cause," replied Gay, "the bears was all fat-
ted up already for winter, and was n't hungry."

"It was fall, then, was it?"

"Yes; and Ferdy and Bel wanted something
comfor'ble for winter, an' one morning when
they were out walking they happened to meet a
wolf, an' he said to them quite polite, 'Good-
morning; how do you do?' and they answered
good-morning, that they were quite well.
'Where are you a-going?' asked the wolf."

It seemed both to Marcia and to Lucy that
this had a strangely familiar sound, but by great
effort they kept quiet. Gay went on rapidly :—

"They told him they was looking for a
boarding-place for the winter, an' the wolf said
he knew of a nice old lady who would be glad
of their company."

Marcia could not repress an exclamation.
Gay opened his eyes, looked at her a moment,
then said, —

"The children went on till they came to the house the wolf had told them about. It had a big door, with iron clamps and a brass knocker. Ferdy was tallest, so he reached up and knocked."

"Somebody said, 'Come in,'" Marcia cried. "They opened the door, and there was the wolf in bed with the old lady's cap and spectacles on."

" 'T was n't so at all," rejoined Gay with high disdain. "Ferdy rapped an' rapped till he was tired. Then Bel, she rapped an' rapped till she was tired. So, thinking everybody had gone out, they pushed open the door and went in. There was a great big fire burning in the chimney, and before the fire was a chicken all roasted, with mashed potatoes an' cranberry sauce, an' the moment the children had entered an' shut the door, what did the chicken an' potato an' cranberry sauce do but jump upon a nice little table laid for two people."

"That was beautiful," said Marcia. "I do hope, Gay, that, no matter what happened afterwards, Ferdy and Bel ate up that chicken and cranberry sauce."

"They did," said Gay. "There was bread an' butter too, an' — an' — an' other good things; they ate everything up clean. Then

they looked round and saw two nice little beds,
an' so each of 'em got into one an' went fast
asleep. Presently came a great knocking at the
door."

"Oh, dear," said Marcia, "this is the ogre.
He comes in and says, —

> 'Fee, faw, fo, fum,
> I smell the blood of an Englishman.' "

"Not a bit of it," said Gay. "It was the
uncle, the cruel uncle. He came back to make
sure that Ferdy and Bel were dead."

"Did he kill 'em as they lay asleep in their
nice little beds ? "

"No, not then. He did n't dare kill 'em
then, for somebody might come in an' find out.
No, he treated them quite polite, an' asked them
to go sleigh-riding with him."

"You had n't said anything about snow being
on the ground," observed Lucy.

"Oh, yes, the snow was almost up to the roofs
of the houses," said Gay, "and the uncle had a
splendid sleigh outside with two black horses.
He put Bel in ; next he put Ferdy in, and then in
he jumped himself and took the whip and the
reins, and off they went, the bells jingling and the
sleigh dashing on as the horses kept going faster
and faster. Ferdy and Bel crouched down under
the buffalo robes and wondered what would hap-

pen next. They could see how scowling their
uncle looked, and how he kept lashing the horses
with the whip. They wondered where they were
going ; through the woods, up an' down moun-
tains, an' over rivers. All at once the horses
stood still an' listened. The uncle laughed an'
said, —

" ' Children, do you hear that noise ? '

" Ferdy an' Bel did hear a howling.

" ' It's a hungry pack of wolves,' said the
uncle. ' Do they make you tremble ? '

" Ferdy an' Bel trembled so they could n't answer. The horses, they trembled ; that is, for a
minute they trembled, then they began to gallop.
The uncle could n't hold 'em in. On they went
rushing, and behind 'em came the wolves a-howl-
ing. No matter how swift the horses galloped,
the wolves was a great deal swifter. First their
howling sounded very far off, but now it kept
sounding nearer and nearer — nearer and nearer.
The hungry pack was close behind now, and
their red eyes was shining like — like — like " —

" Like lamps ? " suggested Dorothy.

" Shining like lamps," said Gay, catching
gratefully at the phrase. " And the uncle, he
could n't begin to hold in the horses that was
raging and tearing. So he stood up and looked
back at the wolves ; he smelt their dreadful

breath ; he watched 'em getting so near he could look into their eyes ; just as they was jumping up to get into the sleigh, up he picked Bel an' flung her out to them."

" Oh, oh, oh," cried Dorothy, " not Bel."

" Yes, he did ; he flung her out ; then he picked up Ferdy an' flung him out. You see the uncle hoped the wolves would be satisfied an' leave him alone. But it was n't so ; the wolves was bound to have him. They kept getting closer an' closer ; up jumped six at once into the sleigh."

" I hope they finished the uncle," observed Marcia.

" Yes, they ate him up, an' when they had got through with him, they devoured the two horses."

" Oh, Gay," faltered Dorothy, " I can't bear to think that Ferdy and Bel were eaten up by wolves."

" They was n't," Gay replied. " Wolves and lions never eat the true princes ; it 's only the false ones. They did n't even bite Bel once. No, the two children picked themselves up an' began to walk back."

" Through all that snow ? " inquired Lucy.

" They had n't far to go," said Gay. " The people of the kingdom that belonged to them was coming after them with a carriage an' a

brass band ; and so they went to the palace an'
reigned happy ever after."

The three listeners sat silent for a moment
taking in this conclusion ; then Marcia broke
the pause by observing, —

" It was n't a bad story, take it altogether.
But somehow it did remind me now and then of
things I had heard before. You did n't quite
make it all up, Gay."

" Wh—wh—wh— " Gay began.

" Count three, Gay," said Lucy.

" One, two, three. Why, what 's the use of
making up stories when there 's such heaps
already ? " Gay burst out indignantly.

" Now, I 've got a story," said Marcia, " that
I made up myself."

" Oh, do tell it," implored Dorothy.

" It 's just a little story," said Marcia ; " but
I thought it every bit to myself. Its name is
' Six Matches.' "

The firelight shone on Marcia's face, and she
gazed back at the fire, and kept her hands busy
braiding and unbraiding the ends of her hair
that hung over her shoulder.

" Once," she began, " six matches lay in a
tray together. One of them was taken by a
servant-maid to make the kitchen fire and she
cooked the family breakfast."

Marcia glanced from one to the other of the three eager faces to be sure she interested her audience.

"A man took another of the matches and lighted his pipe. In fact, he took two, for one would n't light, but broke off."

"That makes three," said Lucy, keeping the tally on her fingers.

"That makes three," said Marcia. "Now the fourth went to light a ball-room, where beautiful ladies with wonderful dresses and necklaces and bracelets and feathers in their hair danced all night."

They all drew a deeper breath. They could tell by Marcia's face that something else was coming.

"The fifth set fire to a city," said Marcia. "It was dropped in a stable and somebody stepped on it. It made a blaze in the straw and everything was burned up, — houses and horses and men and women and children; people at church and people at theatres."

"Oh, Marcia, there 's one more," whispered Dorothy.

"The last one lighted a tallow candle in the cell of a prisoner who had been condemned to death," said Marcia. "The place was very black and dismal, and the light was very poor and dim.

But the man was to be hanged at daybreak, and he was glad even of the tallow candle, for his heart was much oppressed, and he was afraid of the darkness."

"Is that all?" inquired Lucy.

"Yes, that's all," answered Marcia. "How did you like it, Gay?"

"P—p—p—"

"Count three, Gay," said Lucy.

"Pr—pretty well," said Gay. "I—I—I—I think I rather like to know what's coming in a story."

"Marcia will tell it to us again," said Dorothy. "Won't you please, Marcia?"

"Some time, perhaps; not now," Marcia returned. "I've got another to tell you, if you want very much to hear it."

"Another you made up all by yourself?"

"Yes," said Marcia, "all by myself."

"Oh, how do you do it? Oh, tell it, tell it; do tell it."

Marcia looked into the fire silently for a minute, then began : —

"It was a straight, ugly post, — nothing in the world but a straight, ugly post, and it did n't like it. It stood not far from a fine country house, and at first it had been intended to have a dovecote on top, but something happened so

that the dovecote was n't built, and there the
post stood. Nobody even took the trouble to
paint it. Sometimes the owner of the house
said, ' I 'll have that ugly post cut down.' But
the thing did n't get done, and there the post
stood. In winter, it was n't so bad. The trees
and rosebushes were all bare and ugly then ;
their leaves and flowers had dropped off, and the
post tried to believe that there was n't so much
difference between it and them. However, the
trees and the shrubs were always whispering
about how they longed for the summer-time and
the birds and the bees and the flowers. Once the
post thought it would not be entirely left out
in the cold, so it said, ' Summer is on its way
back.' But the trees and the bushes just laughed
and said to each other, ' As if summer made any
difference to a bare pole just stuck down in the
earth without any life or any roots.' You see,
they did n't suppose the post had any real feelings. But it had, and the post just despised
itself for not having any leaves or flowers or
fruit quite as much as the trees and rosebushes
despised it, if not more.

" Well, when spring-time came and everything
else put out leaves, there the post stood browner
and uglier than ever. But something happened.
There was a pretty girl who lived in the house,

and, when the weather was warm, she went about planting seeds and setting out plants. And one day she stopped by the post and said to herself, ' This would n't be a bad place for a moonflower,' and she dug a hole close beside the post and set out a little vine. ' That 's a poor, delicate, sickly thing,' the post said to itself at first. ' I never have any luck. If it had been a climbing rose, that might have done me credit.' The girl forgot the moonflower after she had planted it. Presently it began to grow and looked about for a support. ' If you would lean on me,' said the post, and the moonflower put out one little tendril and then another, for it was glad not to be left to draggle on the ground. It was the first time the post had ever received such an attention, and, feeling rather embarrassed, it stood up straighter and uglier than ever ; for a mere bit of a green vine down at its feet was no great company. But in a week the moonflower was halfway up. ' How you do grow ! ' said the post. ' Oh, this is nothing,' said the moonflower. ' In a few weeks I shall have wound myself all round you, and covered you with festoons, and then I shall blossom. Until you have seen me in blossom, you really have no idea ! '

" Oh, how happy that post was now ! Day and night to have this beautiful thing twining

all round it! Then to see it break out into buds!
Really, the post had no reason to envy the rosebushes or the apple-trees. People stopped and
looked at the post covered with the moonflower,
and said they never had seen anything half so
beautiful. The girl who had planted the moonflower began to watch the buds, and finally she
said, '.They will come out to-night.' The post
really grew so excited that afternoon, it would
have trembled except that it was fastened deep
into a stone foundation. When the sun was going down it was something to look at the lovely
white petals untwisting. Then, all at once, they
were open! It was as the vine had said,—until
it was in blossom, the post really had no idea!
Why, it was hard to tell whether the real moon
and the stars were more beautiful! The post
was a part of the wonder of the night. The
moon and stars nodded and greeted it; the wind
blew round it; great white moths came. Then
finally it grew red in the east and the sun rose
and saw the secret of what had happened! The
birds saw it, too. A humming-bird, up early,
came and found what honey the moths had left
in the blossoms. Then a bee crept into the cup
of one, and, finding it sweet, forgot that moonflowers do not keep open all day and was shut
up in it.

"Well, this went on all the rest of the summer, and until frost came in the fall. The post knew that leaves and blossoms always faded then, but it had a dreadful heartache when it saw that the vine was dying. Day by day its hold was looser. Finally it all shriveled up and fell to the ground quite dead. 'It will come back,' the post thought, trying not to be too wretched, for the rosebushes were in the same plight. 'Wait till spring and I shall have my beautiful vine and moons and stars again!' However, just before Christmas a man was going round the house trimming up the place, and he chopped down the pole. 'Just right for kindlings,' he said, and put it under the great Yule-log which was to be lighted Christmas eve.

"'I shall have great sport,' the post remarked to itself. 'There are six of me now.'

"Just then the fire was lighted, and the post thought when it saw the blaze that it itself was bursting into blossom.

"'I always did believe I should do something at last,' it whispered as it burned away vigorously. Next day its ashes were carried out and put round an apple-tree."

"Oh," said Dorothy, drawing a long breath.

She was about to tell Marcia how delighted she was with the story, but Miss Hester came in from the hall, where she had been sitting, and told Marcia, Gay, and Lucy that it was tea-time, and that they would be expected at home.

Then Dorothy ate her hot bread and milk, was put to bed, and went to sleep.

# CHAPTER VIII

EVEN in the midst of winter there comes now and then a day when there is such a shining of the sun, such a soft stirring of the wind, that one has a new feeling, and knows that spring is on the way.

On such days the children always said to each other that it would soon be time " to go to the spring-lot."

Dorothy loved to go to the " spring-lot " almost better than to do anything. It was such a delightful place. The spring itself was halfway up a hill that sloped to the southeast. The clear water boiled out of white sand, filled the basin to the brim, then overflowed and made a gay little rivulet, which went dancing down the hillside and lost itself in the river. Around this spring grew the finest, thickest, greenest grass, like velvet ; and all along the course of the brook the grass kept green almost all winter. The spring was always a fresh miracle to Dorothy. What made the water boil up ? Surely

not the heat, for, unlike other boiling water, this
was icy cold. They had all tasted it, and, besides, Dorothy had once fallen into the spring,
and might have said, as a great poet did of a
different pool, —

> " I 've measured it from side to side,
> 'T is three feet long and two feet wide."

However, the spring was but one attraction of
the spring-lot. The really wonderful and delicious secret of the place was that just at the edge
of a thicket of birches, a little above and to the
side of the spring, there grew the earliest wild
flowers. When not a flower was to be seen in
any other spot, here could be found the blue
liverwort and the white stars of the bloodroot,
and these blossoms were soon followed by
anemones or windflowers, dogtooth violets, and
troops of others. As for blue violets and Quaker
Ladies, not to say dandelions, the grass was
soon so full of them it was like a picture.

Then the walk to the spring-lot was such an
enjoyable experience. It was along the lane,
which was really a part of the Dundas place,
and had, in the old, prosperous days of the
family, been a cow-path to and from pasture.
Thrilling incidents belonged to this lane, which
was bordered with tall ferns and elders and
brier-roses. The children had once seen a snake

there; then, again, they had encountered a large and very fierce-looking mud-turtle. Dorothy had been startled by a rabbit whisking across, and something else had scuttled away as she advanced, something big and bushy-tailed, which Bert Lee thought was probably a woodchuck. The lane led to the bridge over the Swallow River, which here meandered through a wide, open meadow. It was such a pretty river. Just where the bridge crossed it the water spread out wide and shallow, and any one driving horse or oxen was apt to ford it. It was said that Bert Lee had waded across, but then Bert did such wonderful things. Dorothy and Lucy and Gay, even Marcia as well, were quite contented to cross by the bridge, which was some twenty-five feet wide, made of planks, with, on either side, a huge log, which seemed made to sit down on and loiter away almost more time than could be spared, listening to the murmur of the river, or the bees that buzzed in the blossoms of the old willow-trees which grew at the west end of the bridge. Beyond the river the lane became a mere cart-path, and led to Wolf Hill and the great woods, but when one was going to the spring-lot, one skirted the pasture, or the "rye-lot," and so gained the spring.

This winter had been one of intense cold and

deep snows.   March not only came in but went
out like a lion, and roared through storms and
tempests.   Finally, however, the sky was clear;
the sap was running from the sugar maples;
the catkins of the willows were bursting their
sheaths; the sunny slopes were growing green.

"I am sure it must be time to go to the
spring-lot," said Dorothy to Marcia.

"We will go next Saturday," Marcia answered, with her little nod which always settled
things.

All that week Dorothy could think of nothing
else but the little blue and white stars blossoming on the edge of the thicket.   The idea of
them got into her reading and writing and
spelling and geography, and the multiplication
table.   When lessons were over she sat with
Mrs. Bickerdyke and knitted two rounds on a
stocking; then Jerusha overlooked her while she
pieced three blocks of a silk quilt.   Thus life
went on Monday, Tuesday, Wednesday, Thursday, and Friday; but Saturday dawned at last.

"Don't tell, John," Dorothy whispered to
John Pearson that morning when they were
looking at the daffodils and narcissi and hy-
acinths and crocuses in the beds which he was
at last uncovering.   "We are going to the
spring-lot this afternoon."

"DON'T TELL, JOHN"

" 'T ain't likely you can get there," John answered. " River's too high. Never know'd it so high before in all my born days."

Dorothy speculated as to what it might mean that the river was " too high." She did not find out that day, for on that Saturday afternoon, when Dorothy came out of the house to set forth on the walk, Marcia met her.

" Lucy and Gay can't go," she said.

" Oh, dear!" answered Dorothy. " Why not?"

" It's Bert. It always is Bert," said Marcia. " His father told him to pile the wood, and he has bought up Lucy and Gay, and made them do it. They always feel so proud when Bert lets them do anything for him."

" Oh, dear!" Dorothy said again. " What shall we do?"

" Go without them?" asked Marcia.

" They will feel so unhappy," faltered Dorothy. " Perhaps if we wait a little they will go."

" Let's go and see," said Marcia, and going through the wicket they entered the Lee place, and soon found Gay and Lucy hard at work carrying the sticks of wood, freshly sawed and chopped, into the shed.

" Can't go till it's all piled," said Lucy.

"We 're p—p—piling it as fast as we can," said Gay.  "P—p—p—"

"Count three, Gay," called Lucy warningly.

But Gay could n't stop to count three just then.

"P—p—p'raps," he spluttered, "we shall get through in time."

"Would n't your mother let you go, if I asked her?"

"Mother might, — it 's Bert we 're afraid of," explained Lucy.  "We promised him we 'd do it, if he would let us have part of his garden."

"Where is Bert?" inquired Marcia.

"He went over to aunt Morris's to spend the day."

"Oh!" Marcia said in a significant tone.

"He gave us some peanuts besides," remarked Lucy.

"A—a—a—" Gay began.

"Count three, Gay," said Lucy.

"And his knife, too," gasped Gay.

"Marcia," suggested Dorothy, "if we helped Lucy and Gay"—

"Let 's," said Marcia.  "I 'll pile the sticks, if you children will bring 'em."

"You shall have some of the peanuts," Lucy hastened to promise.

"I 've got some taffy, too," said Gay.

Whatever Marcia did she liked to do well. Accordingly she began by pulling all the wood down and piling it from the beginning. The peanuts and taffy furnished a pleasant occasional refreshment. The time passed. They all talked a great deal. Then, too, one has to rest when one is worn out. Lucy's way was to take two sticks and go backwards and forwards very rapidly. Dorothy tried to take four, but was apt to drop one. Gay remembered what big armfuls Bert carried, tried to follow his example, and constantly tripped himself up, or, falling over the dogs, who constantly got in his way, would drop his whole pile and tumble over it.

When the last peanut was eaten, and the last stick piled, it was almost six o'clock, and, of course, going after wild flowers was not to be thought of that day. They all expressed bitter disappointment, but they had all had a capital time, and Marcia was as proud of her straight rows of sticks as if they were a work of art.

Next day came a deluge of rain, and for four days it poured. Oh, what black skies! what dark, late mornings! what early evenings! But on Friday, after an interval of twenty-four hours when the rain had ceased, but the northeast wind had not relaxed its grip, it finally cleared off. Then, next day it was Saturday,

and now it really was to happen that the children were going to set out for the spring-lot.

It was a bright, sunny day, and, although
there was a cool edge to the wind, in protected
places it was really warm.  Not one of the children had so far seen even a dandelion blossoming in a door-yard, but still they all felt sure
that there would be a gush of flowers under the
birches in the spring-lot.

It was so pleasant to be really doing something, going somewhere, after the long winter.
Carlo and Flossy were of the same mind.

Few leaves showed yet, but the buds were
swelling, and some of the maples hung out tas-
sels.  There were a great many birds — crows,
blackbirds, robins, and bluebirds — flying hither
and thither, and certainly it must be spring if
the birds had come.  They all ran ; they jumped ;
they dabbled with sticks in the little pools they
met.  The dogs, as well, felt the joy of being
in the lane ; they had run races with each other ;
they had far outstripped the children, when suddenly they stopped short.

In another minute, Marcia, Dorothy, and the
twins came up standing.

" Oh," said Dorothy.

" Oh, dear me," said Lucy.

" Is n't that a shame ? " ejaculated Marcia.

Gay really could n't utter a word.   He had to set to work counting to himself.

" I suppose that's what John meant by the river's being high," murmured Dorothy.

" It's a freshet," Gay now observed sagaciously.

" I declare, I do think it's too bad," exclaimed Marcia again.   " Two Saturdays we had to stay in because it was stormy.   Then last week we helped Lucy and Gay, and now " —

" There's always something in the way," said Lucy, who was easily discouraged.

" And now it's the river," said Dorothy, almost ready to weep.

It was the river, sure enough, that was in the way.   It was no longer a pretty, shining little river, with laughing ripples tinkling over the pebbles on the bottom, but a river that stretched out like an ocean.   It had flooded the whole pasture, and flowed up the lane to their very feet.

"On Jordan's stormy banks I stand,
And cast a wishful eye
To Canaan's fair and happy land,
Where my possessions lie."

That was Dorothy's thought, and her coveted possessions were the flowers blossoming away in the spring-lot, feeling lonely, and wondering why she did not come to pick them.

" I don't mean to give it up," said Marcia.

The three children always expected something fine and heroic from Marcia. The dead calm and nothingness of giving up helplessly before the rushing river might have suited them, but Marcia found no evil without its remedy. Her spirit rose. She liked the spice of danger.

"Why not cross on the fence?" she suggested.

"Why, yes," said Dorothy. "Why not?"

"Is it s—s—s—afe?" inquired Gay.

"I would n't be so prudent as you are for all the world," said Marcia, with high disdain for safety.

"Mother would n't want us to go if it was n't safe," Lucy now remarked.

"It's perfectly safe!" declared Marcia. "We've all walked on fences. It's just as safe to do it over water as over dry land."

There was, of course, a fence on each side of the lane. That on the north would have been the desirable one to cross by, for it led straight up to the bridge. But bushes grew against it, and thorns and briers were plentiful. Thus the fence on the south side, being clear of any hedge, or any sort of impediment, was the one to be attempted. Yet, even when the river was within its banks, it would have been a difficult and dangerous enterprise, for, as we have seen, there was a ford, and the fence spanned the river some fifty feet below the bridge.

Marcia, however, had n't thought this out.

" You 'll try it, won't you, Dorothy ? " she said coaxingly.

" Oh, yes, I 'll try it," answered Dorothy, only too eager to get over.

" And of course, Lucy, you and Gay will go if Dorothy will. She 's so much younger than you are," pursued Marcia.

Gay had looked at Lucy, and Lucy at Gay. Lucy was prepared to take a high moral tone and insist that her mother would not approve, which was most certainly the case. But what Gay thought of was how Bert would despise him for backing out, for Bert always said, —

" A man does n't back out, you know."

So what Gay said was, —

" We 'll go.   Lucy, we will go."

" All right," exclaimed Marcia. "Here, Dorothy, you are the lightest ; you go first."

" I go first ! " repeated Dorothy, a little surprised, and opening her eyes very wide.

" Of course ; you are the lightest, so you go first. Then, Gay, you follow, and Lucy after you. I 'm heaviest, so I 'll go last."

Marcia's orders always carried a logical convincing quality along with them. Dorothy

obeyed. The fence had four rails, and by putting her feet on the lowest rail, she grasped
the upper one tightly and securely, and could
advance sideways by putting one foot and one
hand over the other. When she came to the
post she drew a long breath, for there she had to
reach round and get hold of a new and untried
rail. But, after all, it was not a very difficult
undertaking ; and she did so long to reach the
flowers, any road to them was welcome, no matter how hard. So she looked back to the others
with a nod and smile, calling, —

" I shall get there first."

Gay was following her, putting all his might
into the task, and Lucy was following him.

" Hurry up," called Marcia.

So on went Dorothy, putting hand over hand
and foot over foot. She needed to give all her
attention to the task, for the rails were rough
and uneven. Her mind soon became completely
absorbed in the mere mechanical operation of
changing her position at each moment without
ever releasing her hold upon the rail. She felt
in a hurry, lest she should get in the way of the
others and hinder them. Then, too, the sound
of the water kept growing louder and louder.
It must also be getting deeper and deeper, for
all at once, not to get her feet wet, she had had

to mount to the second rail. At first, too, the water had been quiet. Now, it swept along with a strong current, and was so full of life and motion she would have liked to stop and watch it swirling and eddying beneath her, if there had been time. The wind, too, kept blowing harder and harder and colder and colder. If the others had not been within hail, she might have thought this was more than she had bargained for. As it was, she rather liked the excitement of feeling that she was leading the way.

"I must be almost across by this time," she said to herself, and stopped for one second to give a look. She had not looked before. What she now saw almost took her breath away.

The waste of waters about her seemed endless. They broke into waves; they foamed and eddied; here and there were actual whirlpools, in which sticks and branches swirled round and round in circles. She heard such curious voices in the water: there were cries and calls, it seemed to her, and a loud babble as if dozens of people were talking at once.

"Oh, dear," said Dorothy to herself, "I don't think I quite like this."

She now turned her head and glanced behind her. She was about to ask Marcia if she had better try to go on. But where was Marcia?

Dorothy rubbed the mists off her eyes. Where
were Gay and Lucy? She could see nobody;
she could see nothing, — that is, nothing but
water. She could not even see all the fence by
which she had come. Some of it was gone, and
the rails were floating in the water.

"Dear me," Dorothy thought to herself, "I
hope this fence won't tumble over with me
on it."

Perhaps, if there had been time, Dorothy
might have been alarmed about the possible fate
of her companions who had been on that fence.
But there was no time to think. She was conscious of a sudden terrible disturbance in the
water; also of a rushing and a roaring wind.
There was a loud, crashing noise just behind her.
At this same moment, the rails she was holding
by began to sway and totter. She clutched at
a fresh support, not knowing what it was. But
with everything giving way under her feet, it
was a comfort to get hold of something.

What she had caught was the branch of a
tree which, dislodged from the bank a mile away,
had floated downstream two days before and
caught under the bridge. There it had stayed,
twisting its roots and branches among the stones
and boards. The time had come, however, for
it to go on its way. The wind blew hard through

the arch of the bridge ; the fierce, strong current beat through. The tree had to move ; once outside, it turned over and over, then planted itself vigorously in midstream, turning itself down towards Dorothy, who, just as the rail fence toppled, was able to seize hold of the branches. Dorothy had no particular idea of what she was doing. In fact, she was so dazed, so exhausted, so blinded by the spray, and confused by the roar of the water, she could never afterwards tell just how it happened that she .presently found herself sitting quite cosily, almost at ease, among the branches of the tree, high above the water.

What she experienced was an intense surprise. She was almost curious to see what would happen next. The wind blew ; the waters seethed and roared. Overhead flew a flock of crows, and it sounded to Dorothy as if they cawed derisively. She began to feel as if everything were moving, — the clouds above her, the waters opening in a deep gulf beneath her, the tree to whose branches she was clinging.

" Now we 're sailing," she seemed to hear somebody say out of a story she had read.

It was just at this moment that she caught a different cry.

" Hulloa! " said a voice ; " hulloa! "

"Why, John, is that you?" said Dorothy, turning round. "I hoped you 'd come."

"Wa-al, I never!" said John Pearson. "Wa-al, in all my born days I never see the like o' this!"

John was in a wagon, — a wagon drawn by a stout horse. The water was already about up to the seat of the wagon, and he did not know how to venture deeper into the stream. He sat looking at Dorothy, and Dorothy in the tree looked at John.

"I think this tree is going on, John," Dorothy suggested. "I feel it move."

"Oh, thunder," said John. "Git up, git up, I tell you." This was addressed to the horse, who, feeling his way carefully, advanced slowly a little nearer and then a little nearer to Dorothy.

"Can you jump?" inquired John gruffly.

"I don't know," said Dorothy. "I think the branch is in the way."

"Oh, thunder," muttered John again. "Git up, git up, I tell you."

The horse obediently pushed on. By this time he was swimming and the wagon was floating.

Dorothy could now reach John's extended arms, and in another moment she was sitting cross-legged on the seat beside him. They could not turn back, so were obliged to go on, the water flowing into the wagon, the horse swimming on bravely, trying all the time to find a footing.

"Here we be," said John; and in another minute the horse was toiling up the bank.

"Why, we really can go to the spring-lot," said Dorothy.

"I guess not to-day," answered John.

He gave a smile, as he looked at Dorothy. She was smiling, too, but she looked pale.

"Was n't you frightened any?" he inquired.

"Oh, I don't know," she answered, and then she began to cry.

"Don't cry, now it 's all over," said John.

"That 's what makes me cry," said Dorothy.

John had been letting the water out of the wagon by taking out the tailboard.

Now he clambered in again by Dorothy's side, turned the horse, and they went slowly and carefully over the bridge and then down the slope into the lane, where the water was twelve to eighteen inches deep. Dorothy could see the rails of the fence floating in the water. It all grew dream-like to her. It was like a dream, also, to find Marcia, Gay, and Lucy, and the dogs standing waiting for her where the dry land appeared in the lane.

" Oh, Dorothy," said Marcia.

" Oh, Dorothy," said Lucy.

Gay was counting to himself, that was evident, but no sound escaped him. He looked a little ashamed of the way he had kept safe on dry land.

" Oh, Dorothy," Marcia said again, " I thought for a minute " —

" So did I," said Lucy.

" Oh, was n't I glad that John Pearson came along! " said Marcia.

" Ef I had n't a-started to cut pea-brush," said John, " I dunno — I dunno what would have happened."

" It was all my fault," said Marcia magnanimously. " I should be glad if you would all run pins into me."

" Run pins into you? " repeated Dorothy, quite amazed.

" I don't mind your running pins into me," said Marcia tragically. " I deserve it,— I know I deserve it. What I do mind is your telling Miss Bickerdyke, or Gay and Lucy's telling their mother. For, if they know, they will never, never, never let any of you play with me again."

" Oh, we won't tell," said Dorothy.

" I won't tell," said Lucy, " and Gay won't tell, either. Will you, Gay? "

" N—n—no," said Gay.

Marcia turned to John Pearson.

" You 're such a dear, good old John, you won't tell."

" 'T ain't right," John replied.

" But you won't tell? "

" You 'd ought to be punished, Miss Marcia Dundas."

" I *am* punished," said Marcia.

# CHAPTER IX

## KEEPING CHICKENS

Mrs. Deane came for a little visit at Easter, when the weather was really spring-like, and she and Dorothy planted flower - seeds together. Then mother and child bade each other good-by for a good many months, for Mrs. Deane was to go to Europe in June, for the summer, with some of the pupils of the school where she taught. Thus it was a comfort to Dorothy to have a new interest and a new enterprise.

Jerusha had grown up on a farm in Maine, where, of course, hens and chickens were kept and eggs had been abundant. She had for years petitioned Miss Hester to allow her to keep hens. To Jerusha's way of thinking, having hens meant thrift, abundance, economy. She could do so much more if she had all the eggs she wanted to use. Besides having eggs for boiling, poaching, frying, scrambling, and omelette making; eggs for cakes, puddings, mayonnaises, there were other uses still for eggs, — chickens came out of them. Miss Hester reflected that Mrs. Bickerdyke was fond of chickens, and that, moreover, nourishing food like chicken was good for the old lady.

" What do you think, John? " Miss Hester inquired of John Pearson.

" All I say is, hens must be kept off my garden."

" They'll be kept off his garden," Jerusha promised. " Well-fed and well-tended hens won't want more than their own yard."

" Do you suppose, Jerusha," proceeded Miss Hester, " that they will pay for themselves? "

" Pay for themselves? They will make you rich," said Jerusha.

Miss Hester finally yielded. She had not asked Dorothy's opinion on the matter, for she knew that Dorothy would be perfectly happy if they kept chickens. Dorothy had not had many pets of her own. Once she had found a half-dead bird in the lane, its wing slightly injured, and had brought it back to life by holding it against her warm throat. She had begged Miss Hester to let her keep it for her own, and Miss Hester — who recognized the bird as a rose-breasted grosbeak, that probably had hurt its wing flying against a wire when it was on its way south for the winter — had consented. Dorothy had made all sorts of beautiful plans about

herself and the bird. She had not quite decided
when she went to bed what his name was to be,
but she knew exactly how she was to tame him;
how he was to come to her and perch on her finger; how he was to live in her room and sing at
night, for the grosbeak is a night warbler. Yes,
Dorothy went to bed very happy and woke up
very happy. Rory O'More, however, was up
before her, and by the time the little girl had
opened her eyes, Rory O'More had eaten up the
rose-breasted grosbeak.

It had been very hard for Dorothy to go on
living with Rory O'More. Sometimes, even now,
when she saw Rory lying on his cushion in the
chair before the range, so white, so soft, blinking his eyes and purring, Dorothy would suddenly burst out with a wail, —

"Oh, Rory, I can't help loving you, and
yet I don't want to love you! I feel as if I
ought not to love you — you were so wicked,
Rory! It does sometimes seem as if you had n't
any conscience!"

No, as long as Rory had a soft, warm place
and plenty of milk to drink, nothing troubled
him very much. Dorothy went on being fond
of him because she loved everything and everybody, and pined for more things to love. Over
at Gay's and Lucy's there was an endless suc-

cession of pets, and an equally endless succession of disasters. The rabbits burrowed their way out of their inclosure and utterly vanished; battles, murders, and sudden deaths finished off birds of all sorts, guinea-pigs, and squirrels. At present, Carlo and Flossy were the only pets belonging to any of the four children; thus Marcia and the twins were almost as much interested as Dorothy herself in the chicken enterprise.

The little shed outside of the stable was to be used as a hen-house. The hens were also, to some limited degree, to be permitted to have the run of the stable itself with its old corncribs. Some hens, Jerusha said, were never satisfied unless they could steal a nest. But for sensible, well-conducted hens, John Pearson arranged a row of neat boxes well raised from the floor; cosy, comfortable, and inviting. Outside shed and stable was a yard some thirty feet square surrounded by a high fence of wire netting. Never had preparations for the comfort of chickens been more perfect. Miss Hester had bought three white brahma hens and a cock. Then Mrs. Fuller had sent six of her own hens as a present to Dorothy. The white brahmas were beautiful, slow, majestic-looking fowls; Mrs. Fuller's, of no recognizable breed, were spotted, speckled, parti-colored, certainly not handsome,

and seemed a distinct species from the sleepy
thoroughbreds, as if their struggle for existence
had been more fierce and their hardships had
made them eager and hungry.

Dorothy at first adopted the brahmas as her
favorites, but Jerusha was on the side of the
plainer fowls. " They 'll lay two eggs to one
of the white ones," she said.

John Pearson gazed at them all with a shake
of his head ; but in answer to Jerusha he observed, —

" Should n't wonder ef Mis' Fuller was glad
to get rid of them speckled critters.   They look
lively — a'most too lively."

John accordingly looked round for a roll of
wire netting to carry his fence higher.

If only the dear, beautiful creatures need not
be penned up !   That was the feeling of all the
children.   Of course, they named all the hens.
The three brahmas at first looked so precisely
alike it was no easy matter to distinguish one
from the other ; but presently Dorothy saw that
one was the handsomest ; she was Blanche.   Another had a refined, mincing way ; she was Lady
Jane ; and the third was White Lady.   The
cock was left to Herbert Lee to name.   Bert
said, " Oh, call him — call him —   Oh, I don't
care.   Call him what you please."

" I — I — I — was going to say, M—M—
M—" said Gay.

" Count three, Gay," said Lucy.

" Mikado," said Gay.

" Well, Mikado is as good a name as another," Bert condescended to admit; so the cock
was Mikado.

Mrs. Fuller's hens, not belonging to the
brahma class, had to take up with common
names. One was Speckle; the second, Topknot; the third was Dappy; the fourth, Biddy;
the fifth, Fantail; and the sixth, Dot, for she
was black and round and little.

Mikado, Blanche, Lady Jane, and White
Lady were beautiful creatures to look at; but
Speckle, Dot, Dappy, and the others were so full
of life, character, and whim, Dorothy was soon
almost ready to agree with Jerusha that one of
them was worth two of the big, sleepy creatures.
They were always on the lookout for Dorothy,
and, naturally, such signs of affection pleased
her. The truth was, however, that the problem
of how to make a living was the one that concerned them. They scratched, they dug; they
were on the watch incessantly, not only for their
regular meals, but for any sort of miraculous
dispensation in their behalf. In a few days they
had devoured every blade of grass in the hen-

yard; what had been turf became a mere gravel-
bed. They had even undermined the roots of a
small apple-tree growing there.

However, they carried the same energy into
the laying of eggs, and their shrill, triumphant
cackle resounded from seven o'clock in the
morning until long past noon. Jerusha was as
proud of the eggs as the hens themselves. She
loved to give Dorothy a pleasure, so she let the
children hunt for the eggs. The brahmas' eggs
were large, a perfect oval in shape, and of a
rich cream color. They were set aside and kept
for hatching. All the eggs were dated. Dorothy was soon able to recognize the egg of each
individual hen. Speckle's had funny little dark
marks like speckles in the shell; Dot's were
small and round and clear white; Dappy's long
and slim. Each had its own distinct traits.

"Oh, grandmamma!" Dorothy would break
out at breakfast, "that is one of Topknot's
eggs you have got, and aunt Hester's is Fantail's."

"Nonsense, Dorothy," Miss Hester would
say; "it is not possible to tell one egg from
another."

Not possible to tell one egg from another!
If Dorothy had not known it was impolite to
contradict, she could have proved that no two
eggs were exactly alike.

The children knew. How they gloated over the eggs! They had seen eggs, eaten eggs all their lives, but the real meaning of an egg had never before dawned upon their minds. Tennyson wrote about the music of the moon lying hidden in the eggs of the nightingale. That faintly suggests what Marcia, Dorothy, Lucy, and Gay saw in those piles of eggs.

If only the hens would be sensible. Dorothy's first idea had been to have the name of the hens printed in black ink on the boxes, so that each hen, knowing her own place, might always go to it, so avoiding all confusion; and, indeed, if the hens had only carried out this excellent idea of Dorothy's, it would have been of inestimable advantage to all parties concerned.

" I suppose," Marcia observed, " that the hens have their ideas just as we have ours."

This was, of course, a sympathetic and charitable view to take of the matter. The hens did seem to have original ideas. When any one of them started off to begin her laying, she was almost sure not to do what was expected of her. When nice, comfortable nests in boxes had been provided, why should Blanche drop her eggs about casually, as it were, on the ground, on the floor of the hen-house? Why should Dot fly up and lay her egg on a high beam, so nar-

row that she could hardly balance herself on it
when she was sitting down? Really it was difficult even for Dorothy to have patience with
these stupid, idiotic, absurd proceedings; although when John Pearson said (when asked
to mount the ladder and put a box up on the
beam for Dot), "Hens is all born fools," she
begged him with tears not to say such dreadful
things.

Four hens insisted on having their nests together in the corncrib, which was accordingly
filled with hay and given over to them. These
were White Lady, Speckle, Dappy, and Topknot. Blanche finally concluded to try her
luck in one of the regular boxes. Lady Jane
had her nest at the bottom of a barrel.

"Does n't it seem too bad," Marcia said one
pleasant day, "that they can never come out of
that dreary little cooped-up place?"

"Does n't it?" Dorothy exclaimed. "I do
feel so sorry for them. They must get so tired
of being shut up."

Lucy and Gay gave each other a glance.
Their gardener highly disapproved of Mrs.
Bickerdyke's having chickens at all, and was
constantly uttering dire threats as to what would
happen if one of the hens was to invade his
premises.

"I — I — I —" said Gay.

"Count three, Gay," said Lucy.

"I— don't believe they mind being shut up," said Gay.

"Should n't you mind?" demanded Marcia. "Should you like to be shut up from one week's end to another?"

Jerusha, too, sympathized with the hens, and the result was that one soft, balmy afternoon, after John Pearson had gone home, Mikado and the hens were invited to come out. Gay and Lucy were picketed so as to head off any invasion of the Lee place. Jerusha mounted guard over John's garden. Marcia and Dorothy were to take care of the flower-beds, while Carlo and Flossy, in the highest spirits, appointed themselves general skirmishers. Mikado strutted forth, and, with congratulatory chuckles, invited his spouses to come on, making straight for the bed of freshly planted annuals. Dorothy and Marcia rushed at Mikado and Blanche and Lady Jane; Carlo and Flossy chased Dappy out into the street, and across the way, into a neighbor's yard, while Dot flew straight over the hedge into the Lees'. It was, however, Jerusha who had the worst time. She fought with Speckle, Fantail, Biddy, and White Lady, until the sun had gone down and the shades of night

had gathered. Then slowly and reluctantly the
hens, one by one, took their way back to the
roosting-place. Even Dappy turned up, minus
some tail-feathers. How Jerusha and the children trembled at the thought of what John
Pearson would say! All agreed that henceforth
the hens should be kept shut up. But, having
once tasted the delights of liberty, they were
always pining for it. They escaped whenever
they could, and, with one fell swoop, descended
upon John's garden.

Thus it was a most welcome sight to Jerusha
and Dorothy when, after a few weeks, certain
of the hens began to go about clucking and ruf-
fling their feathers, sitting on their nests for
hours at a time, and altogether showing that
they were bent on settling down to be quiet family hens. Blanche was the first to be given
fourteen beautiful creamy eggs. The children
looked on in awe, while John Pearson lifted the
great white clucking creature, and Jerusha arranged the eggs beneath her ample breast and
wings. Next, all four hens in the corncrib went
to sitting. It was a beautiful sight to see them,
each in her own corner, with her head down, her
feathers widespread, all the thirteen or fourteen
eggs beneath her well covered; each one intensely quiet, yet each with an air of subdued

excitement. Lady Jane soon followed suit. Six hens were now sitting.

" Three hens on fourteen eggs and three hens on thirteen eggs makes eighty-one chickens," Marcia announced after long battling with the figures.

" Eighty-one chickens ! "

" Then suppose Dot, Fantail, and Biddy go to sitting, and each has thirteen eggs, that will be thirty-nine more. One hundred and twenty chickens ! "

" One hundred and twenty chickens ! "

" Don't count your chickens until they are hatched," said grandmamma Bickerdyke.

" Don't count your chickens until they are hatched," said Miss Hester.

" Don't count your chickens till they 're hatched," said John Pearson ; and even Jerusha, who was in high spirits over her enterprise, also uttered the same warning. It had sounded familiar to the children, even from the first, like " Haste makes waste," " One thing at a time."

" Don't count your chickens till they 're hatched." Dorothy repeated it to herself, trying to see the virtue of the saying. Why not count them now when there was time ? By and by, when the one hundred and twenty chickens were hatched and running round, it might not be so easy a matter to count them.

The hens had been sitting about a week, when one morning when Dorothy went to take a peep between lessons, she found that something had happened.

She ran back to John Pearson and Jerusha, who were looking at the beans just up, or, as John described it, " a-busting the ground."

" Oh, John ! " cried Dorothy. " Oh, Jerusha ! "

" What has happened ? " " What 's the matter ? " John and Jerusha exclaimed, looking at Dorothy's face, which had grown pale, while her eyes seemed starting from her head.

" I don't know what 's happened ! I don't know what 's the matter ! " cried Dorothy wildly. " Come and see ! "

She led the way, and pointed at the corncrib in the stable.

" Well, I never did ! " said Jerusha.

" Did you ever see the beat of that ? " said John.

Nobody could tell what had happened ; nobody could tell just what was the matter, but the sight that met their eyes was this : instead of, as yesterday, each of the four hens being quietly and decently ensconced in her own cor-

ner over her own eggs, all the eggs from all
four nests, except a few which had strayed, were
gathered into the centre of the box, and on these,
in a sort of a pile, were grouped the four hens,
all alike bristled up sullenly, and each sitting
with an evident fury of intention to hatch all
the eggs for herself.

"And they've left five eggs out in the cold,"
said Dorothy.

"I ought to ha' knowed more," said John,
with an air of intense disgust, "than to have
let you set them four hens so close together, and
so ought you, Jerusha."

"I always heard from my youth up," said
Jerusha, "that hens stick best to the nest they
choose themselves."

Dorothy looked wistfully from one to the
other as they spoke.

"I'm blest if I feel sure what's the best
thing to be done," said John.

"I know what's going to be done," declared
Jerusha, with an air of determination. "Each of
them hens is a-going back into her own corner,
and there she's got to stay till she hatches her
eggs, even if I have to sit here all day and all
night and watch her."

John shook his head, not so much in denial,
as if hopelessly perplexed before the situation.

Jerusha's plan was acted upon, however. Jerusha lifted two of the hens, John lifted two, and Dorothy proceeded to count out fourteen eggs into White Lady's original nest, and thirteen into each of the others.

There was no doubt about the accuracy of Dorothy's count, for she carefully laid out each egg before the eyes of John and Jerusha. Singular to relate, however, when she had put fourteen into one corner and thirteen into each of the other corners, there still remained nine eggs in the centre of the bin. She gazed at them aghast. It seemed like a juggler's trick.

"Now, where on earth did them nine eggs come from?" queried John.

"They must have gone on laying after they went to sitting," said Jerusha.

"But what shall we do?" demanded Dorothy, indifferent to theory.

There was only one thing to be done, apparently, which was to divide the extra eggs fairly between the four hens. Each, indeed, was ready to expand her feathers to meet any demand. Each hen, too, had settled anew to her duty with a conscientious air, which seemed to promise better conduct for the future. Jerusha kept watch; John Pearson kept watch; Dorothy, Marcia, Gay, and Lucy kept watch; Carlo and

Flossy longed to keep watch, and had to be carefully restrained from stealing into the stable. Nevertheless, by the day after the morrow, all the eggs were in the centre of the corn bin again, and the four hens were again mounting guard over them. There were by this time sixty-five eggs.

" I 'm going to give each one of them hens a box to herself," said John Pearson. " That 's what they want. White Lady shall stay here in the corncrib, and I 'll rig up three other boxes, and put 'em next to it."

This was a sensible arrangement, but Dappy, Speckle, and Topknot declined to coöperate; they persisted in leaving their own eggs to get stone cold and going back to sit with White Lady.

It was Miss Roxy Burt who was called in to give advice.

"Put all the eggs back into the big nest," she said. " Let the hens have their own way. They know more than you think they do."

There was some comfort in this definite statement; but everybody's calculations had been upset. It was discovered presently that each time Lady Jane returned to her nest in the barrel after her morning's feed, it was her habit to break one or two of her eggs. Dot went to

sitting, not in the box John had arranged for
her comfort, but on a place higher up, which
nobody but a winged creature could have inves-
tigated. Fantail had hidden somewhere; nobody but herself knew the secrets of her retreat.
Biddy, like Blanche, conformed to the laws of
good sense and personal comfort, and had taken
a box.

But everybody's faith in the hens and confi-
dence in the one hundred and twenty chickens
was shaken. Jerusha was depressed; John shook
his head, and said he never had taken any stock
in the enterprise. Not even Marcia ventured to
predict what would happen. Against a hen's stu-
pidity the best efforts seemed to be powerless.

The only thing to do was to watch the al-
manac and await events.

Blanche had been brooding over her eggs
nineteen days. It was a Saturday; a beautiful soft day in May when all the sky, and earth,
and tree, and flower, and springing seed suddenly thrilled with the touch of tender, stirring
life.

"It's Saturday, Jerusha," said Dorothy.
"Just think, — *perhaps* on Monday!"

She did not say any more, at least in words.
She needed to say no more. Was not Jerusha
also counting the days?

Dorothy went out and gave one look. Blanche appeared as usual, — calm, majestic, and undisturbed, not as if she was in the least degree upset by the idea that her eggs were on the point of hatching. The other hens also all seemed quiet and self-possessed, except the four in the corn bin, who, as usual, had an air of excitement as they sat in a heap together. At this moment Speckle happened to be on top.

Dorothy glanced at them and shook her head. She was saying to herself what stupid, naughty, ungrateful hens they were, when all at once something startled her. She looked, advanced nearer, listened an instant, then drew back ; she looked again, then fled to the house shrieking, " Oh, Jerusha, Jerusha ! "

In less than five minutes, Jerusha, John Pearson, and Miss Hester were all on their way to the stable.

What Dorothy had heard had been a soft, faint little " peep." What she had seen had been a bright-eyed downy little creature looking out at her from the breast feathers of one of the circle of hens.

" It can't be," Jerusha was saying. " Them hens hain't been setting but eighteen days. I did n't give 'em any eggs till twenty-four hours after Blanche had hers."

" 'T ain't in natur'," John Pearson had insisted.

But those four hens in the corncrib had managed all through to compass the unexpected. There were actually four beautiful little white chicks out of their shells, two of them bright, alert, and eager to be fed. Although Jerusha said it was incredible, and John Pearson maintained it was impossible, the miracle had happened nevertheless.

" You must have made a false calculation," said Miss Hester, at which suggestion Jerusha actually snorted in indignation.

The other children had to take Dorothy's word for it about the four chickens for two days more. Then Blanche came off her nest with twelve beautiful little creatures of her own, and the four from the corn bin were added to her flock. No more had been hatched, and not one of the four hens was disposed to adopt these stray nestlings ; each being afraid, perhaps, that the least concession to them might put her claim to the whole pile of eggs in jeopardy. It is not often that a hen has some seventy eggs under her, and a mere matter of four small chicks is not worth looking after.

Blanche was placed in a coop out on the clean green grass. She was an easy, comfortable-going mother, and was perfectly willing to have the children sit down and watch her and her chickens from morning until· night. Nothing in the world is so perfect and so wonderful as a chicken just out of its shell.

There are some people who think it is a superior sort of thing never to wonder. I would n't, myself, give a pin for a child who never wonders. There 's a dreadful lack of understanding and sympathy behind that superior attitude of thought and mind.

Dorothy, Marcia, Lucy, and Gay experienced not only wonder, but delight, and an almost greater puzzlement, over the chicks and their mother. How could little balls of fluff, just out of the shell, possibly know so much? It was painful to see that they were as selfish and greedy among themselves as if they had been hard at work getting their living out of a cruel, hard world for years. But how pretty they were! How deliciously full of fun and spirits! What soft little voices they had, and how many different notes in their voices! And what a delightful little crooning song they sang when they nestled under their mother's feathers at night!

When they were only four days old the chickens recognized the children, and would come running towards them.

"I suppose it's only because they want to be
fed," Marcia said; "but it's awfully cunning
all the same."         .

"I don't believe it's because they want to be
fed," Dorothy insisted. "It's because they're
so glad we have come."

Carlo and Flossy, at first, were full of curiosity and eagerness about the chickens. They, too,
wanted to have their fun with them, and, alas!
it was death to one chick. The dogs repented
in sackcloth and ashes. They were talked to
by the hour. "Poor little chicken!" one of the
children after another would say in accents of
displeasure and pointing the finger of scorn at
them. Flossy had no heavy sins on his conscience, but Carlo felt it to the bottom of his
soul, and would whine, lie on his back, and put
up his paws in supplication. After a little, he
refused to come near the brood at all.

In the course of a week seven more chickens
were hatched in the corncrib; but still the
four hens continued to sit on. Finally the nest
had to be broken up; the corncrib was covered
over. Even then, White Lady and Dappy continued to sit about in dejected attitudes near
the place where they had brooded with so many
fond hopes.

The hen on the beam had it all her own way

for a while ; but one day she flew down clucking beseechingly and authoritatively, and was
followed by ten little white and black chicks.
Lady Jane came out of her barrel with eight,
and Fantail had twelve.

Dorothy had learned, by this time, what the
proverb meant about not counting chickens before they are hatched. But the fact was that
with some forty or fifty there were as many as
the place could hold conveniently.

# CHAPTER X

NOTHING had really happened for a good
while when Marcia began to talk about her picnic. They had done a good many things : had
made expedition after expedition to the "spring-
lot;" they had watched brood after brood of
chickens; had named each individual one ; they
had gathered wild strawberries, to say nothing
of eating berries of all kinds that came within
reach. But all had been easy, safe, and generally acceptable. Now the weather had become
very warm, and one hot afternoon the children
had carried some of Jerusha's cakes up to the
top of the hill, where they had coasted on that
moonlight night, and they were pretending to
have a picnic.

"I should like," said Marcia, " to have a real
picnic. What I want is to know what is on the
other side of those woods."

Green and cool and grand stretched the line
of forest at the west, crowning the swelling up-
lands beyond the Swallow River. The sun set

there and the moon ; there too the stars went
down. Thunder-storms came up from behind
that horizon. Now, each afternoon, when a
shower was hoped for, everybody looked to see
if white, fleecy clouds were showing their heads
above the sky-line of those tall trees.

Dorothy had had an idea that the world ended
on the other side of those woods. After a long,
long tramp in search of chestnuts the autumn
before, they had reached the outskirts of the
forest, and had peered in, trying to see daylight
through the long vista of trunks of trees. But
the shade grew more and more dense ; there
was no sign of an opening. And this thought
of going through the woods was one of those
wonderful thoughts which could only have occurred to Marcia.

" And we are all not only going through those
woods," she went on, " but we are going to
find out what is on the other side."

" How could we ever get there ? " demanded
Lucy.

Marcia gave a little nod.

" I mean to borrow Pocahontas," she returned.

" I — I — I 'll drive him," cried Gay.

" Not you, Gay," said Marcia.  " Miss Roxy
would never lend him to you, — never in the
world."

This was true, and Gay, after a moment's feeling of rebellion that he, a boy, must be driven
about by a mere girl, gave in to logic and reason. Somehow, it always was so. The sting of
it lurked in Bert's disdain of Gay's going about
with a " lot of girls." But then, as Lucy explained, Bert was not " a twin." The fatality
of it lay in Gay's being a twin.

More than once, when Miss Roxy Burt had
been sitting with Mrs. Dundas listening to the
last accounts of what " poor Paul " was doing in
South Africa, Marcia had been permitted to
drive the pony for half an hour. Nothing could
better have shown Miss Roxy's leaning to Marcia. Pocahontas was not a mere pony; he was
a sort of personage. He had been trained for a
circus, and had been one of a company of per-
forming ponies, until, most unluckily, while going through some exercise, the tendons of his leg
were injured by a rope. Thus, considered useless,
he was offered to any one who would buy him.
It was Miss Roxy Burt who out of pity made a
bid for the poor creature. He was turned into
the meadow behind the Burt place, and after a
few months' grazing defied prediction and got
well. This had happened years ago, and by this
time Pocahontas had waxed old in Miss Roxy's
service, and she and he and the phaeton were

known for miles around. She did not set up to be a doctor, but always carried about a case of homeopathic remedies, and administered little white pellets to any one willing to become her patient. Not only pellets, but sympathy, care, nursing, and good food, which sometimes did as much good as doses of aconite, belladonna, and nux vomica.

Poky (short for Pocahontas) was to Miss Roxy's mind a very knowing creature. Having been trained to the circus, he persisted in believing that all the world's a circus. He could not get the ideal of respectable private life into his head. He was always waiting for the signal to begin his performance. Not given his cue, how could he possibly know what to do?

Miss Roxy, with her wide-brimmed straw hat well off her head, her gray curls on each side of her face, and spectacles on nose, would mount into her phaeton, gather up the whip and reins, one in each hand, give a twitch, and say, —

"Now, Poky! Get up, Poky!"

Poky, however, with his head down, his feet set stubbornly, apparently declined to make a start.

"Now, Poky!" Miss Roxy would plead. "Why, Poky! Poky! Did you hear me say get up, Poky? Why, I really am surprised

at you, Poky! Do you think we can wait here
all day, Poky? You can't be tired, Poky!
Now, Poky! I say, Poky!"

Miss Roxy would stop for a moment to peer
over her far-sighted spectacles at the reluctant
Pocahontas.

"Now, Poky," she would begin again, "don't
you remember what I said, Poky?" at the same
time touching his flank with the butt end of her
whip. He was waiting for this signal, and off
he would start. Miss Roxy always believed it
was the force of her reasoning that had overcome his obstinacy.

She never really whipped him. At the sound
of the crack of the whip or the touch of the lash
the creature was capable of the oddest antics.
He loved to describe a circle. Any wide open
space brought back early associations. Miss
Roxy would never have dared tell her sister,
Miss Amelia, or her brother, the Rev. Dr. Burt,
how, more than once, the pony had insisted
on traveling round and round a large empty
place near Bristol Basin, where four roads met.
Once, when the Rev. Dr. Burt (now retired
from active service) was officiating at a funeral,
in the absence of the parish clergyman, Pocahontas (whom Dr. Burt was driving at the head
of the procession), catching sight of the circular

drive before Dundas House, insisted upon entering the grounds and making the circuit.

These pranks of Poky's of course pained Miss
Roxy, but, as she said, the bad tricks we learn
when we are young are apt to stick to us all
our lives, and ponies need not be expected to be
wiser than human beings. However, Pocahontas had nowadays waxed old and lazy.

Marcia made her plea for a whole long afternoon with Pocahontas and the phaeton in this
wise : —

" Oh, Miss Roxy, I am so fond of Poky."

Marcia said this standing at the pony's head
and rubbing his nose. Miss Roxy, naturally
pleased, replied, —

" Poky is an excellent pony. Such a really
sensible pony."

" I really think," continued Marcia, " that
Poky knows me."

" There is very little that Poky does n't know,
— I mean, of course, things that he has an
opportunity of knowing," said Miss Roxy.   .

" And I think," persisted Marcia, " that Poky
likes me, — likes me rather particularly."

" I dare say. I like you, Marcia; I like you
rather particularly, and Poky and I are apt to
be of one mind. I don't hear quite so much
good of you as I should like to hear, Marcia,"

Miss Roxy added, glancing kindly at the girl over her spectacles, "but I always say that you are well-meaning, — that your faults come from your high spirits."

Marcia always listened to strictures upon herself with the imperturbable air of the old Dundases. Miss Roxy said to herself now that, although Marcia resembled her mother, she could see traits of Paul Dundas about the brow and eyes.

"Miss Roxy! dear Miss Roxy!" Marcia proceeded, "will you do me a very great kindness?"

"Why, my dear child, — I have so little in my power. For your father's sake — if there were anything I " —

"Just let me have Poky and the carriage for one whole long afternoon," pleaded Marcia.

After explaining, arguing, promising, listening minutely to every sort of detail relating to the proper way to manage Pocahontas, Marcia got what she asked for. Miss Roxy consented to send Pocahontas to Dundas House at half-past one on the following day.

It did really seem a wonderful coincidence that Mrs. Bickerdyke and Miss Hester set out that same Wednesday morning to spend a night at North Swallowfield. It was such fine weather

Mrs. Fuller had sent over a comfortable carriage for her mother just after breakfast, asking her and Miss Hester to come and enjoy the late strawberries, which were now in perfection. There was some question as to whether Dorothy should go, but as the little girl had not been expressly named in the invitation, it was decided, much to the relief of Dorothy herself, that she should stay at home with Jerusha, who was left in charge.

" Now, Miss Marcia Dundas," said Jerusha, " will you promise not to be up to no mischief if I let Dorothy go ? "

" Mischief ? " echoed Marcia. " I don't know what mischief means. I've got to take good care of this pony, — that's all I know, — to keep him from being up to mischief."

It was quarter to two. The phaeton and pony were standing in the grass-grown drive behind Dundas House. Lucy and Gay had a lunch of bread and butter packed in a box; this was stowed away on one side under the seat. Jerusha had toiled over with a huge hamper, and this was placed in the middle. Dorothy carried a blue and white wicker basket, which was tucked in the only bit of space left. The phaeton was low and wide and comfortable. There was plenty of room in it for two grown persons,

so of course four half-grown would have room
and to spare.

Carlo and Flossy were running backwards
and forwards, expressing great interest in the
expedition. The question had been discussed
whether the dogs should or should not be permitted to go, but Carlo decided the matter by
not allowing himself to be caught and tied up.
Carlo was wiser in his generation than Flossy,
the child of light, and when a certain gleam of
fun appeared in Carlo's eyes, he was too much
for Gay or for Lucy.

The first idea, that all four could find room
on the seat, turned out not to be quite prac-
ticable.

" You 'll have to sit on the floor, Gay," said
Lucy.

Gay was staring hard at Marcia, who had
taken her seat and grasped the reins ; and Dorothy squeezed in between her and Lucy.

" Sit down, Gay," Marcia said, " I 'm going
to start."

He looked so full of worry and anxiety that
Dorothy pitied him.

" I 'll change places with you when you get
tired, Gay," she said.

" I— I— I— I— " spluttered Gay, pointing
to Marcia.

"Count three, Gay," said Lucy.

Gay struggled with himself silently a moment, then burst forth, —

"People don't sit on that side when they drive."

And, droll to relate, Marcia was sitting on the left side.

"What difference does it make, anyhow?" said Marcia. But they unpacked themselves, and packed themselves up anew, and Gay could now sit down contentedly on the hard floor, saying to himself that girls did not know things. They might think they knew; they might put on airs and pretend to know, but they did n't.

"Now, Poky!" said Marcia. "Get up, Poky."

And, strange to say, Poky did get up. Off they went down the drive, between the rows of maple-trees; out of the open back gate into the lane; down the lane towards the river. Before they crossed the railroad track they paused, as Jerusha had directed, looked up, looked down, waited, and listened. The dogs, too, stopped short, cocked their heads on one side, and looked and listened. Nothing was to be seen; nothing was to be heard.

Across the track they went. Here they were safe in the fern-bordered lane. All four of them

now looked at the others and smiled. Oh, how
delightful this was ! Usually they toiled along
this road on foot. This was promotion. They
knew exactly how kings and queens felt in a
royal progress. It was perfectly blissful to sit
squeezed up on the rather high seat, — and then,
when one could no longer endure to have one's
legs dangle down without reaching the floor, to
stand up a little, in order to get the queer feeling out of them.

"Is it nice down there, Gay ? " Dorothy inquired.

" P—p—pretty nice," murmured Gay ; and
presently, rather to Marcia's and Lucy's relief,
Dorothy said she, too, would try it. Down she
went on the floor beside Gay.

" They 've mended the fence," she observed,
and then they all laughed. They had made
more than one expedition after flowers since
that first in early April. In fact, they had almost forgotten about the time of the freshet.
But to-day the recollection came back, and they
all laughed. The Swallow River was a very
quiet little river to-day. As they clattered up
the ascent to the bridge, Dorothy and Gay stood
up and looked out at the clear, bright water running over the sparkling stones, and at the long
branches of the willow-tree swaying in the ripples.

They did not like to confess, even to themselves, that their legs got cramped with sitting, but pretended that they liked to watch the dogs. Carlo and Flossy had run to the edge of the river as they approached, lapped a little water, and waded in to a certain distance, perhaps to cool their legs, perhaps to try whether they could ford it. It was too deep ; so out they came, up to the bridge, crossed over, then ran down to the other bank, again lapped a little water, and waded in as before.

So far it was familiar, well - known ground. Usually the children's expedition branched off here across the fields to the " spring-lot." Not so this afternoon. On they jogged towards Wolf Hill. The pasture-lands on each side of the river ended ; the grain - fields began. Tall rye, nodding oats, and Indian corn, not yet tasseled, stretched out on either side as far as the eye could reach. They had not known, until this minute, how hot the day was. Everything began to give out heat and glare ! — not only the sun, but the sand of the road, the stones in the sand, and the rocks piled up on either side. A sort of green flame with little points of white light seemed to play over the grain-fields and emit sparkles. Now and then a breeze would make a long, slow, beautiful billow over the rye

and oats, but no cooler breath of air reached the
party in or outside the phaeton. The dogs hung
out their tongues, panting. The children were
all engaged in discussing what Wolf Hill was
and where Wolf Hill began. Just ahead were
three great hickory-trees. The trees threw a
shade over some rocks beneath them, and really
the nook did look invitingly cool.

" I see raspberries ! " cried Marcia.  " Whoa,
Poky !  Let 's get out."

Dorothy and Gay were very glad to get out.
Pocahontas was ready to take a rest; he stood
perfectly still, put his legs out as far apart as
they would go, and went fast asleep.

The children clambered over the rocks and
picked the raspberries, just ripening, with great
satisfaction.  Anything to eat, somehow, does
seem to add attractions to a place.  They ate all
the ripe raspberries; also all the green raspberries.  There were a few strawberries in the
grass, very small ones, but they were devoured
with keen relish.  Finally they sat down and
enjoyed the shade and coolness, although the
rocks, all at a steep slope, were most uncom-
fortable to sit on.  They decided that this was
Wolf Hill, and that probably wolves used to
congregate here.  Gay suggested that perhaps
they had better get out their bread and butter,
and have a lunch.

This remark reawoke Marcia's ambition.
There were the woods they were to traverse,
looking not so very, very far off.

" No bread and butter till we have got a good
deal farther on than this," she said. " Come,
wake up, Poky. Jump in, children."

She picked up the reins, hanging loose, as she
spoke. The children were about to obey, when
Pocahontas began to back, then, of his own accord, was about to turn the phaeton round.

" He thinks we 're going home," observed
Lucy.

Marcia, quite indignant, ran forward, seized
the bridle, and brought the pony back to position.

" Hurry up," she called ; " he wants to start."

This was quite true. Dorothy, Lucy, and Gay
clambered in, Marcia followed, took the reins,
and called, —

" Now, then, Poky ! "

Pocahontas again made a movement as if to
turn about.

" You are not going home, Poky," said Marcia, tugging hard at the reins. " You 're going
up to those woods, and through those woods.
Get up, Poky."

The dogs began to run forward and back,
barking, to show the pony the way.

Pocahontas, not permitted to turn round, put down his head, planted his feet deeper in the sand, and declined to budge.

" Oh, dear ! " faltered Lucy, who was timid.

" Now, Poky ! " Marcia began, with something of Miss Roxy's bland habit of persuasion, " now, Poky ! Get up, Poky. This is n't proper behavior, Poky. We want to go through those woods, Poky."

" Please, dear Poky ! Try to do as you 'd like to be done by, there 's a good Poky," said Dorothy.

" You shall have a nice cake if you 'll go on, Poky," said Lucy.

" G—g—g— "

" Count three, Gay," said Lucy.

" Give him all the cakes," said Gay.

Pocahontas did not move.

" I 'm really surprised at you, Poky," Marcia began once more. " Miss Roxy will be very sorry to hear how naughty you have been, Poky. She said you were so sensible, Poky. Do you call this sensible ? She told me that the whip was the very last resort, Poky ! I don't want to whip you, Poky. It would hurt my feelings very much to whip you, Poky, but " —

At the mention of the whip Gay had drawn it out from its safe receptacle beneath the leather boot and began gently to flick the lash.

"Be careful, Gay," said Marcia warningly. "Don't touch him with it until I tell you."

Gay perhaps intended to be careful, but wishing to let Pocahontas understand that the whip could at need be forthcoming, he went on flourishing it in the air until, presently, it gave a loud *cr-cr-crack !*

The pony turned back his ears, threw up his head, tossed his mane, kicked out his legs, and set off at a pace so astonishing that the reins dropped from Marcia's hands and Gay fell backwards against Lucy, who caught him in her arms. They fairly flew on, Pocahontas showing by the motion of his head and the spirited fling of his mane that he was not without some personal enjoyment in the cutting of these capers. The way, for some distance, lay straight and comparatively smooth between banks ; but after the run had lasted about a half mile, the road forked suddenly, the right turn leading to the woods, and the left, a mere cart-path, opening into a rough clearing given over to berry bushes, rocks, and half-decayed stumps of trees. Pocahontas took the left, making so sharp a turn that the children had to cling to the seat in order not to be thrown out. Their cries of "Oh, Poky!"

"Now, Poky!" "Poky, stop!" "Whoa, whoa!"
only seemed to make the pony increase his
speed. And as he was all the time gathering a
little more and more rein, he became more and
more rampant. When the cart-path ended, on
he went, prancing and curveting, into the waste
of huckleberry bushes.

"Oh, what shall we do?" cried Marcia.

"I — I — I — " Gay began, at the same time
leaning over the dashboard, whip in hand, to
make an effort to fish up the reins, when the
phaeton was suddenly brought up with a terrible
jolt. The right wheel having lodged in some
bilberry bushes and the left made fast against a
rock, Pocahontas's mad career was checked. Having accomplished so much, the pony yielded to circumstances, and seeing some fine herbage at the
base of the rock, he began peacefully to nibble.

"I'll get out," said Marcia.

"I — I — I — I — I was just going to stop
him myself," remarked Gay, but nobody listened. Lucy and Dorothy were clambering out,
each looking a little pale.

"Suppose he had broken the carriage all to
pieces," said Marcia. "I do just wonder what
Miss Roxy would have said to me then." With
a knowing air Gay examined the wheels and
shafts. Fortunately no harm had been done.

"I'll tell you what we will do," Marcia announced. "You three children get in again, and I will lead Poky the rest of the way."

"Oh, please let me walk, Marcia! I should a great deal rather walk," pleaded Dorothy.

"So should I," said Lucy.

"I — too," said Gay. "I—I'm st—st— stiff with riding so long."

"I don't like horses," said Dorothy.

"Nor I."

"Or ponies, either."

"Particularly ponies," said Lucy.

Marcia had gone up to Pocahontas, and, taking him by the bridle, backed him away from the rocks and bushes.

"Do you know," she called to the others, "he is regularly grinning at me, the beast! He thinks it is good fun."

The dogs also thought it was good fun. They had not been quite easy and contented in their minds at seeing the children in the phaeton, instead of being on foot as usual. Now they dashed forward, then ran back, jumped up and down, barked at the pony, and altogether acted as if they had lost their heads.

Oh, how the sun beat down in that open, unshaded place! Marcia walked on one side of the pony, holding the bridle, and Gay on the

other. Dorothy and Lucy lagged behind the
phaeton, trying to get a little shade from the
cover. Had it not been for Marcia's indomitable
resolution to go through the woods, they would
all have given up, — that line of deep shadow
looked so far, far off. By Gay's little silver
watch it was only ten minutes past three. Not
even Gay believed it. They had started at a
quarter before two. Dorothy said it seemed
a day ago. Lucy declared she knew it was a
whole year ago. It was certainly incredible
that all these events had happened in less than
an hour and a half.

But Marcia behaved as if she found the experience delightful. And if Marcia really did
like it! That was the way with Marcia. Diffi-
culties that robbed others of spirit seemed to
give her a sort of passion of enjoyment. Anything to be done was to be done, and personal
discomforts were not to be thought of. On she
went in the full glare of the sun, her torn straw
hat far back on her head, her hair clinging in
little wet curls to her forehead and temples; her
great eyes shining; her cheeks and lips red as
crimson cherries, — all the time laughing and
talking. The pony, every few rods, would decide that he did not like this sort of thing at
all; he would stop short, plant his forefeet

in the turf, and drop his head between his
legs.

"Poky, my dear Poky," Marcia would say,
addressing him with arguments and remon-
strances; "it is not worth while for you to put
on those little airs, Poky, for you are out on a
picnic, — a whole long afternoon picnic! We're
not going home till almost sunset, Poky. Do
you hear? There are the woods, and we are
going through those woods. You can't stop and
rest till you are on the other side of those woods.
Then, dear Poky, you shall have a perfectly
beautiful time," and she would pull him along
almost by main force.

They toiled on. The forest, which from a distance had had a uniform color, began to take on
different shades of green. They could make
out trees standing singly and in groups on the
border. A little more and they were under the
lengthening shadows, enjoying grateful coolness.

How glad they all were! Everybody, except
Marcia, had lost spirit; the pony had stumbled
along at a snail's pace; even the dogs, with
lolling tongues, had finally slunk under the
phaeton and panted on quite discouraged.

Here they actually were beneath the great
dome of foliage, and it seemed, compared with the
glare of the open meadow, as if they had passed

into a dimly lighted church. They all stood
still, looking up at the green arches of the roof.
Here, on the edge of the forest, light streamed
in and fell on the white, feathery flowers, the
moss, and the fine, scanty grass. But this was
the daylight they were leaving behind. Ahead
all was dark and cool and colorless ; the wide
cart-path was the only open vista.

"Isn't this worth coming for?" demanded
Marcia. Her eyes had grown dark and pensive,
but she was smiling, and her teeth shone like
little pearls.

"It makes me just a little bit afraid," said
Dorothy in a hushed voice.

The dogs, too, made up their minds that they
had better wait and see what sort of a strange
place this was. There were so many soft noises
in the wood: a stir and rustle in the branches
above them ; something seemed to be creeping
through the thickets and the undergrowth. Accordingly, not quite liking it, Carlo and Flossy
kept very close to the children, for suppose there
should be strange beasts!

"I — I — I —" Gay began.

"Count three, Gay," said Lucy.

"I — I — I don't believe there are any bears
in these woods," Gay finally announced, with
some swagger.

"Bears!" Marcia repeated, with just that expression of scorn in which few could excel her. "There may be a squirrel or two."

And, as if to reassure them, a red squirrel at this moment ran across their path not ten feet away. Carlo and Flossy, slinking behind, tails down, their hair stiffening along their dorsal column, thinking of bears, no doubt, and lions and tigers, at the sight of this enemy regained heart and courage. Up went their tails; with a joyful bark they dashed forward just in time to see the squirrel run up the trunk of a tree, where, gaining a safe degree of elevation, he gazed down at them with his bright little eyes, then, chattering, retreated to a still higher bough and vanished.

It really was a wonderful wood; an enchanted wood. Quite reassured, Carlo and Flossy ran hither and thither, following up scents, investigating holes and hollow tree trunks, now and then making something scurry into the deeper thickets. They crossed and recrossed the path in front of Marcia and Gay and the pony and phaeton; with Lucy and Dorothy bringing up the rear.

Dorothy had gradually recovered from her fears, although, somehow, her heart beat as she looked about her with wonder and surprise, and

listened to the soft sigh and rustle in the leaves.
Now and then sounded the note of a bird, — a
persistent, soft note. Dorothy thought to herself, " Oh, if I could only see that bird ! " She
strained her eyes to look far up into the green-
gold glimmer of the roof of the wood. While
she still looked up, her quick ear caught a sound
in the undergrowth beside her. She turned ;
there was a little gray bird ; silver-gray, with
feathers preened to the softness of satin. Its
eye, too, was gray, set in a ring of white, and
with its little gray eyes it looked at Dorothy,
and Dorothy gazed back at it. It evidently
wondered about her and did not seem afraid,
and as she went on, it flew silently from twig to
twig, and followed her, always regarding her
with that soft, inquisitive eye.

" Oh, dear ! " Dorothy whispered, " it makes
me almost feel as if I had done something
naughty."

" Oh, dear ! " cried Marcia, so loudly that the
little gray bird flew away, " there 's a fallen
tree across the path."

" Oh, dear ! " said Lucy, " we shall never get
through this wood. I 'm sure we shan't."

" I — I — I — I — f—f—feel like M—M—
Moses in the wilderness," said Gay.

Luckily the obstacle in the path was not a

whole tree, only the branch of a tree which had splintered down the side of a great chestnut in the storm of two days before. Marcia lifted the end of it and tugged hard; Gay lifted and tugged; so did Lucy and Dorothy. The dogs desisted from their sport and came and looked on, as if to help. Only the ungrateful pony, the object of all these labors and pains, made no attempt to get the obstacle out of his own path, but after blinking, and rather grinning, fell to cropping the thin green blades of grass which pushed their way through the rich mould.

Finally, after four pairs of arms were pulled almost out of their sockets, the obstruction was removed and the way was clear. Marcia once more took Pocahontas by the bridle; the children followed, and the dogs began to frisk about. Dorothy caught sight of a white flower and went aside, out of the path, to look at it. It was a pipsissewa, growing at the foot of an oak-tree among the leaves of last year, half-eaten acorns, little sticks, and moss. As she stooped to look closer, something flew up, knocking against her cheek, and making a loud whirring noise. And under her feet? What were these little things that moved? Had the brown leaves suddenly come to life?

"Oh, oh, oh," cried Dorothy. "Oh, Marcia! Is it chickens?"

When Marcia and the others came running towards her to see what she meant, Dorothy was standing looking perfectly bewildered, staring at the ground.

"I don't know," she said. "One minute I saw speckled chickens — ever so many of them — then all at once " —

"They must have been partridges," observed Marcia.

"But what became of them?" demanded Dorothy. "One minute they were right here — I was almost stepping on them — then, in another minute " —

Alas! Carlo and Flossy knew something about that family of partridges. Carlo had seen one of the old ones go whirring up past him to find safety on the bough of a tree. Flossy, meanwhile, had made a grab at the other as she scuttled off into the bushes, but he had missed her. Carlo was more sure : there was one pounce, a shake, and then the poor, faithful mother partridge was just a limp heap of feathers. Flossy contented himself, meanwhile, with one of the pulpy young ones.

"S—s—see there !" cried Gay.

Dorothy followed the direction of Gay's finger and uttered a shriek of indignation.

"Oh, you bad dogs !" 'she screamed, running

towards them. "Oh, you horrid, wicked, cruel dogs! You 've killed both these poor, beautiful creatures! Oh, how naughty you are! Oh, these poor birds! I wish I had never seen you, you bad, heartless, wicked dogs! "

Dorothy had pressed the poor dead things against her breast, and was stroking their feathers gently. The other children looked at her and at the partridges with solemn eyes. Lucy began to cry. Gay would have liked to cry, but that would have been like a girl, so he began to kick at the dogs, who, suddenly pulled up in their mad pranks, were quite surprised and in dismay at this burst of fury on the part of their master.

"It is a shame," said Marcia. There had been a good deal of cold water flung on her enthusiasm that day. "Dear, pretty little creatures." She, too, passed her hand over the soft plumage. "I would n't have had them killed for anything ; but now that they are killed, may I have 'em and cook 'em for mamma, Dorothy ? "

"Cook them ? " repeated Dorothy, bewildered.

"They 'll be good for mamma," said Marcia. "She 's not strong, you know. She loves birds, but does n't often get them."

Dorothy, all alive with pity and drawing every breath in pain, still looked horrified.

"Why," said Marcia, "if a man had killed them with a gun and taken them to market " —

Gay pulled at Dorothy. "They 'll do her good," he suggested.

Dorothy, still bewildered and disenchanted, yielded up the birds to Marcia.

"Oh, yes, if they will do her good."

The dogs, quiet for one moment, now at some fresh sound cocked up their ears and were about to dash off again, when Dorothy flung herself upon them, and, seizing Carlo by the ears and Flossy by the tail, gathered them both under her arms.

"No, no, no," she cried, "I will not let you go killing some more beautiful things."

It was no easy matter to go on holding the dogs by the ears and tail. Still Dorothy felt she must hinder any more wicked mischief. Accordingly, it was decided to put Carlo and Flossy in the phaeton and tie them to the seat. The extra hitching-rein was slipped over the rail of the dashboard, then each end was buckled to the collar of the dogs. After a few moments of surprise and insubordination, Carlo and Flossy accepted the inevitable, and, with some natural pride in such elevation, sat side by side on the seat of the phaeton, looking for all the world as if they considered themselves superior creatures

taking an airing, while inferior creatures went
on foot.

The children had all taken hold of Pocahontas's bridle, and were pulling him on at a rapid
pace. The afternoon would not last forever, and
they were beginning to think longingly of the
contents of the baskets, and of the comfort it
would be to sit down and have their picnic. It
was evident that they were nearing the end of the
wood. The air, which for a time had been damp
and cool, grew warmer. Tall, feathery ferns
began to show in great masses, and instead of
the vistas before them being dim and dark, there
came a sudden brilliance, and long shafts of
sunlight made their way in.

" Here we are ! " shouted Marcia. Even Pocahontas, sniffing the scent of fresh pastures, set
off at such a gallop that the children could
hardly keep up with him. As they emerged
from the shadow, they were all dazzled by the
light. The sun was shining straight in their
faces out of a brilliant blue sky. They stopped,
shaded their eyes with their hands, and gazed
about them. What they saw was a very green
and fertile-looking field, which, descending in a
gentle roll, met the banks of a brook fringed
with alders. Beyond the brook the ground rose
again into a hill, and above the hill was a high

mountainous ridge, whose dark fir woods showed heavily against the sky line.

This was the promised land.

"I knew it would be worth coming for," Marcia now observed with a complacent air, as if she had arranged the meadow and the brook and the hill and the notch in the mountain, where the sun was to go down. "I felt sure it would be a beautiful place to have a picnic."

"I should love to come here in the spring after wild flowers," said Dorothy.

"L—l—let's have our p—p—picnic right off," said Gay.

"So I say," Marcia rejoined. "Lucy, you and Dorothy find a place to sit down, and Gay, come and help me unbuckle Poky, so that he can graze comfortably."

Dorothy and Lucy regarded each other with peculiar satisfaction at the thought of the picnic.

"This will do," said Dorothy, pointing out a flat rock where a stony ledge cropped out of the soil.

"Yes, that will do," Lucy agreed. They turned to look at the phaeton, from which Marcia was leading Pocahontas away.

"Where are the dogs?" inquired Dorothy, suddenly remembering. "Gay, what did you do with the dogs?"

Gay had not seen the dogs. He and Marcia turned and looked. Where were the dogs? While the others were staring about in surprise and alarm, a sudden suspicion smote Marcia. She dropped the pony's bridle, dashed back to the phaeton, and looked in.

"They 're at the baskets!" she cried. "They 've eaten up our picnic! Oh, was ever anything so perfectly ridiculous!"

This was the fact: The two dogs, sitting bolt upright on the seat of the phaeton, like Mr. Punch's knowing little beast, had at first been so surprised and pleased by this novel form of attention, they had kept perfectly still. Gradually Carlo's keen sense of smell detected some odor which did not belong to this wild, untamed forest: it was not balsam, or pine, or squirrel, or woodchuck; it was something pleasant and familiar. Accordingly, just simply to investigate the matter, Carlo first put his head under the seat, then his forepaws, finally his whole body. Flossy followed suit. Here was a wicker basket, with the cover carefully tied down with a string. What were paws made for? They knew now what it was that smelled so nice! Cakes! Jerusha's cakes!

# CHAPTER XI

MARCIA'S excursion had so many climaxes, we were obliged to leave off before we came to the picnic. At the end of the last chapter it really did seem as if the picnic were to be exclusively Carlo's and Flossy's. Although Marcia was probably as hungry as any one of the party, when she saw Carlo and Flossy looking out at her from under the flap of the cushions, each with his mouth full of Jerusha's cakes, she sat down on the grass and laughed! As she said, it was so perfectly ridiculous! She had carried the dead partridges in her hand all this time, thinking that the dogs might scent them if she put them in the phaeton, but she had not been alarmed about the safety of the baskets and their contents.

The others were amazed to see Marcia overcome with amusement. It did not seem to them a laughing matter that the dogs had eaten up their picnic. Dorothy climbed in, untied the two, scolding them all the time, and turned them

out ; then she went down on the floor and looked
under the seat, to find out the extent of the
disaster. There was the little blue and white
wicker basket overturned, — indeed, almost torn
to shreds, — and only here and there a crumb of
cake left. Nevertheless, she came up smiling
and tugging at Jerusha's hamper.

"Never mind!" she cried. "Never mind!
They have n't eaten up everything. Here, Gay."

Carlo and Flossy, released from captivity,
stood beside the phaeton with expectant, hungry eyes. Gay was admonishing them with up-
lifted finger.

"Sh—sh—sh—" he began, over and over
again.

"Count three, Gay," said Lucy.

"*Shame on the dogs!*" Gay now burst forth.
Having once uttered the phrase, he repeated it
half a dozen times. "*Shame on the dogs!*"

"Never mind!" said Dorothy. "Here 's the
big basket, Gay. They have n't touched that, or
your box of bread and butter, either."

It was, indeed, a big basket, — so big it might
be called *the* basket. In fact, the cakes which
the dogs had devoured had been extras.

It was Jerusha's way to begin by saying that
nothing was so wholesome for the children as
bread and butter. After packing an ample

supply of bread and butter, it would occur to her that, poor little things, they were growing so fast they needed to have their strength kept up; accordingly a couple of sandwiches apiece, with a bit of cold ham or tongue, were added. Then a little bread and butter and jam is never amiss, and, finally, four little turn-over gooseberry tarts somehow got themselves baked and put in. Thus the hamper had grown, and here it was!

Gay needed all his strength to lift it out of the phaeton. He set it down on the flat stone beside Marcia and Lucy, the dogs following his every motion wistfully, and seating themselves on their haunches in an attitude of impatient expectation.

" Shame on the dogs! " Gay now exclaimed again. " Shame on the dogs! "

Pocahontas, on being released, had turned a blinking, surprised glance behind, and, stepping forth free, lay down on his back, pawed the air, looked at the sky while uttering whinnies of satisfaction, then finally stood up and went to grazing.

Gay was still saying to Carlo and Flossy, —

" Shame on the dogs! "

He explained to Marcia that he had lately read a story about a collie-dog that entered his master's kitchen and stole an oat-cake. Making off with his plunder, his master caught sight of him and exclaimed, " Shame on the dog ! " at which the collie dropped the cake, and, in great shame and distress of mind, hid himself for two days, and never afterward was able to bear the sight of an oat-cake, and by no entreaty could be brought to eat one.

Again Gay apostrophized Carlo and Flossy, " Shame on the dogs ! " hoping similarly to rouse pangs of conscience in them.

Carlo and Flossy, it was clear, had no pangs of conscience whatever. It is not certain, indeed, but that they thought it was the children who were without heart or conscience. They, Flossy and Carlo, had been established in the carriage along with the baskets, and naturally took it for granted they were expected to fall to and help themselves. They had only just begun to fall to when they were interrupted, and now what had happened ? Here were Marcia and Dorothy, Gay and Lucy, sitting down comfortably to eat up their (the dogs') picnic ! As if that were not enough, every other minute Dorothy would say, puckering up her face, and screwing up her lips in order to look severe, " Naughty Carlo ; naughty Flossy ! " To Carlo's and Flossy's thinking it was most cruel and unjust. Pocahontas had grass and clover, the children had sandwiches, but they, two worthy, excellent, and knowing dogs, had nothing at all. They lay down at a little distance, with their heads on their front paws, and looked at Dorothy with such an earnest, agonizing gaze, she really could not go on eating her sandwich.

"Oh, I must give it to them," she said, almost with tears. "They do look so hungry!"

"I'd let them look hungry," observed Marcia.

"So would I," said Lucy; and Gay nodded as if to express his conviction that the dogs ought to beg in vain. But when they transferred their glance of entreaty to him, Gay gave in, and like Dorothy insisted that the dogs should have a fair share of the good things, for there was enough and to spare. For as soon as Marcia's hunger was satisfied she began to be curious about this new world that she had discovered, and was in a hurry to explore. Dorothy as well turned a quiet, thoughtful glance all round, and smiled at Marcia.

"I don't suppose," she said, "that anybody was ever here before we came."

"No," said Marcia. "It has been waiting for us."

Gay shook his head and pointed to the fence. "Somebody had to make that," he declared.

"No," Marcia declared, "the fence grew and the stone wall too."

Lucy and Gay insisted that fences and stone walls were made with hands, but Marcia said that she knew nobody had ever been through that wood before and come out on this side, because the grass was so green and the mountain so blue. They all went down to the brook where Pocahontas was quenching his thirst.

"If anybody had ever been here before," Marcia persisted, "the water would n't be so clear. See, it is as blue as the sky."

Lucy was easily convinced, but Gay would not give up his point. Girls never understood, he said to himself. Why, there was the stump of a tree! He pointed it out to Marcia, trying to make her see that some man must have cut it down with an axe. But Marcia would n't listen. She was strolling on, looking at the little brook which slid quietly along between two very green banks, with here and there a clump of alders bending over it, until presently the stream seemed to vanish in a wide, marshy place full of sweet-flags, cat-tails, and lily-pads. Two or three yellow cow-lilies were in bud, but there was no way of getting anywhere within reach of them, for the whole ground had turned into a quaking bog under their feet. How wonderful it all was!

The joyous fever of discovery had its hold upon each one of the four. children, and the dogs contentedly followed them.

" I — I — I wish we might live here always," said Gay.

They all echoed the wish except the practical Lucy, who inquired what they would live on.

Marcia was full of expedients. There were berries and nuts, and the woods were evidently full of squirrel and partridge. Dorothy objected. She would prefer to starve outright rather than harm the dear, beautiful, little wild creatures.

" And where should we sleep ? " demanded Lucy again.

" Oh, sleep! " said Marcia, as if that were the smallest possible matter. " I should n't want to sleep. I should want to sit up all night and see the sky."

" There goes the sun," exclaimed Gay. And, indeed, the sun had dropped into the notch in the mountain behind the feathery tops of the tall pines. Of course it was n't actually sunset, for the trees of the forest were still bathed in the full glow of sunshine ; but the sun had gone so far as the meadow was concerned. Everything took on a different tint, — the greens turned bluish ; color and brightness vanished.

"WE MUST GO HOME"

"We must go home," said Lucy. They all had a feeling of being suddenly overtaken by night, although Gay found by his watch that it was only half-past five.

"Six o'clock will do to start," Marcia decided. They had no fears about Pocahontas being slow in getting back. Miss Roxy had told Marcia that he could manage himself on the home-stretch.

Gay asked Marcia to let him catch the pony and put him in the traces, and Marcia consented. Pocahontas, having eaten and drunk his fill, stood meditatively rubbing himself against the elder-bushes by the brook. He probably had his own ideas about this picnic, but at this moment was in a bland mood, and, when Gay approached, permitted his nose to be rubbed, his mane to be twitched, and showed himself so docile that Gay suddenly jumped on his back.

"Why, Gaynor Lee!" exclaimed Lucy.

Gay had plenty of spirited capabilities, which, somehow, had little chance of coming to the surface. The girls were so used to ordering him about, they had almost forgotten that he belonged to the stronger and more daring sex. But there he was astride Pocahontas!

"Oh, Gay," cried Marcia, "that is splendid!" When anything was going on, it was so

natural for her always to be in it, to be part of
it. "I tell you," she went on, with sparkling
eyes, "let's play circus. I'll be ring-master."

Pocahontas was a trifle startled, even a little
displeased, to feel the unsuspected weight on his
back. He stood still for one minute, not quite
sure what to do; backed a little, then ran a few
steps, and stood still once more, Gay all the
time holding on manfully.

By this time, however, Marcia, suiting the
action to the word, had run to the phaeton after
the whip, and now stood in the centre of the
field cracking it. Pocahontas had just lowered
his head and was prepared to kick up his heels,
when his sensitive ears caught the once familiar
signal. Up came his head; he tossed his mane;
out he threw his legs and tail, and off he went,
taking the circuit of the meadow in large, easy
circles. Gay was somewhat surprised at finding
himself prepared to witch the world with noble
horsemanship. The pony's back was so low and
broad, it had been an irresistible impulse to
jump on it. He had not expected to stay, but
by clutching the silky mane and digging his
feet into the animal's sides, Gay was really holding on very well. Every now and then, when
the creature described a sharper curve than
usual, the rider's seat became precarious, but by

putting his arms round the neck of Pocahontas
he contrived to avert the danger. Perhaps Gay
did n't quite like it, but the pony liked it, and
Marcia liked it. She played the part of ring-
master very well, cracking her whip and calling,
" Well done, Poky ! " " Hold on, Gay ! "
" Just one more ! " " Now, then ! " and the like.

Dorothy and the dogs looked on with equal
surprise. The dogs were astonished and rather
displeased. Dorothy's eyes grew bigger and
bigger, her mouth rounder and rounder, and her
cheeks redder and redder, as she watched the
performance. She was so bewildered. It seemed
like a dream. She could not feel quite sure
that it was not wicked, particularly as Lucy
was weeping, and kept saying in a weak voice,
" Oh, Gay ! Don't, Gay ! Stop, Gay ! "

Perhaps Gay would have been glad to
stop, but, more and more, all his attention had
to be given to the difficult task of holding on.
He was growing a little giddy. His cap had
long since fallen off, and now one of his shoes
was gone. The pony had all the time pranced
round in a regular circle, but, never quite coming back to the original starting-place, had gradually gone farther and farther afield, until presently his easy, ambling strides had brought him
close to the bog. At the same moment that he

felt, instead of the firm sod beneath his feet, the
ooze and slime of the morass, Marcia's voice
rang out like a shot, "Look out!"

Whether she addressed the warning to the
pony or to Gay did not appear. But it was
Pocahontas who looked out for himself. Putting down his head, he flung back his hind heels
vigorously, and alighted on dry ground. He
was safe, but not Gay, who was thrown clean
over the pony's head and into the very middle
of the quagmire.

"Oh, Gay, Gay!" cried Lucy, running towards him. "He'll be drowned! Oh, Marcia,
save him! He'll be drowned!"

Gay had fallen face downwards, but now
came up spluttering.

"Is it deep?" called Marcia anxiously.
"Can you touch bottom?"

Gay was apparently experimenting, for down
he went again, then floated up like the bubbles
he made. He was by this time clutching at a
tuft of bulrushes.

"N—n—n—not quite!" he gurgled.

"Hold on," said Marcia. "I think I shall
have to run back to the wood and get a log."

Almost before the words were out of her
mouth, however, Gay, who was as light and as
nimble as a cat, had drawn himself up by the

rushes; next he grasped the lily-pads, and sup-
porting himself first by one clump of the lush
vegetation and then by another, he presently
seized a branch of alder and swung himself
across to the bank, where Lucy and Dorothy
were waiting, ready to pull him up.

There he stood dripping, his feet bare.

"Oh, Gay," said Lucy, looking at him with
streaming eyes, "you've lost your shoes and
stockings."

"I don't care," said Gay recklessly.

"I'm glad they were n't your best shoes,"
said Lucy.

"Should n't mind if they were!" retorted
Gay, feeling as if he had for once in his life
successfully escaped from feminine domination.

"Here's one shoe," said Dorothy, who had
picked it up and now offered it to him, along
with his cap. "Oh, Gay!" she. faltered, as
their eyes met. "Oh, Gay, I'm so glad!"

She did not say what she was glad of, but
Gay knew what she meant. He, too, was glad
he had scrambled so easily out of the cold, damp,
clinging weeds and grasses, which had seemed
to pull him down. But all the time there was
a certain proud satisfaction in the thought that
he had ridden Pocahontas, also that he had been
in danger. Even when Lucy had made him

strip off his wet jacket and knickerbockers, and
wrap himself in the woolen carriage rug, there
was still something heroic about his feelings.

Marcia had by this time caught Pocahontas
by the bridle and was buckling the harness to
the shafts of the phaeton. Then she turned
pony and chaise in the direction of home. The
empty basket was put in front ; Gay was established on top of it, the dogs one on each side
of him (Dorothy was afraid they would waylay
some innocent creature in the wood) ; the three
girls piled on the seat, and off went Pocahontas
as if he were the most sensible and obliging
pony in the world. Oh, how delightful it was
in the wood ! They wished Pocahontas was not
in such a hurry, for from the high upper
branches of the trees came the notes of birds.
A hermit thrush was singing, oh, so beautifully !
as if it was breaking its heart with happiness.
Then, when they were through the wood, what
wonderful lights lay on the valley below them,
the little winding river, and the village beyond.
The church spire and some of the houses seemed
to gleam with points of ruddy fire. The dogs
were now compelled, much against their inclina-
tion, to get out and walk the rest of the way.
Still, they had a feeling that their picnic, upon
the whole, had been rather a successful affair.

Gay, on the contrary, could n't quite get over
the feeling that Carlo and Flossy had been
weighed in the balance and found wanting. In
any book about dogs, these animals are noble,
conscientious, heroic. Carlo ought, when he
saw his master in the fen, to have jumped in,
seized him by the sleeve, and drawn him out.

No, the dogs had not acted up to the possibilities of the occasion. Nobody could even write
a book about the splendid feats accomplished by
Carlo and Flossy. Still, after the children had
each described what the two animals ought to
have done, they decided that they loved them
just the same.

How easy, how pleasantly, how wonderfully
swift, the way was home! Pocahontas dashed
along as if running a race with the dogs. When
they reached the river, Marcia said, —

" Let 's ford it."

She had had it in her mind all the time that
they could go through the water instead of over
it on their return. She could not be quite sure
how deep the stream was, but she liked the
excitement, the risk of finding out. It really
seemed for one instant, when they were halfway
over, as if it were going to be up to the bottom
of the phaeton! Oh, how strong the current
was ; how the water swirled past the wheels and

the pony's feet ; what a queer grinding and roar the stones made on the bottom ! Then in another moment it was all over. But there were Carlo and Flossy swimming across ! That was their great feat.

Really, taking it altogether, Marcia, Lucy, Gay, and Dorothy decided they had never had such a good time in their lives.

The children got out at their back gates. Dorothy was ecstatically pounced upon and greeted by Jerusha, but Lucy had a chance to smuggle her bedrabbled twin up to the nursery, and to set him up in shoes and stockings, not to say dry knickerbockers, without being seen.

Marcia had some natural pride in returning pony and phaeton, safe, sound, and unharmed, to Miss Roxy, who had not been without her misgivings. Riding on the crest of the wave that threatened to overwhelm her was the phase of existence that Marcia best enjoyed. It was something to make life satisfying and worth acceptance that she had had such a variety of experiences with Pocahontas.

It was just sunset when Marcia entered her own house, and gave the birds to old Chloe to pick.

A little later, upstairs in Mrs. Dundas's room, there was a small table drawn up to the lounge where Mrs. Dundas was reclining, and on the table were the partridges that the dogs had run down. Marcia was telling her mother all that had happened, and they grew quite merry. Marcia acted sometimes the part of the pony, sometimes of Gay, sometimes of the dogs. She described how Gay had put on one moment the aspect of a fearless rider, and the next had clung to the neck of Pocahontas.

Marcia's big black eyes were full of fun and frolic; she had shaken her hair about until it was as rough as the pony's mane; she wore an old gingham frock altogether too short to have pleased Miss Hester; but Mrs. Dundas, as she ate the bird, not so much that she was hungry as to oblige Marcia, said to herself, —

"Oh, how I wish her father could see her!"

# CHAPTER XII

" PEOPLE who live together," said Mrs. Bickerdyke, looking over her glasses at Dorothy
rather sternly, " ought to tell each other everything. Don't you think so ? "

Dorothy's face had grown rather red, but
then she was bending down very much engaged
in putting the angles of her piece-work together.

" Oh, yes, grandmamma," she replied.

" When people do not tell each other all they
have done and are going to do," Mrs. Bickerdyke proceeded in her deliberate, solemn way,
" very strange things sometimes happen. Now,
once there was a young man who lived with his
mother and two sisters. They were excellent
people, but they were very silent, and hardly
ever spoke unless it seemed really necessary. It
happened that the young man was going to be
married. So he had a new suit of clothes made,
and when they came home he tried them on.
When he sat down to supper he said, ' I find
my trousers are two inches too long, and I

should be obliged if one of you could shorten them for me.'

"Well, his mother and sisters did n't say anything; they never did say anything unless they felt really obliged to speak. As soon as supper was over, the eldest sister, who was very prompt, went upstairs to her brother's room, took the trousers, cut off two inches from the bottom, and then hemmed them up again. Well, she did n't tell anybody. Then after all the others had gone to bed, the mother, she took the trousers, and she cut off two inches, and she hemmed them up again. Next morning the youngest sister, who liked to do things bright and early, she went and got the trousers, and cut off two inches, and hemmed them up again."

Dorothy dropped her work in distress.

"Oh, grandmamma, what did he do?" she said, with a little shriek. "Why, how could he possibly be married? Was he going to be married that very same day?"

"I think he was," answered the old lady. "I never heard that part of the story. What I told it to you for was on account of the moral, — that is, never to be silent and mysterious with the people you live with; but open and frank as the day."

"Yes, I know," said Dorothy; "but just think,

grandmamma, six inches off the bottom of his
trousers! Why, what could the bride have said
when she saw him?"

"You think too much about the story itself,"
insisted Mrs. Bickerdyke. "It is the moral I
want you to lay to heart."

"Oh, I do, I do," said Dorothy, with a pro-
found sigh. "Only I do think it was lucky that
there was n't a larger family. If there had been
five sisters, he would n't have had any trousers
left at all."

Mrs. Bickerdyke shook her head severely at
Dorothy and frowned. "When I tell you a
story," she said, "it's the moral you must lay
to heart, — not the story."

"Oh, yes, grandma," said Dorothy; "I keep
thinking about the moral."

This little sermon of Mrs. Bickerdyke's and
its illustration referred to the fact that Dorothy
had not told her and Miss Hester everything
about Marcia's picnic, the incidents of which
had, in one way or the other, leaked out. Gay's
lost shoe had to be accounted for. Marcia told
Miss Roxy about the pony's behavior, and finally
all was known. Dorothy had confided everything
to Jerusha and to John Pearson; but somehow
it was so hard to find courage to tell it to grandmamma and aunt Hester, who were certain to

say, " Ah, that Marcia! It needs only that girl
to make strange things come to pass."

When Jerusha and John Pearson said the
same thing, Dorothy could argue with them.
How could it be Marcia's fault that Gay lost
one of his shoes and both stockings in the bog?
How could the fault be Marcia's, when the pony
cut capers and the dogs killed the partridges?

Marcia came out of any such trial triumphantly
clear to the minds of Dorothy, Gay, and Lucy.
There could be nobody in the whole wide world
so delightful as Marcia. And the fact was, that
the three had plenty of time to discuss her per-
fections, since for the six weeks following the
picnic they were almost wholly cut off from her
society. Just at the moment when Mrs. Lee.
and Miss Hester Bickerdyke were discussing the
question whether they ought to permit the children to see so much of Marcia, Marcia took the
initiative and renounced the children.

For Marcia's aunt Mary, her mother's sister,
whom they had visited at Christmas, came to
Dundas House, bringing her two daughters, girls
of fifteen and sixteen, their governess, and three
servants. No more flags floated from the window of the tower ; no more delicious feasts were
given the children in the kitchen of Dundas
House ; there was no more running in and out.

Dundas House was quite reclaimed from its
easy-going ways, — at least for those long, tedi-
ous six weeks.

How insignificant Dorothy and the twins felt
in comparison with Lil and Bel Stuart, — for
these were the names of Marcia's young lady
cousins. "I 'm sorry I can't ask you to come
over," Marcia had explained ; "but we have so
many things to do, and you 're such children in
comparison with *us !* "

Dorothy and Lucy and Gay crept around like
whipped dogs after this rebuff. They knew they
were children. Bert, not to say the other bro-
thers and sisters, all frankly despised them for
being children ; but to have Marcia look down
on them ! The iron entered their souls. That
Marcia had up to this time regarded them with
kindliness instead of contempt was simply her
goodness. Oh, how heavy, how dull the time
was without her ! All three felt half ashamed of
the childish games they played together. What
was it to pretend to be building a house, —
that is, to put pebbles in a row and make flower-
beds with shells and moss ? Then, when Gay
decided to set up for a druggist and make pills
out of bran, and Lucy and Dorothy came to buy
them, telling a story about their children being
ill ! What dreary work ! Paper dolls, too, palled

upon them. The fact was that Marcia, with that easy superiority of hers, came into their petty little world and brought them up to her higher level, infusing life and spirit into the simplest thing. When they caught a glimpse of Marcia nowadays there was an air of painstaking, of scrupulous neatness about her, which depressed them. She was evidently acquiring the distinctions and graces of Lil and Bel. Oh, it was hard to bear! She had not used to care about these worldly adornments. What she had hungered and thirsted for had been free, easygoing, shabby ways.

I really do not suppose Dorothy and the twins could have endured this dreary interval at all, had it not been that they nursed the hope of · having one happy day.

When Mrs. Bickerdyke and Miss Hester were over at Fuller Farm the day of Marcia's picnic, Mrs. Fuller had said to her mother, —

" Since Dorothy did not come with you now, send her over some day with the Lee twins to eat fruit and play about the place."

This was told to Dorothy, who naturally repeated it to Lucy and Gay, and for the next fortnight they would say to one another every day, " Do you suppose it will be to-morrow ? "

Certain ideas do so contrive to stick in the

memory! Now, it was an easy enough matter
to forget other things; for example, people were
always saying, "It is very bad for children to
eat between meals;" "Always wipe your feet
carefully on both mats before coming into the
house;" "When you have on a nice clean
frock, sit down and read a book, instead of playing rough games;" and these and similar exhor-
tations went in at one ear and out at the other.
But Mrs. Fuller's hospitable invitation was
never out of the children's minds for one instant
while they were awake. The Fuller homestead
was to Dorothy's imagination a land flowing
with milk and honey. Oh, the fruits that grew
there! one variety succeeding another in rich
profusion. Strawberries were not gone before
raspberries and cherries came; blackberries,
apricots, peaches, plums, pears followed, not to
say apples. There was one tree to which the
Fuller children (now men and women with fam-
ilies of their own) used to race out in early summer dawns, since the first-comer had a right to
the mellow fruit lying on the dewy grass. Dorothy thought that those apples, at any rate,
must be ripe by this time.

It was so strange that what was so much in
her own mind should not be equally in everybody's. Twice Dorothy almost asked Miss Hes-

ter if it was not time to go over to Fuller Farm,
but somehow the words did not quite come out.
However, when there was anything on Dorothy's
mind, Miss Hester was apt to notice the look of
the little girl's eyes, and the downward curve of
the corners of the lips. And finally, when she
observed that Dorothy forgot to eat her supper
and sat staring straight before her, she asked, —

" What is it, Dorothy? What are you thinking about? "

Dorothy's cheeks grew pink; her eyes began
to shine.

" Oh, aunt Hester! " she exclaimed.

" Well, what is it? "

" Don't you think that aunt Fuller will be
expecting us? " Dorothy inquired coaxingly.

" Expecting us? "

" I mean Lucy and Gay and me," Dorothy
explained. " You know she asked us to come
over and eat fruit and play about the place."

" Yes, I remember Lois did tell me to send
Dorothy and the Lee twins over," observed
Mrs. Bickerdyke.

" Oh, mother! " said Miss Hester, " I don't
think it was wise to tell Dorothy what sister
Lois said. That sort of a general invitation
amounts to no invitation."

Mrs. Bickerdyke would not admit that Mrs.

Fuller's had been a mere general invitation.
Accordingly, after some discussion, Miss Hester
agreed that if Mrs. Lee's permission could be
obtained, Dorothy and Lucy and Gay should
go over to North Swallowfield on the following
day. The early apples would be ripe ; apricots
and plums ought to be plentiful; they could
set off soon after breakfast, stay to dinner, have
a long afternoon, and, perhaps, uncle Fuller
would drive them home himself before or after
tea.

"Don't take the dogs," Miss Hester insisted.
"Aunt Fuller dislikes to have strange dogs
come on the place."

This was said when, on the following morning,
Lucy and Gay came over at breakfast-time to
say that they could go with Dorothy. Carlo
stood by listening, with his head a little on one
side, as Miss Hester said this, as if he had his
own ideas about the matter. But John Pearson
was too quick for him. It needed a long head
to be able to manage Carlo, but then John
Pearson flattered himself that his head was long
and deep. Five minutes later Carlo and Flossy
were shut up in John's own tool-shed, and were
to be kept shut up until the children were
safely at Fuller Farm.

John and Jerusha looked the children over

before they set off on their long walk. They were all as neat as wax and were dressed for coolness. Each carried a small basket.

" What 's in the basket ? " inquired John.

" Nothing *yet*," said Dorothy, with little dimples playing all over her face.

" You mean, no doubt, there will be something in the baskets when you come back," observed Jerusha.

" Does Mrs. Fuller know you 're coming ? " asked John Pearson.

" She invited us to come some time," returned Dorothy.

" Some time," repeated John dubiously. " Some time 's no time."

" She said we were to come," Dorothy insisted, " and eat fruit and play about the place." She lifted her basket. " This is to bring back the fruit we can't eat."

The three children went up the street together, Lucy and Gay hand in hand. They all felt in the most wonderful good spirits. It was the first time they had had any experience really to enjoy since Marcia's cousins came.

" If only Marcia were going with us ! " Dorothy said, with a little soft sigh.

" She was n't asked," observed Lucy. " Mrs. Fuller said the Lee twins."

"I forgot that. But I'm sure aunt Fuller would be glad to have her."

The clock struck nine just as they passed the church. They had a two mile walk before them, but it was a plain and easy way, and it gave them a sensation of freshness and freedom that they had started early and could be as long as they chose on the road. It was a charming day; a soft rain had fallen in the night, and the air was delightfully cool. The sky was blue, with soft, fleecy white clouds traveling across it. It was a day of days; just the day for the visit.

"I think," said Dorothy, after a time, "I shall give some of mine to Marcia." She was alluding to the fruit she was to bring home in her basket.

"I, too," Gay hastened to add.

"I shan't," Lucy observed, in her quiet, deliberate way. "Marcia does n't care anything about us nowadays."

"I don't mind that," said Dorothy; "I care just as much about Marcia."

"I, too," declared Gay.

"If you give Marcia your fruit, Gay," observed the practical Lucy, "you 'll be wanting some of mine."

"Why, yes, of course," said Gay, turning a soft, surprised glance at his sister.

" Well, I'll try to get a good deal," Lucy remarked.

They had to walk through the upper part of the village, past a church and a store and houses ; then came a burying-ground, and after that the real pleasantness of the way began. The Swallow River had one of its many turnings here and came almost up to the road ; a brook flowed into it and went under the bridge. At one place there was quite a thick wood on each side, and birds were flying in and out of the cool depths of shadow ; butterflies fluttered high and low; dragonflies darted hither and thither.

" It makes me feel a little sorry," said Dorothy, " to think of poor Carlo and Flossy shut up at home. They would have liked this so much."

Yes, the dogs would have enjoyed it ; they would have been running forward and back ; no sober walking along the road quietly and properly for them. They would have explored the wood as far as they dared to go ; waded in the brook ; dashed after everything that rustled and stirred ; in short, would have kept the children occupied in watching them, calling to them, scolding them. Dorothy really missed the dogs, and felt a little remorseful at the thought of

them in the tool-shed, having such a dull time
and mourning the absence of their friends.

"We shall be there very soon, now," Dorothy presently announced. The river meadows
were passed. On each side houses began to
appear, — not set very near together, but in
the midst of orchards and gardens.

"There it is ! That's aunt Fuller's place ! "
Dorothy cried, pointing to a large, comfortable
square house, painted white with green blinds.
A long wing extended towards the east.
"That's the dairy," she went on, and told how
a stream of spring water flowed beneath it.
There were whole rows of shelves covered with
pans of delicious cream ; there were cheeses, too,
and the smell was delicious ! It really made her
hungry to think what a delicious place that
dairy was !

"Once, aunt Fuller gave me a little round
cream cheese to take home," Dorothy whispered,
and at this each of them smiled. Now that they
saw the house, the great, substantial looking
barns, the general air of solidity and thrift,
their baskets seemed so very small. Gay was
thinking of a wonderful wallet he had read
about, which, although it was so tiny you could
hide it in your pocket, would open at need wide
and deep enough to hold all you wished to put

inside of it. Surely, just such a wallet was needed to-day.

The gate stood wide open. On each side of it was an elm-tree with branches that offered a welcome shade. It made an excuse to loiter there a moment. Dorothy was conscious of a little fluttering of the heart.

"See," murmured Lucy, "there is a row of beehives."

"Oh, aunt Fuller has loads and loads of honey," said Dorothy.

"I — I wish she'd give us some b—b— bread and honey," gasped Gay. "I'm so hungry."

They all laughed; and as they laughed, they turned away from the direction of the house towards the road they had come. Two dots, one white and one black, seemed to be moving along it at a rapid pace.

"R—r—rabbits," said Gay, pointing. He was a little near-sighted.

"Rabbits!" repeated Lucy; "it's dogs!"

"It's Carlo and Flossy," cried Dorothy. "It's Carlo first and Flossy following after him."

"Oh, dear," said Lucy.

"It's too bad," said Gay.

The twins looked rather anxiously at Dorothy.

" Do you think your aunt will care very much ? " Lucy inquired.

" I think," Dorothy replied, " that when we tell her that we did not mean to bring the dogs, she won't mind so very much."

It had been a quarter-past eight o'clock when John Pearson put the dogs in the tool-shed. At a quarter-past ten, Jerusha let them out, having heard, at intervals, for two hours, Carlo's short, indignant, interrogative bark, — a bark suggestive of surprise, incredulity that they were apparently shut up, — shut up by mistake. It was now half-past ten, and the dogs, exceedingly pleased with themselves and in the highest spirits, were jumping up and down round the children, trying to lick their faces in glad recognition.

It was at this same moment that Mrs. Fuller, happening to glance out of the window, saw her three visitors and their two dogs on the drive.

" Bridget," she called, " you just step out and tell those children we don't want any berries. We have almost more than we can eat ourselves. I don't want them coming any nearer with those dogs."

Bridget, a portly, red-faced Irishwoman, stepped forth.

" You may just take yourselves off this minute," she called. " You 'll sell no berries here. We want no berries at all, at all. We 've more than we can ate. It 's ourselves as is fading the pigs with thim. And as for thim dogs, it 's me honest duty to declare to you that there 's a mastiff here tin times the size of both, who would rather eat thim than look at thim."

Bridget stood facing the party, stopped midway in the drive, rather enjoying the surprise and horror of the three terrified little faces.

" Be off wid ye," Bridget said again, addressing, we will hope, Carlo and Flossy, who, breathless and exulting, were dashing forward.

Dorothy advanced a step.

" Oh, please," she said in a trembling little voice, " I 'm Dorothy Deane."

" And who," demanded Bridget, " may Dorothy Deane be ? "

But Mrs. Fuller had caught the name, and now bustled to the doorway.

" What, Dorothy ! " she called. " Is that you ? "

Dorothy gladly ran forward, and along with her Carlo and Flossy.

" Why, it is you, Dorothy, is n't it ? " said Mrs. Fuller. " What in the world brings you over ? Surely mother is n't ill ? "

" No, ma'am," said Dorothy under her breath.

" Or your aunt Hester ? "

" Aunt Hester is n't ill, either," faltered Dorothy.

" Who are those other children, pray ? " Mrs. Fuller demanded, while Bridget, skeptical and still belligerent, stood by longing for fresh orders to disperse the enemy.

When Dorothy, instead of answering, gave a little half sob, and while Gay held down his head, blushing, Lucy, quite self-possessed, called out, —

" We 're Mrs. Lee's twins, Gay and Lucy, Mrs. Fuller."

" Well, well," said Mrs. Fuller, as if trying her wits at an insoluble riddle. " How did you all get over here ? " She looked from one to the other. " You don't mean to say you walked ? "

At this moment came the sound of a crash.

" An' will you look at that ? " cried Bridget.

Carlo and Flossy, being thirsty after their long walk, had run to the well-trough to slake their thirst. A tortoise-shell cat was sunning herself on the curbstone, but at the sight of the intruders retreated, putting up her back. The first thing to be accomplished was to slake their thirst; that done, Carlo, with a loud bark, started in pursuit of the cat, and Flossy after him. The cat had by this time gained a safe

altitude at the top of a brick wall, against which
rows of milk pans, pails, and cans were drying.
As the dogs pressed closely up, as if determined
to scale the wall and seize the cat, one of the
milk-cans was knocked down, and the whole
shining row of tins went down like a set of nine-
pins and with a terrific clatter.

"Goodness!" Mrs. Fuller exclaimed, "see
what those creatures have done! You might
have left your dogs behind, at any rate."

Having set off in this free-and-easy way, Carlo
and Flossy, quite intoxicated with the novelty
of the situation, and seeing fowls in the distance, were bounding towards them, when they
caught sight of something coming round the
corner of the brick wall; something large, yellow, black-faced, — something to take their
breath away.

It was Bunch, the mastiff. Carlo and Flossy
stood glued to the spot. Bunch walked slowly
towards them, not with eagerness, but with an
air of knowing that things waited for him. The
dogs waited, — Carlo with his hair bristling
along his spine, Flossy with his erect, plume-
like tail uncurled and between his legs. Bunch
did not condescend to approach very near. He
eyed them and walked twice slowly around
them ; then, having made it clear to the dullest

canine understanding that this was his place, that was his cat, and those his chickens, he quietly sank down on the turf, picked up a casual bone, and began to gnaw it.

The children had for a moment or two been frightened out of all the senses they had left by the apparition of Bunch. Mrs. Fuller, however, seeing the anguish of terror on the three little faces, was good enough to reassure them.

"Oh, Bunch won't touch such little dogs," she said. "You need n't be a bit alarmed. You have n't told me yet what your errand was." She looked questioningly at Dorothy, whose little flushed face with its tearful eyes was now turned towards her. "What did you say?" Mrs. Fuller asked, as the little lips quivered as if trying to form a word.

She bent her head closer.

"We just came over to see you," whispered the shame-faced Dorothy.

"Well, well," said Mrs. Fuller, laughing, "just came over to see me! You must have been at a loss for something to do, and I should think your elders would have known better than to let you heat yourselves up this warm day. You all look like red peonies. I'm sure I don't know what to do with you. You've come to a busy place. Company's expected to dinner, and here is Bridget with twelve pounds of jam on the fire. How should you like to go into the garden and pick some peas? Ann can't stop, and I was just thinking of blowing the horn for one of the men to come up from the fields to help us out."

" Oh, please let us pick the peas, aunt Fuller," said Dorothy.

Bridget had gone back to her jam, but, fully acquiescing in the idea that the children should be made useful, now came running out with three good sized baskets, led them towards the garden, and pointed out the particular crop of peas to be picked. The dogs slunk away from the vicinity of Bunch and kept pace with the children, Carlo every now and then giving a rigid sort of glance behind him, to make sure that he was not followed. Once in the garden, Dorothy and Gay fell to picking the peas with a sort of fury, their melancholy and dejection working itself off in that way. Lucy was hurt and angry; and crying softly to herself, as her way was, decided that she would do as little as possible. Not one of the three felt like talking, but Lucy did say to Dorothy in an injured tone,

" You told us she wanted us to come ; " and Dorothy replied with a little, soft sob, —

" Grandmamma Bickerdyke said she did."

When Dorothy had picked her own peck basket full, and Gay his, they began to fill up Lucy's.

" If there 's c—c—company to dinner," questioned Gay, " will she want us to st—st—stay ? "

" Oh, yes," said Dorothy hopefully. " I 'm sure she will. I wish she would let us have a little table to ourselves. Once, some of us had when we came to a family tea-party."

" That would be nice," Lucy observed, and the last basket was soon filled up ; and, with a clear sense of duty performed and a consciousness of good deserts, they walked up the long garden-path towards the kitchen. As they approached, Bunch trotted lightly round the house and alighted in their way as suddenly and unexpectedly as a bird, uttering a low growl. Gay dropped his basket of peas and threw his arms round Flossy, while Dorothy did the same for Carlo.

" Bunch, Bunch," Mrs. Fuller called warningly from the house. " Come here, Bunch. Don't mind him, children ! He 's jealous ; that 's all." She came out and dismissed the big, black-nosed creature. " Do you mean to say you 've picked three pecks of peas already ? " she continued. " Why, you are dabsters at it. I wish I had such helpers every day. Now, if you 'll sit down and shell them for me, I shall feel as if there was some chance of dinner 's being on the table before two o'clock."

Accordingly, Mrs. Fuller brought three pans, and the three children sat down in the wide doorway and began the task. It was a cool place, facing the north, and the outlook was very pleasant. But the children were tired ; they were hungry, too, and the shelling of the peas seemed one of those monstrous and unending labors which no mere human power can accomplish. The dogs had squeezed themselves in under the children's feet, — not for comfort, but for the sake of security. Who could tell from what quarter Bunch might next descend ?

Gay, conscientiously opening one pod after another, soon became interested in his work. Most of the pods held seven full-sized peas ; a few had only six and a little one ; here and there one mammoth growth had eight. Gay would make a guess how many peas each pod he took up would hold, and the occupation soon offered a mild excitement. Dorothy, too, tried to make a guess, but something seemed to be gluing her eyes together. Once it seemed to her Marcia was talking.

It turned out to be Mrs. Fuller, who was saying, —

"Come, children, wake up! At this rate, those peas will never be ready! I'll sit down and help you a little, presently, as soon as I get the ice-cream going."

The children were wide awake now. Even Lucy flew at the peas, and showed herself the most dextrous of them all. The idea of ice-cream had wreathed their faces with smiles. How pleasant it was to be sitting here in the doorway and looking over the garden into the orchard.

"I see apples," whispered Dorothy!

Oh, how their mouths watered for early apples! How their teeth longed to nibble at them, just as a preparatory relish before they sat down to fricasseed chickens, green peas, and ice-cream!

Mrs. Fuller was as good as her word, and presently her capable hands helped reduce the piles of pods in each pan to empty shells. She had too many irons in the fire, as it were, to give much attention to her little visitors, but her calls and orders to her subordinates were in themselves interesting bits of conversation, opening up fertile vistas to the imagination. For example, —

"Ann, keep turning that freezer. Don't let it have a chance to stiffen too much in one place. That makes it coarse."

Or, "Bridget, that sponge cake must n't get a scorch."

And again, "Better put the jelly as close to the ice as you can. There 's no danger of its being too firm."

Really, this was being in the centre of things, — turning on the very axis of events.

"Children, I 'm very much obliged to you," said Mrs. Fuller. "Many hands make light work."

She had risen, had gathered up the three pans, and now pouring the contents of all into one, was much pleased to see what a fair provision it made for the coming dinner.

The children, too, rose in a modest but conscious sort of way, blushing with pleasure at being appreciated. The dogs found their feet, but they stood still suspicious and on guard.

Mrs. Fuller, possibly a trifle embarrassed, but meeting the three glances of pleased expectation, kept running her hands through the peas.

"Why, I do declare," she said, giving a sudden glance at the clock, "it 's almost half-past twelve. You 'd better run home, children, as fast as you can. You 'll be late for dinner."

It was more than half-past one, and Jerusha had just cleared the table, put on the sweets,

and gone back to the kitchen, when there came
the sound of a loud exclamation to the ears of
Mrs. Bickerdyke and Miss Hester.

"What is that?" cried the old lady. "Oh,
Hester, what can have happened?"

"I hear Dorothy's voice," answered Miss
Hester; and in another moment Jerusha ushered
in a little girl with a very flushed, tear-be-
smirched face.

"Why, Dorothy!" said Mrs. Bickerdyke,
"what's the matter?"

"Nothing," Dorothy replied; "that is, nothing much."

"Is aunt Fuller sick?"

"Oh, no, grandmamma, aunt Fuller isn't a
bit sick."

"Why did you come home so soon?" demanded Miss Hester.

"Because aunt Fuller told us to come," answered Dorothy.

"But why did she tell you to come?"

"She didn't exactly say," replied Dorothy,
"but I guess it was because she didn't want
us to stay to dinner."

Mrs. Bickerdyke and Miss Hester both recognized a note of indignation in Dorothy's voice,
and a flash of fire in her eyes.

"I suppose," Miss Hester now suggested,

" that aunt Fuller gave you a nice lunch, with lots of good things."

" No, she did not, aunt Hester. It was Bridget that gave each of us two cookies. And then she asked us if we should like a glass of buttermilk."

" Did you drink the buttermilk? "

Dorothy shook her head.

" We all said, 'No, please, we don't like buttermilk,' " she returned, with some pride. " And I gave my cookies to Carlo and Flossy. Gay and Lucy did n't want to eat theirs, but they had to, they felt so hungry."

While Dorothy was telling her story, Jerusha had freshened up her face and hands with a wet sponge. Now she established her in a chair and brought a plate of green-pea soup.

" When we first got to aunt Fuller's," Dorothy went on, " Bridget rushed out and ordered us off. She thought we came to sell berries."

Mrs. Bickerdyke sat back in her chair, and raised her hands.

" Thought you came to sell berries! " she ejaculated.

" Yes, grandmamma," said Dorothy. " She told us they had so many berries they were feeding the pigs with them. We did n't see one single one," she added significantly.

"Well, well," observed Miss Hester, "that will do. I don't quite understand it, but we will not talk any more about it."

"Grandmamma says," replied Dorothy gently but firmly, "that people who live together ought to tell each other everything."

"Yes," said Mrs. Bickerdyke, "I did say so. I told Dorothy she ought to be frank and open."

"I said to myself coming home," Dorothy explained, "that this time I meant to tell grandmamma every single thing."

Miss Hester was obliged to give way before this laudable determination to be candid and open. She and Mrs. Bickerdyke heard the whole story of how surprised Mrs. Fuller had been; of how she wondered anybody could have permitted the children to come out in the heat; of how Bunch frightened them; of how they were set to picking three pecks of peas, and shelling them afterwards; and then how they were summarily dismissed just as it was getting dinner-time, and when they knew exactly what there was going to be for dinner: fricasseed chicken, new potatoes in cream, green peas, and summer onions; lettuce and kale; then berry pudding, ice-cream, and sponge cake.

Dorothy had had a good deal of self-command during the greater part of this recital, but as she enumerated the good things they had missed, her face began to pucker a little, then a little more; her eyes filled with tears, and finally, great sobs burst forth.

" Oh, grandmamma," she cried then, " I could have stood it better if it had n't been for the ice-cream."

# CHAPTER XIII

## A STEW OF MUSHROOMS

MRS. FULLER accounted satisfactorily — at least satisfactorily to her mother and sister — for her lack of hospitality to the children, by saying that she had been expecting her daughter Amelia and her visitors from Boston, seven people in all, to dinner that day. She promised to make it all right for Dorothy and her little friends another time.

To Dorothy, Lucy, and Gay, " another time " sounded very, very far off. Three weeks had passed since their visit to Fuller Farm, and nothing more had come of it. It was now the middle of August. It had rained for two days; then, instead of its really clearing off, warm, damp, sultry weather had set in. In the morning, fog and mist shut out the landscape ; when the sun was fairly shining, the mists broke away into great white woolly masses. But after midday, real clouds would come up, threatening rain, and the afternoon would go on, first darkening, then brightening, then darkening again.

Sometimes a few drops of rain would fall; finally, just before his setting, the sun would blaze forth, lighting up the world with a last gleam of splendor.

" Real dog-day weather," Jerusha and John Pearson explained it.

Dorothy and Gay and Lucy had not heard or seen anything of Marcia for some time, when one afternoon John Pearson observed to Dorothy that he supposed now that the company was going away from Dundas House, Miss Marcia would be preparing some fresh pickle for them all.

" Are her cousins really going away ? " demanded Dorothy.

" So I heerd," said John.

Dorothy was on her way over to play with the twins, and she lost no time in slipping through the wicket and running towards " the children's play-room," where they had spent most of the time through the wet weather with their dogs, their books, dolls, blocks, and tenpins. Dorothy now found Lucy sitting on a stool cutting paper dolls, and Gay lying on the floor, his head propped up by his hands, reading, with Carlo asleep on one side of him and Flossy on the other.

Dorothy was not slow in communicating the news.

"Oh, I do wonder," said Lucy, "whether she will let us play with her again when her cousins have gone away."

"I think she will," said Dorothy.

"I — I — I hope so," exclaimed Gay.

A row of pears was ripening on the beam. Gay brought three of the yellowest and mellowest, and they all nibbled at the fruit while they discussed the chances of Marcia's once more bestowing her friendship on them. She had of late looked so superior, so grown up, so remote, so aloof from them, that they had felt she was lost to them forever.

This was the same sort of unpromising looking afternoon that I have described. The sun was first in, then out; the air was heavy and oppressive in the narrow, confined place. Still, there was a general brightening of spirits now that the children had something to talk about. The pears, if not perfectly ripe, were toothsome. Life once more seemed to be growing interesting; and all at once, when a shadow crossed the window and the dogs sprang up wagging their tails joyfully, the three children turned and beheld Marcia.

"There you are!" said she. "I wondered what had become of you. I've been looking for you all day."

They all stared in surprise.

"Why, did you expect us to go over?" asked Lucy.

"Did n't you see the flag flying?"

The three children regarded each other in dismay. It was a long while since they had thought of looking for that flag.

"We only just heard that your c—c—c—cousins were going away," Gay explained.

"Going?" said Marcia. "They 're gone, — went last night, bag and baggage. Aunt Mary, Lilly, Bel, Miss Brown, cook, chambermaid, and waitress. Don't you see my old clothes?"

Marcia had at first perched on the window-sill with her legs hanging down outside. By one easy wriggle she now transferred them to the inside and stood before the children.

Yes, they saw the dear old clothes that they knew: the red frock with holes burned in it, holes torn, and holes worn; the red cap thrust jauntily on one side of her head; the great flapping braids tied with red. Even the split in the side of her shoes was familiar.

"You don't suppose," she now went on, "that if aunt Mary were anywhere within hail I should have these things on."

"I think you look real nice in them, Marcia," said Dorothy.

"I know I feel so," returned Marcia. "How about those pears?"

The pears were instantly put at her disposal. "They're pretty green," she observed. "However, I'm hungry."

Oh, how delightful it was to see her sitting on the window-sill, swinging her legs in the old way, her great elfish eyes sparkling, her red lips smiling, and her little, white, even teeth gleaming.

"But I mustn't forget," she said presently; "I'm going for mushrooms."

"Mushrooms?" repeated Dorothy.

"M—m—may I come?" inquired Gay.

"I'm afraid it will rain," said Lucy.

"It's just precisely the right weather for mushrooms," said Marcia. "I don't believe it will rain. But anybody who is made of sugar or salt may as well stay at home."

Three minutes later all six, counting the dogs, were outside the window, having scrambled over the sill. They might have left the place by the door, but the door of the play-room opened on the drying-yard and the laundry, and the cook, not to say the man mowing the grass, might have seen them. The window, on the contrary, commanded a retired spot close by the arbor vitæ hedge which separated the Lees' place from

Dundas House.   Once on the grounds of Dundas House they could scurry on like rabbits.

Inside, it had been hot, close, dismal.   Here, with the south wind in their faces, the air seemed fresh ; their bodies felt so light, as if they could almost float !   It was the sort of wind that made a loud swish through the trees.

" Oh, how nice it is to go out without Miss Brown," cried Marcia.   " It was ' My dear, don't,' ' My dear, don't,' all the time.   Why should I run, when there was time to walk ?   Why should I stand, when there was a chance to sit ?   Why should I perch on a rail, when there were chairs and sofas ? "   She paused and nodded at the children.   " Miss Brown does n't know what fun is ! " she added

Oh, how grateful they were to Marcia for not caring about Miss Brown !

" Then Lil and Bel," she proceeded ; " they thought everything was ' odd.'   How odd not to have the house repaired !   How odd that the nice gardens were all overgrown with weeds !   How odd that we did n't always have three servants !   How odd the piano had n't been kept in tune !   Oh, it 's so nice to be ' odd.'   I 've done the oddest things I knew how to do all day."

They would not have dared believe it ; they never could have believed it unless she had told

them ; but looking at Marcia now, from the tassel
on her red Tam O'Shanter cap down to the
holes in her shoes, they were enabled to grasp
the fact that she was n't changed, thaṫ she
had n't become an elegant, finished young lady.

" Where are we going ? " inquired Lucy.

" I know," said Marcia.

If Marcia knew, that was enough. They
would gladly follow her through fire and water.

" Miss Brown was n't so very bad, after all,"
Marcia now observed. " She made the girls
study four hours a day and practice three, because aunt Mary wanted it. But she knows lots
and lots of things, — about botany, for instance.
She taught me a great deal."

" I — I — I — I want to know about b—b—
botany," said Gay.

" Oh, it is n't so easy," returned Marcia. " I
don't feel sure I like it. It 's all rather nice
when you want to know what true mushrooms
are, but not so easy when it 's just saying, for
instance, that the crowfoot is a large family,
and includes many species where the pistils are
closely packed together. Now, when I see a
buttercup or a cowslip or a hepatica in blossom,
I can sit and smile at it for a week. I don't
care a bit that it belongs to the crowfoot family.
But it 's different about mushrooms ; some are

good to eat, and some are poisonous. So it's important to know the true mushrooms."

"I — I — I know what mushrooms are," said Gay.

"But do you know them when you see them?" Marcia demanded triumphantly.

"What are they, Gay?" Dorothy inquired.

"I don't know what mushrooms are," observed Lucy primly. She was often surprised, almost hurt, that Gay knew about more things than she did. But then Gay was always reading, and ideas grow in books. At this moment, however, he had not fully got hold of his idea. It eluded him.

Marcia knew mushrooms and that was enough. She went on describing the different features of her aunt's stay with them, — regular meals, flowers in the centre of the table, all the old Dundas silver and china out. It had been a liberal education, of course, in the way of civilization and refinement; but Marcia had, it was clear, been a little cramped and fettered. Not only Miss Brown, but aunt Mary had had nothing but "don't's" for her.

"Don't eat so fast, Marcia."

"Don't bite your bread, Marcia."

"Don't come to the table in tearing haste, as if you were too hungry to wait."

"Don't seem impatient between courses."

Then, in return, Dorothy and Lucy told Marcia about their visit to Mrs. Fuller.

"If I had been with you, I should have stayed to dinner," Marcia said. "I should have gone to the orchard, and I should have filled my basket with apricots and plums."

She would have done it; they all three felt sure of it.

"Grandmamma says we can all go over when the fall apples are ripe," Dorothy said.

"C—C—Carlo won't want to go," observed Gay.

Carlo and Flossy were frisking about, but now turned and looked inquiringly at the sound of Carlo's name.

"B—B—B—" began Gay.

"Count three, Gay," said Lucy.

"B—Bunch is coming, Bunch is coming," said Gay.

Carlo uttered a low whine, looked around fearfully, his hair standing up along his back. Even Flossy was a little frightened.

"You shouldn't tell Carlo what isn't true, Gay," said Dorothy. "Bunch isn't coming, Carlo. Bunch is at home. Bunch never comes over here."

But, all the same, the very name of Bunch cast a gloom over Carlo.

They had run down the lane as far as the railroad track, but instead of crossing it, Marcia took a narrow footpath which led up to the top of a hill, through which a cutting had been made. Then down they went again, and soon reached a wood of young trees growing up very straight, slender, and tall, out of a dense undergrowth. They had to pick their way through brambles and briers for a little time, but presently felt repaid, when, after crawling between the bars of a rail fence, they emerged in a park-like place. Here the trees grew singly, or in clumps of three or four. They were all very old and very fine trees, mostly oaks and beeches. There was also one very tall tulip-tree. Whether these great trees had killed out all seedlings and saplings, who could tell? but, for some reason, the whole place was given up to these giants. One huge oak was entirely dead, and this dead tree was encircled by a belt of the finest, softest grass. On the tree itself they saw three or four beautiful gray and white woodpeckers creeping up the branches, and making repeated blows that sounded like fairy hammering.

Dorothy had taken hold of Carlo's collar and had put her arms about him. He should not run down any birds to-day; no, not even if she had to call Bunch.

The sky had been completely swallowed up in
blue-black storm-clouds almost ever since they
left the house, but just at this moment the va-
pors parted and the sun shone out brilliantly.

" I felt sure it was not going to rain," Marcia
now observed.

Rain ! The idea of its raining out of this blue
sky !

What a lovely place it was ! Dorothy could
see liverwort leaves and strawberries ! Oh, how
pleasant to come here in the spring !

Marcia was peering about in the soft, rich
mould.

" Do you see these ? " she called. " Come
and look."

Lucy, Gay, Dorothy, and the dogs answered
her call. The ground was broken up by masses
of whitish, pinkish, brownish knobs.

" Fairy umbrellas," said Dorothy.

" F—f—f—f— " Gay stuttered.

" Count three, Gay," said Lucy.

" Fungi," Gay now continued to say.
" They 're fungi."

" I call them toadstools," said Lucy.

" Toadstools ! " exclaimed Marcia, crushing
Lucy with her disdain ; " they are mushrooms ! "

Gay looked bewildered.

" I — I — I thought m—m—mushrooms were

a sort of aristocracy," he said, looking questioningly at Marcia.

" What 's an aristocracy ? " demanded Lucy.

" I thought," said Dorothy, peering closely at
the queer little fairy umbrellas, — " I thought
mushrooms were good to eat."

" They are," Marcia affirmed.

" I — I — I suppose when people are c—c—
cast away on a desert island they eat them,"
said Gay.

" Mushrooms are a very great delicacy," Marcia declared, almost with indignation.  " Now,
children, I 'll show you."

She picked half a dozen of the fungi, and
pointed out the distinguishing traits of the true
mushroom : how the gills ought to grow clear
and free from the stem ; how there was a little
ring at the base.  Really, it was very interesting.  Marcia had brought a basket, and the
children all began to gather the mushrooms with
a will.  Sometimes the funny little knobs (which
Lucy still to herself called toadstools) grew in
circles.  It was so easy and pleasant to pick
them ; they broke off as if they liked it.  And
some of them were so pretty, with such soft, delicate colors that each new one was a fresh
study.  The dogs had, so far, stood by, not quite
understanding what it all meant, but with a sus-

picion that there was something to eat coming;
but now, catching sight of the vanishing whisk
of a squirrel's tail on the fence, they started off
on a foray.

Dorothy looked up in affright.

"Bunch, Bunch, Bunch," she called. "Carlo,
Bunch is coming!"

At the same moment Marcia, also lifting her
eyes, was startled to see what a change had
come over the face of things. The clouds had
gathered in a mass like a curtain, which covered
all the sky except a streak in the east. And
even over this the fringes of cloud were dropping
ominously.

Carlo, at the mention of Bunch, had desisted
from the chase. Perhaps in any case he would
have stopped short, for suddenly the dogs, as
well as the children, became conscious of a peculiar hush. The wind, which had been blowing
a soft gale through the woods, no longer made
even a murmur; the birds that had been twitter-
ing were silent; not a blow sounded from the
woodpeckers.

"How still it is all at once!" said Marcia.

She gave another uneasy glance up at the
canopy of clouds.

"Perhaps we had better go home," she now
observed. "Any way, the basket is almost full."

Lucy looked up at the signs of the weather. "Oh, Gay, Gay!" she cried; "come! Do come! We shall get wet!"

Lucy tugged at Gay, who was still stooping to pick the mushrooms. Marcia and Gay both tugged at the basket, and Marcia taking hold of it by one hand and of Dorothy by the other, they all four scrambled over the fence, then through the wood, from which they were glad enough to emerge with only a few rents and scratches.

As they reached the open, the dogs stood still and cocked up their ears.

"What is that noise?" murmured Marcia. It was a strange sound, as if something were coming towards them; it grew louder and louder; nearer and nearer; a steady tramp, tramp!

"It's the rain!" cried Gay.

"Let's hurry over this hill," said Marcia. "If we can only get into the lane, I don't so much mind."

They clambered up the slippery bank, reached the top, and could see that the rain-cloud had swallowed up all the west and south. Down they toiled. How glad Marcia was to be safely over that perilous place! Now they had only to follow the narrow footpath for five minutes, and

then they would be in the lane. It had grown
almost as dark as night. One big, plashing
drop fell, then another and another; still the
real shower had not yet reached them. They
were just saying to each other that perhaps,
after all, they could reach home without getting
wet, when, all at once, with one tremendous
swoop, down came the deluge. They felt, for a
moment, as if they were swallowed up in it.
The rain made a solid wall all around them.
They kept walking on mechanically, all holding
on to the nearest hand, but they were blinded,
they were deafened, they could not see where
they were going. Luckily they were in the lane,
where they knew every inch of the way. They
could make no mistake, and could feel that
every step told in the right direction. They
were walking through a running stream of
water; water was in their eyes, their noses, their
mouths. It was like being under the falls of
Niagara. Nobody had breath to speak, but if
any one had spoken, nobody could have heard.
The rain descended with a noise like the roar of
artillery.

But not being the falls of Niagara, presently
this tremendous burst of rain from the low
clouds was spent. Then came a lull. It only
rained in a sensible, every-day sort of manner.

"Now, then," said Marcia, "let's run home by the short cut."

It was not too easy a matter to run with all their clothes clinging, dank and chill, to their bodies; nevertheless, in another five minutes the four children and the two dogs were all gathered in the warm, comfortable kitchen of Dundas House, which old Chloe had only lately deserted.

Marcia surveyed the three little dripping, shivering creatures with all her wits alert.

"I'll make up a roaring fire," she said, "and you must take off your clothes and dry them."

Carlo and Flossy, who had cowered along close to the children, were shaking themselves violently. Rills of water ran off everybody. It was a miserable moment. The only comfort to Lucy and Gay was that Gay hadn't lost his shoes this time. He had taken them off and buttoned them up inside his jacket. Dorothy was glad that she had somehow kept hold of Marcia's basket of mushrooms, so they were safe. But everything else was sheer misery and gloom. Marcia, after stirring up the embers of the fire and piling on logs, had left them. The logs did not burn; the dogs were sprinkling everything in the kitchen in their agonizing efforts to dry themselves. It all seemed like a horrible dream, — a nightmare!

Then, in another minute, back came Marcia,
herself freshly dressed, and with a pile of garments on her arm.  Gay was sent into the pantry to array himself, and Lucy and Dorothy,
stripping off their brown holland frocks, snug-
gled into the warm and comfortable things.  By
this time the wet clothes were hung up on the
line above the fire, which had become such a
solid core of heat that it was certain to dry the
wettest things in no time.  The dogs were steam-
ing away as they lay pressed up close to the
ashes.  Gay appeared with a jacket and trousers
much too big for him, and they all burst into fits
of laughter.  What had been a little while before
a state of things to weep over was now great fun.
All had their adventures in the rain to tell.

How lucky that they had got away from the
woods and the railway cutting before the storm
came!  After they were in the lane there was
really no trouble.  They had had a lucky experience; nobody had lost a shoe; as for being
wet, all their shoes had been wet before.  It
was odd to think how cold they had felt, for
now each was in a glow from head to foot.

"And hungry?" Marcia inquired.  Hunger
feebly expressed what they felt.  They had
been hungry before.  This was stark famine.

"Now, then," said Marcia.  She put on her

cook's cap and apron. She brought out the very largest copper saucepan, two bowls, and a beating-spoon and a knife.

The three children, with all their heart in their eyes, watched her. How pleasant it was to be in the kitchen again! It was not worth while to have any misgivings, any thoughts about getting away, for the rain, after a brief lull, had now set in harder than ever. It was impossible to see anything outside but the white solid wall of falling drops.

" How it does rain ! "

" No matter."

Marcia was cutting up the mushrooms. " They 're beauties," she announced, with an air of understanding the subject, dropping them as she spoke into a bowl of water. Then she added, —

" You may as well be setting the table, Gay."

Gay had not forgotten how to set the table in the kitchen at Dundas House. First, a fringed towel, then four little plates, four little knives, forks, spoons, and glasses, and the thing was done. No furbelows, no scallops; just the right sort of table. This task accomplished, Gay could sit down with Dorothy and Lucy and watch Marcia. Watching Marcia was, to their thinking, entertainment of a high order.

First she put a piece of butter, half the size of an egg, into the saucepan, stirring into it smoothly a tablespoonful of flour. To this mixture she added a generous pint of milk.

" Gay," she called, " just stir this gently, very gently, until it boils."

Hitherto the evaporation from the wet garments, as Marcia turned them this way and that before the fire, as if she were broiling them, had made its distinctive odor felt. It might not be delightful, but at least it was a promise to the children that perhaps after a time the clothes would be dry enough to put on and wear home; but, nevertheless, when they began instead to smell the simmering milk and butter, it offered an agreeable variety.

Gay soon lifted a scorched face.

" B—b—b— " he began.

" Count three, Gay," said Lucy.

" It boils."

At this Marcia, who had been bringing out bread and butter, and arranging the tray for Mrs. Dundas, instantly took possession of the spoon and began dropping the mushrooms into the saucepan.

" Now you 'll see," she said, with a little nod of satisfaction.

Lucy whispered to Dorothy, —

"Are you going to eat those — those" —

"Those mushrooms?" returned Dorothy. "Yes, of course, if Marcia cooks them for us. Are n't you?"

"I don't want to; that is, I don't want to very much," said Lucy.

"I don't think," observed Dorothy earnestly, "it would be polite to say we would n't eat them."

"Perhaps it would n't. They smell nice."

"Oh, don't they?"

Of course Marcia had not heard this conversation, which had been carried on in a whisper. Now, raising her face, with its sparkling eyes, red cheeks and lips, she cried, —

"Oh, are n't they delightful? Don't they make your mouth water?" Gay nodded, so did Lucy, and, naturally, Dorothy. They were all three interested, intensely curious, and, besides, they were so hungry! And nothing ever at once so stimulated and yet so gratified the appetite as did this peculiar, delicious aroma of the mushrooms. It was the sort of savory smell which makes one glad one is hungry and tired; which laps one round with the idea of approaching comfort; which makes one think how happy one is going to be presently; which almost satisfies while it rouses the keenest sense of expectation and desire.

Then to see Marcia bending over the stew, whisking that long-handled silver spoon ! How could she know how to do it ? How could anybody possibly know everything like Marcia ? Who but Marcia would have thought of going into the beautiful woods and gathering those strange and wonderful things ? Not Gay, nor Lucy, nor Dorothy. But Marcia had done it. The dogs now waked up, and began to have the most sincere curiosity and interest in what was going on. They two were watching Marcia with their soul in their eyes.

" Why don't you talk ? " called Marcia.

But they had nothing to say. It was enough to look at her.

However, Dorothy did manage to exclaim, —

" See how hard it pours ! "

" Does n't it, though ! "

" We could n't possibly go home, even if we tried."

" No, indeed ! "

Going home was an event far off, hazy, remote. Some time, doubtless, they would be obliged to go home, but something delightful was to happen first. The odor grew richer.

" They are done," said Marcia almost solemnly. " That is, I think they 're done. I will taste."

She tasted.

"Oh, they're simply delicious!" she declared. "Gay, please hold this saucepan just there till I come back."

She had poured a portion into a little covered dish. Putting this in the middle of the salver, she set off for her mother's room, was absent five minutes, then returned. Nothing had stirred in the kitchen or uttered a sound in this interval. Gay had continued to hold the saucepan just above the coals; Dorothy and Lucy and the dogs had sat watching him.

"Mamma had caught the odor," cried Marcia joyfully. "She said it had made her feel hungry. I know it has made me feel hungry."

Oh, how hungry everybody was! How hungry, above all, the dogs were! Marcia gave them each a bone.

Four chairs were brought close to the table. The mushrooms were poured into a big, round dish. Marcia sat down, and the children also took their places.

"Now, then, taste 'em," said Marcia, as she helped everybody liberally.

They tasted.

"Aren't they good?" she continued.

They had never in all their experience tasted anything so good. They had bread and butter

too. There were also crackers, — a really royal
meal.

"Aunt Mary's cook taught me how to stew
them," Marcia was generous enough to concede.

The three children had not the least doubt in
the world that Marcia could do everything better than aunt Mary's cook. This sense of their
exclusive privilege deepened their love for her;
they admired her all they could already. They
had lost her for six weeks; now they had her
again, and they all looked at her and smiled.
They felt as if they had never in their lives
been so happy before. This was their ideal of
happiness: to go on eating mushrooms forever
and looking at Marcia. They had each had
two helpings. They had eaten all the bread
and all the butter; now they had fallen upon
the crackers. Crackers were excellent to sop
up the rich, plentiful sauce.

There was now just one mushroom left in the
bottom of the dish, rather a large one, which
somehow had not been sliced.

Marcia cut it in three pieces.

"Here's one little bit for each of you," she
cried.

They begged her to take it. No, it would
give her more pleasure to see them eat it. Dear,
good, generous Marcia!

They had all had enough before, but this little additional piece, with a teaspoonful of sauce and a cracker, was just the delightful too much which gives the feeling of completeness to a meal. They ate, smiled, and loved everybody.

It was over. The rain, too, had spent its strength and was falling only in a fine mist, with the light from the west shining through it. Alas! not even eating stewed mushrooms, and feeling that nothing can possibly happen, lasts forever. It was a point of honor with the children that each should clean up his and her own plate, knife, fork, spoon, and glass. Gay's extra duty was to scour the saucepan, for Marcia liked everything left shipshape. Everybody babbled now. The sun was breaking through the clouds outside; the birds were singing and taking baths in the pools of water left on the stone flagging. Lucy and Dorothy were discussing the knotty point of whether Dorothy had done wrong in making Carlo think Bunch was coming. Dorothy had found fault with Gay for doing the same thing, so Lucy argued. Dorothy explained that Gay had tried to frighten Carlo with the idea of Bunch just for fun, while she, Dorothy, had done it to check him in his pursuit of the squirrel.

While Dorothy was advancing this plea, she suddenly put her hand to her head, then sat

down.   She had grown a little pale, — particularly about the mouth.

"What's the matter, Dorothy?" demanded
Marcia.   "Don't you feel well?"

"Oh, yes," said Dorothy, jumping up.   "I
feel well, only I was dizzy for a moment."

"It's so warm here," murmured Lucy, whose
face was very red.   "I think I feel a little dizzy,
too."

Marcia flung both doors wide open.   The
clouds had retreated towards the east.   The sun
was shining brilliantly; the west wind was astir.
It blew across the kitchen with a life-giving
freshness.

"*You're* all right, aren't you, Gay?" questioned Marcia.

Oh, yes, Gay was all right.

"Are you better, Dorothy," Marcia said.

"I'm better, but I don't feel quite well,"
answered Dorothy.

"I don't feel well at all," murmured Lucy.

"I'm afraid," faltered Dorothy, — "I'm
afraid I ate too many mushrooms."

"I didn't," said Gay; "I could eat as many
more."

Marcia, however, saw something in Gay's face
which seemed to contradict his words.   He, too,
was growing pale.

"Oh, children!" she exclaimed, conscious that with the very best intentions things did somehow turn out calamitously, "perhaps we'd better not say anything about the mushrooms."

Limp as they all were, they promised.

Marcia was taking down the dried garments.

"I'll put these on you," she said; "then I'll take you home."

Getting dressed was hard enough; but the getting over to the play-room, although it was only about a hundred yards away, was the hardest journey Dorothy and Lucy and Gay had ever undertaken.

"Of course," said Mrs. Bickerdyke, "it was those green pears."

Miss Roxy Burt and Pocahontas had chanced to be passing by the evening before — having been detained by the storm — just as John Pearson returned from a fruitless expedition after Dr. Barnes, who was six miles away. Accordingly, Miss Roxy had tied the pony to the post, and had gone in to see the three children, whom John Pearson (when Miss Hester had sent him for Dorothy at six o'clock) had found on the floor in the play-room, all alike in a state of collapse, — pale, spent, and speechless, — with not a word to say except that they had been "so sick."

Miss Roxy had ordered each warm drinks, a warm bath, and had seen them put to bed. Next morning, although still a little languid, they were all better.

" It was the pears, no doubt," Miss Roxy said to Marcia, who was hanging about, very eager for news. " The gardener said he put a whole basket of pears to ripen in the play-room, and now they are all gone but three."

Yes, it must have been the pears. Everybody said it must have been the pears, because there had been nothing else to eat. Jerusha and John Pearson thought that the children must, too, somehow have got their feet wet. It had rained in at the open window of the play-room.

But Marcia and Dorothy and Lucy and Gay could n't help suspecting that it was that one last mushroom which Marcia divided between them which had done the mischief.

# CHAPTER XIV

MRS. DEANE and Dorothy had planted flower seeds together at Easter. By this time the sweet peas had blossomed and died ; the candytuft had gone ; the cornflowers were ragged ladies indeed, and the larkspurs faded. The nasturtiums still made a dazzling show along the edge of the borders and also clambered riotously over the fences and the trellis, while the Japanese morning-glory had wound itself round the wistaria and was setting off the vine with its great blue stars.

Mrs. Deane had told Dorothy that very day, while they planted the seeds, that she had been asked to go to Europe for the summer with two of her pupils and their mother, to coach the girls and look after the party, so that she could not see the flowering of the sweet peas and the early flowers.

" But before the asters and marigolds are out of bloom I shall be back, I hope," she said.

Thus, when, one morning in August, Dorothy

was walking round the garden with Mrs. Bickerdyke, and saw that the marigolds and asters were all full of buds, she gave a little cry, and said, —

" Oh, mamma must be coming home very soon, now! "

" Not for four or five weeks," said Mrs. Bickerdyke. " In fact, I doubt if she will be here before the first of October."

Still, Dorothy thought to herself, the first of October was coming !

So long as Marcia's cousins had been staying at Dundas House, time had seemed to creep ; but now that they saw Marcia all the time, the remaining days of summer were spinning away like a top. The first of October would soon be here. Dorothy would see her mother's loving eyes, hear her mother's loving voice, — but still — It was n't all quite joy that the summer flowers were going out of blossom and the autumn ones coming in ; for, at last, Marcia's mother had had the great, good news ! Paul Dundas was ready for his wife and child, and by the middle of October they were to go to England, where he was to meet them and take them to his wonderful new home in South Africa.

One is so often pulled two ways, — towards pleasure and towards pain ; one so often plucks the bitter along with the sweet. Dorothy could n't quite decide whether she longed more to have her mother back or dreaded to lose Marcia. Even when her mother was home from Europe, she would not live at Swallowfield, while Marcia was here, ready to tell stories, to chase butterflies, or fight buffaloes ; to do anything and everything that turned up, or could be imagined, with all her heart and soul.

Lucy was dissolved in tears whenever the thought came of losing Marcia, while Gay froze up and looked miserably unhappy.

The twins had nothing pleasant to look forward to in October; it would be school-time. No, they wanted the summer to last forever and forever.

Marcia naturally felt the interest and the importance of standing, as she stood now, on the threshold of great events. Then, too, it was a comfort to see her mother so proud and well and happy; so secure in her hopes; so well past her doubts and her alarms ; so eager to meet Paul and belong to his life once more. Nevertheless, what Marcia felt was that she had had, all things considered, a very good time at Swallowfield, and that she loved Dorothy and Lucy and Gay better than anybody else in the world, save her mother and father. They were always ready to

do her bidding, whether to go looking for mushrooms and eating them heroically, or to cross
rivers, to explore woods, and to enter into all
her plans and conspiracies.

Yes, Marcia, as well as Dorothy, was pulled
two ways; with longing for the future, yet with
a desire to say to the passing moment, "Stay,
for thou art so fair."

There was no comfort for any of the children
in Marcia's telling them that just as soon as her
father made a fortune they would come back,
restore the old house, and live there comfortably.    There would be little fun in that, Lucy
and Gay and Dorothy thought; everything in
order; no meals in the kitchen; no scouring of
saucepans and heaping fagots on the fire.   They
had loved the old place just because it was
shabby and going to pieces, and because there
were no cross, pampered servants to interfere
with them.

In September came some rainy days.   Mrs.
Dundas, rummaging among the old trunks and
camphor-chests in the great attics, brought out
all sorts of relics of dead and by-gone Dundases,
and the children played with them to the sound
of rain on the roof.   There was a scarlet riding-
habit which Marcia liked to put on and trail
round in.   It had belonged to her great-great-

IN THE GREAT ATTICS

grandmother, who had been a famous horse-woman, and had a rather imperious way of riding her horse up to people's doors, and, without dismounting, summoning them by a hard rat-tat-tat from the butt end of her riding-whip. Lucy and Dorothy tricked themselves out as well in old-fashioned gowns and spencers and mob-caps, while Gay had a wonderful choice of uniforms and rusty old swords.

Thus arrayed, they used to play the landing of the Mayflower. Grandmamma Bickerdyke's remote ancestor had come over in that ship, and she had told the story over and over again to Dorothy, singing in a quavering voice, —

> " The breaking waves dashed high
> On a stern and rock-bound coast."

Usually Dorothy waited for others to propose games, but the landing of the Mayflower was her own idea.

" First," she said, with her eyes growing bigger and bigger, and with a little smile lurking in the corners of her lips, " first we must have a boat."

They were used to makeshifts. The three men of Gotham went to sea in a bowl, but these four children went to sea in anything, and now, for the good ship Mayflower, took an old clothes-basket with holes in the bottom.

Oh, how that boat rocked and tossed in the waves! Indeed, the voyage was so wild and rough, Lucy fell overboard and had to be saved by having a rope flung out to her. It did really make the dangers of the sea seem very real when she clambered in again.

"Oh, how awfully cold and wet you are!" said Dorothy, clasping the one rescued from a watery grave. "Well, we are almost there. We'll land soon."

"Yes, I see Plymouth Rock," shouted Marcia, who was at the mast-head. "Gay, you must jump out, wade to the shore, and pull us in."

"Yes, that's Plymouth Rock," said Dorothy.

"But, Gay, be careful! You'll be drowned! See how awfully rough it is! I'm afraid the ship will go to pieces before we can land."

And, indeed, there was great danger that there would be a complete wreck, for one of the sides of the basket was in splinters.

"Oh, it's just beautiful!" cried Marcia, entering into the spirit of the thing.

"We're P—P—Pilgrims and P—P—Puritans," said Gay. "We've come over here because — because" —

"Because we want to have a good time," suggested Marcia.

"No, indeed," Dorothy corrected her. "We're

going to have awful bad times.  There's bears
and wolves and red Indians " —

" Lions and tigers, too," put in Gay.

" Lions and tigers if you want them," said
Dorothy, " but grandmamma only told me about
bears and wolves."

How that boat did rock in the surf!

" I'm the first man on shore," cried Marcia,
jumping out, with her red riding-habit gathered
up in her hands.  " I'm planting the flag," and
she flapped a bit of muslin.

They all landed.

" We must all kneel down and say grace,"
said Dorothy solemnly.  Accordingly, all on
their knees, they murmured after her, " For
what we are about to receive, Lord, make us
truly thankful."

Then they rose.

" This is the new world," explained Dorothy.
" There isn't a single house anywhere, unless
you call wigwams houses.  There isn't a single
street or a store or a church or a post-office.
There's nothing but trees and Indians, and wild
beasts going up and down."

" I'll be an Indian," said Gay.  " I'll be a
wild beast, too ; " and from the strange noises he
made, it was clear he meant to be as good as his
word.

"Oh, don't, please, Gay," begged Dorothy. "We have got to build a house first, and you must help us."

They found materials for a house in no time. A bedstead with a canopy, an old quilting-frame, and a few other odds and ends soon enabled them to find shelter. There was even a queer iron tripod with a kettle in which they could cook their first meal.

"Now then, Gay," said Marcia, "you can go and be a wild Indian. Then when we are eating supper, you can come and tomahawk us."

The supper consisted of a dozen of Jerusha's cakes, and Gay demurred. He said he thought he ought to be one of the settlers until he had had his share. Then he would play he was a wild Indian. Marcia told him he would be all the more bloodthirsty for being hungry, and, of course, he could have all the cakes he could rob them of. Gay thought it safer to provide himself with his share in good season. Accordingly, snatching three, he ran off, hid for two minutes behind a beam, then burst out with such blood-curdling yells, Lucy was frightened and burst into tears. Indeed, had such a spirited attack been made upon the original Pilgrims, it is to be feared the Plymouth colony would have been nipped in the bud.

" I will be an Indian, too," Marcia now declared.

Dorothy and Lucy looked at each other in
dismay. To have Gay spring out of the dark
corners with bloodthirsty yells was almost more
than they knew how to endure; but to have
Marcia also lurking in ambush, ready to dash
down upon them,— that was distinctly too
much.

Dorothy and Lucy did not often nurse a
grievance, but it did seem to be taken for
granted that they were always to come off
badly. If, for example, Marcia and Gay played
at being lions and tigers, the two girls stood
no chance at all; they had to fall down and,
to the sound of terrible roarings, be quite
eaten up. But, on the other hand, if Dorothy
and Lucy took the part of lions and tigers, they
fared no better, being pursued by hunters, and
finally brought to bay in the corner, where nothing was left for them to do save to turn over
on their sides and die gracefully from their
many wounds.

Then, too, when they played pirates, it must
always be Marcia and Gay who dressed up in
red sashes and slouched hats and big swashing
boots, and made Dorothy kneel down and beg
for their lives, — beg all in vain, as well. For

never were there more ferocious pirates than
Marcia and Gay, who always decreed that their
unhappy victims should be blindfolded and walk
the plank. Of all punishments, that was the
worst. Dorothy and Lucy shrank and cowered
when they were ordered to be blindfolded and
walk the plank, although they knew the plank
was only two inches above the floor.

Yes, it was always so, they now said to each
other, dejectedly huddling over the tripod and
kettle, which represented the embers of the first
camp-fire. Marcia having, as it were, put on her
war-paint, — that is, stuck two peacock feathers
in her hair, — wrapped herself in a blanket,
and, seizing a bow long since unstrung, led the
attack, and with fierce warwhoops darted down
upon the unhappy Pilgrims, who soon lay quite
dead, with only one eye open to see what was
next to come.

" Oh, is n't it splendid fun ! " said Marcia.

Gay agreed with her, and even Dorothy and
Lucy, coming to life, found themselves in good
spirits, and they all danced a war dance together.

" I do love to be an Indian," observed
Marcia.

" Yes, it is n't so bad *being* an Indian," Dorothy observed gently.

"I tell you," said Gay, "we'll play B—B—Braddock's Defeat."

"What's Braddock's Defeat?" inquired Marcia.

"It happened, you know," explained Gay, — "it happened a long, long while ago. George Washington was in it."

"George Washington?" repeated Dorothy. "You don't mean 'The noble, great, immortal one'?"

"Yes, I do; he was in it. He and General Braddock and a whole lot o' soldiers; they marched through the woods after the Fr— Fr—French an' the Indians; and the Fr— Fr—French and Indians they lay low till they came up, an' then, why, they fired an' killed everybody 'cept George Washington."

"Oh, do let's play it!" said Marcia. "Was it all in the woods?"

"The very thickest woods you ever saw in your life; so thick you couldn't see the sky," Gay returned.

"Now, all of you listen," said Marcia. "This is all deep woods; trees clear up to the sky; great roots down at the bottom, twisting round like snakes. Bushes and vines, too, and all sorts of growing things. Now, Dorothy and Lucy, you two girls are General George Wash-

ington and General Braddock and a whole army
of soldiers! Each of you take a gun or a sword
and be coming along by the path through the
woods, and Gay and I will be Indians and will
be crouching behind the trunks of the trees, and
will just spring out and kill you."

"All except George Washington," replied
Gay earnestly. "He has got to live an' be
father of his c—c—country."

"Oh, Marcia," pleaded Dorothy, with a pa-
thetic break in her voice, "couldn't we be Indians
just this one time?"

"Oh, dear, no!" Marcia replied hastily.
"You wouldn't know how; that is, you wouldn't
know how to be a real, cruel, cold-blooded Indian; we will play a game some time where
there are good Indians for you and Lucy."

"But I never heard of a good Indian," faltered Dorothy.

"Oh, yes, there are heaps and heaps," Marcia insisted. "I'll tell you about them when
the right time comes. But now Gay and I are
going to be awfully bad Indians. Now let me
dress you up." She put an old bear-skin muff
on Dorothy's head, and a three-cornered hat on
Lucy's. "Now," she went on, "run down to
the other end, and both come up, brave and gay,
singing and talking, because, you see, you are

not to have any idea that we are here waiting for you."

" It 's to be an ambuscade," said Gay.

" Well, no matter," remarked Lucy. " I 'm George Washington, so you are not to kill me, either of you."

" No, it would n't do to kill you," said Gay, pondering the matter; " that is, not if you 're really George Washington."

" I tell you," Marcia now explained, " you shall really be George Washington, don't you see, and you shan't be really killed. But then, just to fill out, you can be twenty or thirty soldiers, and we 'll shoot and scalp you."

The trouble was that Marcia always knew her own mind, — knew it in a flash, before Dorothy and Lucy could venture to make up theirs. In spite of her cocked hat Lucy was whimpering when, obeying orders, she and Dorothy withdrew to the farthest reach of the garret and began their march.

" I don't like to be scalped," she whispered. " I don't like to be scalped one bit."

" I don't like it much," Dorothy answered. " But, after all, you know, it does n't really hurt."

" No, 't ain't that it hurts," Lucy granted,

"but I hate it so. And — and — and I don't think it's quite fair."

"I don't think it's quite fair," said Dorothy. "I say, Lucy" — she stopped and put her little face under its bear-skin muff, close up to the other, beneath the cocked hat. "I say, Lucy, *let's not be — killed.*"

"I told Marcia I wasn't going to be, — that I was George Washington," Lucy replied with indignation ; "but she said I was to be twenty or thirty soldiers, and be killed twenty or thirty times, only I could come to life afterwards and be George Washington."

"I don't care," said Dorothy. "The Indians didn't always beat, you know."

"What, not really ? "

"Why, if they had," argued Dorothy, struggling with the idea that the North American Indian did not remain in testimony of his being a survival of the fittest, — "why, if they had always beaten, don't you see, the Indians would be alive and the white people would be dead ; but it's the Indians that are dead and the white people are alive."

"Lots of white people are dead," said Lucy doubtfully.

"There's lots alive, too," declared Dorothy. "Come on. Don't let's be killed."

And they accordingly surprised Marcia and Gay exceedingly. Nobody was killed, although "All day long the noise of battle rolled," until Mrs. Dundas came up to the garret to find out what was happening.

# CHAPTER XV

DOROTHY'S mother was to have sailed from Europe September 19. By the first of October, everybody, except Dorothy herself, was worried over the fact that the steamer had not only not reached New York; but that there was no news of her.

Dorothy picked a fresh bunch of flowers every morning to put on her mother's dressing-table.

" I 'm sure mamma will come to-day," she would say.

" Oh, yes ; she 'll be here as soon as the ship comes in," Jerusha would answer. " But sometimes they do take a fearful time a-crossing."

There was so much to do, the days were so crowded with incidents, Dorothy had very little time to stop and think. To begin with, she and Lucy and Gay were making a book for Marcia's voyage. Each day, on the ocean, Marcia was to tear off a leaf and find under it a letter from one of them. Then, too, Dorothy was making her a bag to tack up by the side of her berth.

And most interesting of all to Dorothy were Mrs. Dundas's preparations : the rugs and cushions ; the natty sailor suit Marcia was to wear ; the trunks, boxes, bags, of their traveling equipment. It seemed to Dorothy as if, seeing these belongings which were to make part of Marcia's new life, she herself could claim a tiny share in it, because she buckled straps, tied knots, and helped pack generally, putting into corners and crevices little reminders, — a rose from her bush ; a bunch of lemon verbena leaves ; a verse written in Dorothy's own rather queer hand, not original, perhaps, but still so full of poignant meaning that it brought the tears to her own eyes, —

> "When this you see
> Remember me."

In one way, Dorothy's whole consciousness was pervaded with the thought of Marcia, and that Marcia was going away. But along with the pang of that cruel loss came all the thrill of glad feeling that her mother was sailing, sailing, sailing towards her every day.

" I 'm sure she 'll be here by afternoon, don't you think so, John ? " Dorothy inquired of John Pearson when she was picking her morning bouquet.

" There 's a west wind," answered John.

" But I should suppose a boat might make some
headway, for it does n't blow hard."

Dorothy looked up at the weather-vane.

" The wind ought to be east," she said.
" That would blow her over faster ; but if it
were east it might be rainy.   She would n't like
that."

They accordingly decided, John Pearson and
Dorothy, that even at the risk of prolonging the
voyage a little, it was better to have fair weather,
particularly as Marcia had only a few days
more at Swallowfield, and that one of these was
to be spent at Fuller Farm.

" It would be a good time, sister," Miss Hester
had said to Mrs. Fuller, " to let Dorothy invite
the children to go over to see you.   It will help
to take up her mind."

And Mrs. Fuller cheerfully sent the invitation.

Dorothy had little idea that the reason Mrs.
Bickerdyke and Miss Hester and Jerusha and
John Pearson, and in fact everybody in Swallowfield, was so good to her just now came from
their dread lest a great sorrow was impending.

" I always thought," Dorothy said, with some
natural pride, when she gave out her invitations,
" that aunt Fuller would really ask us some
time."

Everything, on this occasion, was to be done for the children's comfort. The wagon was to be sent on Saturday at half-past ten. The dogs, even, were invited. Bunch was to be tied up for the day. The early apples and quinces were to be gathered at Fuller Farm; the grapes, too, were ripe, and all the fruit was being boxed and sent off to market. But it had been a great fruit year, and everybody was to eat and carry away all they chose. Now, if the weather would only keep pleasant!

Friday afternoon there came a low bank of violet cloud at the westward.

" What do you think, John ? " inquired Dorothy anxiously. " You don't really believe it 's going to rain to-morrow ? "

John shook his head, declining to commit himself. The sun dropped into the bank of mist presently, but was not hidden, and looked, until it set, like a blot of red sealing-wax. When it was dropping behind the trees, up sailed the moon in the east, almost as red, quite as round, and a great deal bigger.

But in spite of all these favorable portents, when Dorothy looked out next morning, the whole world was veiled in thick mist. It was almost more than she could bear.

However, by half-past nine, when Lucy and

Gay and Carlo and Flossy had come over, and
they were impatiently waiting on the back porch
for Marcia, there came a rent in the mist ; the
top of a maple-tree suddenly showed like a crimson banner ; they had a glimpse of blue sky, and
out came the sun.  Marcia arrived in another
minute, looking so tall and elegant in her new
blue sailor suit and hat, they pressed round her
with admiration.  She held herself like a queen,
they thought, but it was their old Marcia still.
She was laughing, but there were tears in her
eyes.

"Here is the wagon," called Miss Hester.
She was standing at the front door, and the
children all trooped through the house and ran
down the steps.  As it happened, Bert Lee was
walking past at this moment.

"Hulloa," he cried ; "what's this ? "  He was
looking at the wagon and the two great, strong
horses ; but he also saw Marcia with her sailor
hat and dress.

"We're going over to aunt Fuller's," answered Dorothy.  She paused a moment, then
added, with a soft little inflection in her voice,
"Perhaps you'd like to come with us, Bert ? "

"I ? " said Bert, as if he found the idea
incredible.  "I go ? "

"Mamma would have gone, if she had come

last night," Dorothy proceeded ; " you can have her place."

" You 'd better go, Bert," called Miss Hester from the porch.

" Don't care ; might as well," Bert now condescended to say, and clambered up to the seat by the driver, which Gay had spoken for and counted on, but which he relinquished with only one little gasp of discontent.

Carlo and Flossy stood looking up at the party in the high wagon with surprise ; they were almost more surprised when Dorothy said, " Come, Carlo ; come, Flossy," and they were invited to follow after. Such a thing was unexpected ; but they were always expecting the unexpected.

Dorothy blushed all over with pleasure. This was really a party to be proud of. Bert on the front seat with Perkins, aunt Fuller's second man ; then Marcia, looking so beautiful, in the middle seat with Gay ; Lucy behind with Dorothy herself, and the dogs trotting along. If only — if only mamma had come in time ! But then, as aunt Hester said, mamma might have felt too tired to go. And certainly it was an honor to have Bert find anything desirable it was in Dorothy's power to offer. Very possible he might not like it. Nobody had ever

known anything to please Bert. But no matter.

It had by this time not only cleared off, but
it was the most beautiful day October could
give, — which is the same as saying that it was
the most perfect day in the year.

The woods on the hills rose, fold on fold of
crimson, scarlet, russet, and gold. In one field
stood an oak-tree, as green as it had been in
summer, but almost every other tree or bush or
creeper had taken on the richest dyes. Here
and there on the road a single wet leaf burned
like a gem. The banks of the nut-brown sleeping pools, full of reflections of meadow and
woodland, were fringed with yellow and red
leaves. The brook slipped away almost unseen
under its mantle of gay tints.

Dorothy looked and smiled and dimpled; then
she and Lucy, their eyes meeting, would say, —

" Oh, is n't it, though ? "

By which they meant, " Is n't it perfectly
splendid ? "

Marcia, also, at times, turned round and
nodded. They felt this to be kind of Marcia,
for Bert was treating her with very distinguished
attention. She had never seemed to care that
Bert had hardly ever spoken to her all these
three years and more that she had lived in Swal-

lowfield ; she had accepted the enforced loan of his sled with no especial gratitude ; she had piled logs for him without bearing any particular grudge. But something in the way he was staring at her to-day stirred a feeling of mischief.

" I should n't mind it, if I were going to South Africa, myself," Bert had observed loftily.

" Why don't you? " said Marcia.

" I may, some day," he returned.

" But if you don't go now, you will find that I have picked up all the diamonds and nuggets of gold before you had a chance," said Marcia. " I shall have gold rings on my fingers and gold bells on my toes when I come back ; gold bracelets all up my arms and round my ankles ; diamond necklaces on my neck and diamond rings in my ears and nose."

" Oh, Marcia! " cried Dorothy.

" When you live in Africa, you must do as the Africans do," Marcia observed.

Dorothy, Lucy, and Gay recalled the pictures of the native Kaffirs and Dahomeys in their geography, and looked aghast.

Bert was afraid that Marcia was laughing at him, so changed the subject.

" What is there to do when we get over to Mrs. Fuller's? " he inquired in a patronizing tone.

It was at this moment that Marcia made the
discovery that she had dropped her handkerchief. It was only a little way back. She remembered that she had taken it out just when
they passed the bridge. Gay was ready to jump
out on the instant, but that did not suit Marcia.
Nothing would do but that Bert should go back
and find it.

Bert really was surprised at himself. He
would not have supposed it possible. It did
actually seem incredible. But presently he
found himself walking along the road they had
come, looking for that handkerchief. He did n't
want to do it. It seemed absurd that he should
be doing it when Gay or even Lucy might have
done it quite as well. But there was something
in the way Marcia spoke, in the way she looked,
with her sailor hat and her natty collar and
jacket, that seemed to speak the word of com-
mand, as if she had been the centurion.

The others, meanwhile, had driven on, had
entered the gate, and were now alighting before
the hospitable door of Fuller Farm. Mrs. Fuller
came out to meet them, kissed Dorothy, shook
hands with the others, and asked about their
mothers' health. Even the dogs were addressed
and their heads patted encouragingly. Mr.
Samuel Bickerdyke happened to be visiting his

sister, and he, as well, was polite and atten-
tive.

"Now, Dorothy," said Mrs. Fuller, "it is
your party, and you shall do just what you like
and go just where you please. Your uncle will
show you the orchard."

Mr. Samuel Bickerdyke was putting on his
overcoat and rubber shoes.

"I don't think you will need an overcoat this
warm day, brother Samuel," said Mrs. Fuller.

"If you knew as much about lumbago as I
do," replied Mr. Bickerdyke in a mournful
voice, "you would put on your overcoat."

"I am sure it's so dry you will not need rubbers," Mrs. Fuller said again.

"If you knew as much about sciatica as I
do," Mr. Bickerdyke once more answered, "you
would never leave off your rubbers from August
to May."

Nevertheless, Mr. Bickerdyke stepped off
quite youthfully, leading the way. Carlo and
Flossy had kept their ears cocked, and their
eyes had roamed round the place, waiting for
their dreaded enemy, but Bunch was nowhere
to be seen.

"Where do you think Bert can be?" Lucy
inquired anxiously.

"Don't know, I'm sure," said Marcia. As

she spoke she happened to put her hand into her
pocket, and drew out the very handkerchief Bert
was in search of.

" Oh, Marcia ! " said Dorothy, with a sudden
horror.

" Oh ! " said the twins in unison.

" And there comes Bert now," said Dorothy,
as if appalled at the thought of what Bert might
say.

He was sauntering up the drive slowly, ele-
gantly, reluctantly, as if his inclinations were
all against it.

" Did you find it ? " cried Marcia. She shook
out the folds of her handkerchief to wave to
him. " I had n't lost it after all," she said,
laughing. " I suppose I ought to say, I 'm
awfully sorry."

But she did n't say it. She simply laughed,
as if it had been a good joke. Bert did not
seem to mind. He stopped and shook hands
with Mrs. Fuller, then, without haste and with
the air of one to whom all things are equal, he
followed the party, who were now going through
the little gate. When the little gate was passed
they found themselves on the terrace, above the
orchard.

It was a wonderful orchard. The trees stood
each at a sufficient distance from the other to

have the sun and air reach it on all sides. The trees of Roxbury russets, Baldwins, and other late winter apples were still untouched. The others had been stripped of their fruit, which, after being assorted, lay arranged under each tree in three pyramids, — the perfect, the second best, and the third of indifferent quality. Whether little or big, fair or knotted, each pile helped to make part of the picture, and each variety of fruit gave out its own beautiful color: crimson, light red, golden yellow, white, and green. What a rich, fruity smell hung over the orchard !

Mr. Fuller was directing the men who were packing the fruit, and he came down the orchard to shake hands with Dorothy.

" Pretty nice fruit, ain't it, brother Samuel ? " he said, rubbing his hands. " This is a good apple year, and a good apple year means a good deal of money."

Mr. Fuller went on to tell about the late frost in the spring that he had been afraid would injure the fruit; then of the long northeaster in May, which had scattered the blossoms too soon; finally, about the drought in September; but everything seemed after all to have worked together for good.

" Yes," said Mr. Samuel Bickerdyke, " ' Clouds

and wind, the moon, the sun, the firmament, all
are busied that thou, oh man, mayst obtain thy
bread! Only eat it not in neglect.'"

This was an Eastern proverb, and the children accepted it as a sort of grace before falling
to, and each began to nibble at an apple.

"But Dorothy, my dear Dorothy," said Mr.
Bickerdyke, "surely you are not going to eat
that raw fruit!"

"Why, uncle Bickerdyke," returned Dorothy,
"what are apples for?"

"She has you there," said Mr. Fuller. "What
else are apples for?"

"But apples are so very indigestible," pleaded
Mr. Bickerdyke. "I have n't eaten a raw apple
for twenty years."

"Time you did," said Mr. Fuller. "I eat
two every night before I go to bed. I could n't
live without them."

Mr. Fuller went back to direct the apple
packing. Mr. Samuel Bickerdyke and Carlo
and Flossy hung round the five young people,
who were eating apples, looking at them wistfully. It not only made the dogs hungry, but
it made Mr. Bickerdyke hungry. There really
did seem to be something easy and natural
about the way the children were devouring the
fruit.

"Now, please try, uncle Bickerdyke," said Dorothy.

Mr. Bickerdyke, with an air of resolution, accepted the apple Dorothy gave him, looked at it, smelled of it, put his hand into his pocket, drew out his knife, pared it with the utmost nicety, cut it into quarters, then put one into his mouth.

"Why, Dorothy," he said, with an air of having made a discovery, "really it is very good. The flavor is excellent, so fresh, juicy, altogether palatable, neither too sweet nor too sour."

It is only the first step that counts. Mr. Bickerdyke was very warm in his overcoat and very thirsty; the fruit was refreshing. He finished by eating sixteen apples.

How to eat an apple with dignity; how to bite it and munch it without seeming to relish it, had been Bert's problem. His position was a little embarrassing. He had been rather lonely that morning; he had felt left out; then, when he saw Marcia's new sailor suit and hat, there had been a stirring of a wish to join the party. Some things may be done in a half-hearted way, as if the right hand did not approve of what the left hand was doing; but, somehow, one commits one's self when one

eats an apple, particularly when one eats half
a dozen. Bert felt himself to be deteriorating,
but, after all, he had a better time than usual.
Marcia put him to the test more than once.
There happened to be one fine large red apple
which had been overlooked, or else had hung
beyond the reach of the pickers. Nothing would
satisfy Marcia except that Bert should climb up
and get it for her. Really with Bert, as well as
Mr. Bickerdyke, it was only the first step that
counted. After running back to find the handkerchief Marcia had not lost, Bert had grown
more sensible, not to say more human.

I should like to tell about the dinner the children ate; about their visit to Bunch, who was
chained up in the kennel near the stables, and
who lay with his head on his paws and refused
to give a glance at Carlo and Flossy, standing
shivering with terror in the distance.

When the afternoon was waning, Mrs. Fuller
gave the children leave to go to the grapery to
pick grapes to carry home. Bert climbed the
trellis, cut the bunches, and dropped them one
by one into the baskets that Marcia held up.

" Oh, aunt Fuller," said Dorothy, " if I could
only have a little basket with two bunches in it
for mamma ! "

" Oh, yes ; do take all you want," said Mrs.

Fuller. She stooped and kissed the little up-turned face. "I hope your mother will soon be here now."

"I shall keep them till she comes," said Dorothy.

The sun was setting in the west; the full moon was rising in the east. The horses were being put into the wagon to take the party home. It had been a beautiful day. The end of many happy days together. A sad change, a terrible change, was hovering over one of this little group like a hawk over a dove. But they did not know it.

Mr. Bickerdyke was not feeling quite well this afternoon, but he came out to see the children off, and to send a message to his mother.

"Tell your grandmamma, Dorothy," he said, "that I shall probably dine with her and your aunt Hester to-morrow. I am afraid I took a little cold in the orchard this morning; but a good night's sleep" —

He finished his sentence by kissing Dorothy, and then lifted her and her two baskets of grapes into the high wagon.

"Good-by, Marcia," he said next; "you are going on a long journey, I hear."

"Yes," Marcia said, her eyes shining, her cheeks glowing, and her red lips smiling; she

and her mother were, at last, going to join her
father.

" We have been waiting for three years," she
said. " Now, at last " —

She, too, got into the wagon ; Lucy was there,
and Bert and Gay clambered up to their seats.

" Well, children," said Mr. Bickerdyke, " I 'll
give you my blessing for those who go, and for
those who stay : —

" May you be happy ; but whether you are
happy or not, may you be good.

" May you learn all the lessons that books
can teach.

" May you learn all the lessons, too, that books
cannot teach, but which make you simple, self-
denying, honest, and pure-hearted.

" May you be gay, light-hearted ; but may
you shed enough tears to soften your hearts.

" May you live in the world, yet above the
world.

" May you, girls, learn to make good bread,
boil potatoes, broil a chop, and make a good cup
of coffee. And, boys, find the work you can do
best, and do it with all your might."

The horses started, and the children looked
back and waved a good-by to Mr. Bickerdyke,
who stood on the curbstone with his hand still
lifted.

# CHAPTER XVI

Mrs. Bickerdyke had said all that Monday that there was certain to be a frost that night. Sunday had been milder than the Saturday; then at night a little rain had fallen; afterwards it cleared, and the wind came out of the north-west. The old lady was so much in the habit of foreseeing calamity, and of predicting it when it did not arrive, that her prophecies were not always listened to. But it did grow colder, and so, just after three that afternoon, Miss Hester said, —

" Dorothy, grandmamma is afraid the dahlias will be touched by the frost, and perhaps you had better pick them."

Dorothy, accordingly, was fitted out with a basket and a big pair of scissors, and so set forth. Her mother had not come yet, but she felt sure that she would arrive by the five o'clock train. It was nice to be doing something while she waited. As she crossed the lawn, the wind rushed at her with bluff freedom, as if it had been a big dog,

knocked her basket out of her hands, and
seemed to bear her on with its own strength.
But she liked it. John Pearson was carrying
the last bag of potatoes into the barn, and the
hens and chickens were having a good time
scratching in the empty hills. John came
towards her.

"They've got a telegraph over at Mis' Dundas's," he said to Dorothy. "Cablegram, I
think the boy called it."

"I suppose it's from Marcia's father telling
them he's starting to meet them in England,"
said Dorothy, with a little nod. "They've been
wondering why he hadn't sent word."

John carried in his potatoes and then went
home. Jerusha had gathered up the last of the
clothes, and Dorothy had the place to herself.

"Mamma didn't come quite as soon as she
said she would," she thought, as she passed the
bed of asters, quite gone to seed. The nasturtiums still blazed in wonderful flame and vermil-
ion; the moonflowers and morning-glories blossomed all day now; the cosmos tossed in the
wind. Dorothy hated to think that the frost
would kill them all.

"Oh, I don't like to have things die," she
said with the tears starting.

Just then she looked up and saw the blue sky

with soft, downy little clouds like a flock of sheep.

"After all," Dorothy thought, "the sky will stay, and the sun and the wind, and the moon and stars. We shan't be left without anything, for Christmas only comes when it's very cold, and there are snow and ice."

She began to think about Christmas. She hoped that her aunt Hester would give her a great many beautiful presents to carry to people this year. And no matter how many face-cloths grandmamma made, Dorothy would be glad to tie them up. Everybody had been so good, so loving to her lately, she had a very warm, grateful little heart. Somehow, even the chill of losing Marcia no longer made her unhappy. She would write to Marcia, and Marcia would write to her and tell her about the strange, droll, wonderful things in that far-off country.

Then she came to the dahlias. There they stood, straight and tall, with their high color and their prim little quillings, looking too proud and haughty ever to be nipped by any killing frost. Mrs. Bickerdyke was particularly proud of her dahlias.

"But you've got to come down, you splendid great things," said Dorothy, brandishing the sharp steel shears. They were so tall, she could

not reach up to the blossoms, but she could clip
the stems, and pride had a fall.  As the stalks
were cut, they gave out a queer acrid odor.  Let
Dorothy live as long as she may, that strange
scent of a dahlia will bring a clear picture in her
mind of that long-past October afternoon, with
its crisp air, the tossing of the cosmos flowers in
the wind, and the sense of *something about to
happen;* something which touched everything,
changed everything, and ended much.

Lucy and Gay had been taken to town by
their mother to be fitted out for winter.  She
did not expect to see them.  Marcia, of course,
was busy, for, early on Wednesday morning,
she and her mother were to set out for New
York, and on Saturday they were to sail.  Dorothy had filled her basket full of the dahlias
and was cutting the very last, when she heard
a little cry of " Oh, Dorothy."

She turned and saw Marcia.

Dorothy had never seen Marcia cry, or she
would have believed that Marcia had been crying, for her eyes were red and swollen ; elsewhere
there was no color on her face.  Even her lips
were white.

" Oh, Marcia," faltered Dorothy, " what is
the matter ? "

" I was coming to ask you to sit with mamma

while I go for the doctor," said Marcia.
" We 've had — bad — news. Mamma is n't
quite so well. Will you ? "

Dorothy dropped her basket and ran as fast
as she could to the wicket, across the Lees' lawn,
through the gap in the hedge, and gained the
grounds of Dundas House. The kitchen door
stood wide open, and, entering, she saw Chloe
stirring something before the fire.

" Run up, run up to the poor lady. She 's all
alone," said Chloe, who was also crying.

Dorothy toiled up the stairs. Something
seemed to hold her in its clutches. Her little
legs almost bent beneath her, and the way was
very long and steep. The door stood ajar. She
did not wait to knock, but went in softly. There
was the beautiful room, and Mrs. Dundas was
lying on the lounge, bolstered up high with all
the pillows. There was an odd look in her face,
— her lips were blue, but her eyes were wide
open, and their glance clear as they met Dorothy's.

" Did Marcia send you to me ? " she asked
with a little, faint smile.

Dorothy went nearer.

" Oh, I 'm afraid you 're not well," she said.

Mrs. Dundas took the little, warm, outstretched hands between her two cold ones.

"Oh, yes, dear, well enough."

"But you 'll need to be very well to go on that long journey," said Dorothy.

Mrs. Dundas smiled again.

"Marcia did n't tell you, then? We 're not going to South Africa. That 's all over."

Dorothy uttered an exclamation. Mrs. Dundas waited one moment, then said, —

"Poor child! it 's hard for her. Her father is dead."

Dorothy's eyes brimmed over with tears; a sob came.

"Yes, it 's hard for Marcia," murmured Mrs. Dundas. "I had hoped, — yes, I — had — hoped " —

She broke off.

"I don't need to say I ask you all to be good to Marcia."

Dorothy could n't speak. Her face was all a-quiver.

Chloe came with some beef tea. Mrs. Dundas took a few spoonfuls, but Dorothy had a feeling as if no food, no heat, no tender clasping hands could warm or comfort or help that poor woman any more. It seemed to Dorothy as if a long, long time had passed. Her hands had grown very cold, lying between those chilly, lifeless palms.

"I'm thinking" — whispered Chloe, laying her black finger across the blue-veined wrist. But Mrs. Dundas's eyes opened.

"I'm just keeping quiet," she said.

One of the windows had been opened to give the poor lady a better chance for breath. Suddenly, from outside, there came a rumble of wheels, then the sound of an arrival, and Miss Roxy Burt's voice saying, —

"Now, Poky, Poky! Stand still, Poky! Be a good Poky."

And in another instant Marcia came in.

"I couldn't find Dr. Barnes," she said. "I've brought Miss Roxy."

Miss Roxy was just behind her. Marcia had taken Dorothy's place by the lounge. As Miss Roxy came up, she put her hand on Dorothy's shoulder and said, —

"Go right home, dear. Ask Miss Hester to come, and perhaps Jerusha."

It seemed strange to Dorothy to be outside in the wind again, and to see the blossoms of the cosmos tossing to and fro.

She met Miss Hester on her way. Miss Hester had by this time heard the news that had come by cable, that Paul Dundas had died at Johannisburg two days before. A thread

stretches and stretches, but it breaks at last. So
with Mrs. Dundas's heart, worn out with waiting, with hopes deferred. Miss Hester was
hurrying to take what consolation she could
proffer to the poor lady who had lived so near
her, who had struggled so silently, who had
borne so much, — perhaps not wisely, but in her
blind, human way. At this moment Miss Hester
felt, with a pang, that she had tried too little
to help her.

Dorothy picked up the dahlias and carried
them slowly round the house. As she went up
the steps, the door opened before her. It was
Mrs. Deane who opened it. She had just arrived, as Dorothy expected, by the five o'clock
train.

Just as Marcia was losing her mother, Dorothy had regained hers. The steamer had met
heavy gales, had been disabled, and finally had
been towed into Halifax.

Dorothy did not know that she had been in
danger of not having her little mother back
again; but just as if she had known, it was
wonderfully sweet to lie close in those loving
arms. She could not have enough of the comfort
from the touch of those hands and of those lips;
of the look of those eyes. Then the wonderful
thing about it was that henceforth Dorothy was

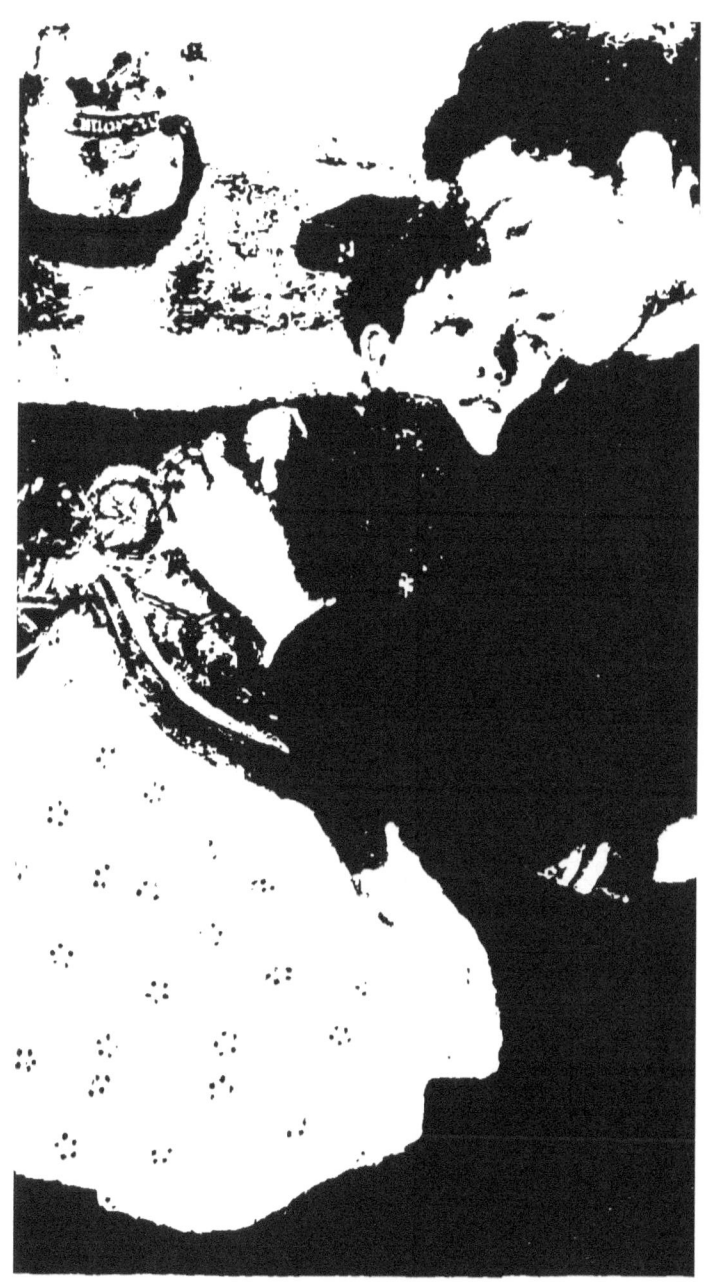

CLOSE IN THOSE LOVING ARMS

always to be with her mother. Strange things had come to pass during the summer trip to Europe. A Mr. Clare, an old friend of Dorothy's father, had been on the steamer, and afterwards had met Mrs. Deane, as tourists do meet in Europe; and Mrs. Deane was to be married to him, and she and Dorothy were to go and live with him at his place near New York.

"I told him," said Elizabeth, "that I could never love him as I loved Frank. But I said that I could be so grateful to any one who gave me a home and helped me to do all I wish for Dorothy, that I believed my gratitude would be almost as well worth having as my love."

# CHAPTER XVII

## "THE PARTING OF THE WAYS"

WINDINGS-UP are always painful, and the end
of Dorothy's life in Swallowfield held, certainly,
some sad moments. She had her mother back,
and she was to have a father for the first time
in her life. He was not so young as he might
have been, but he seemed so wise and kind; his
voice was so pleasant; his face, if not handsome,
was, somehow, so much nicer than handsome,
that she liked him, liked him better and better
every time he came.

But then, poor Marcia had neither father nor
mother any more! Dorothy did not dare to
feel perfectly happy.

Marcia was soon to go away. For two weeks
after her mother's death the children saw her
day after day, looking so strange, so unfamiliar,
so grown up in her black clothes; sitting mute,
motionless, — with a startled look in her eyes,
her lips parted, the upper one with an acute lift
to it, as if she drew her breath in pain.

Her few relatives came and went, settling up

the business connected with the property and discussing the arrangements for the young girl's future.    Everything Marcia had cared for, looked forward to, and believed in, — the fortune her father was making for her and her mother; the life they were to live with him ; the feeling that this father was working for them, thinking of them, day after day, week after week, month after month, and that presently they were to enjoy the result of his labors, — all had crumbled to pieces.    It had been far off, unsubstantial, like a dream at the best; now it was a dream within a dream, for the real life she had had with her mother now had become a dream. No wonder Marcia felt as if between her and the life of the world there was a deep gulf fixed.

The day before Marcia was to go away, Gay came running over to Dorothy.

" D—d—did you see ? " he asked her.

" See what ? " demanded Dorothy, startled.

" She 's p—p—put out the red flag," said Gay.

" Oh, let 's go," cried Dorothy, and she and Lucy and Gay and Carlo and Flossy ran as fast as their legs could carry them to answer Marcia's call.

They found her standing on the grass with her hat on, waiting.

"I thought," she said, "I should like to go to the old places. It's the last time, you know."

She put one arm round Dorothy and the other round Lucy. Gay walked on before, constantly turning back to look; and the dogs, as well, dashed forward, then turned on their steps, ran towards the children, and then frolicked on again, leading the way. They all naturally took the road down the lane to the river. Nobody talked. In spite of Marcia's bright, sweet look, Dorothy and the twins were a little in awe of her. She was older; she had met strange trials; she had reached the zone of deep and terrible feeling; and now they could see in her eyes, in the quiet, controlled lips, that she had taken up her sorrow and was carrying it unflinchingly away into her new life.

"Yes," she said dreamily, "I wanted to go down to the river once more, and over to the spring-lot. We have been so many, many times."

"Oh, Marcia," cried Lucy in a woeful voice, "Dorothy is going away, too."

Marcia did not answer for a long minute; then she said, "Yes, Dorothy has not only got her mother back, but she is going to have a father, too."

As she spoke, she looked straight ahead, as if meeting her desolation face to face. Dorothy blushed and dropped her eyes, feeling that she had more than her share of good things; that she ought to divide with Marcia.

There was a cheerful chirping of crickets along the lane. Now and then a crow flew overhead with a caw, caw, caw, but the other birds had gone with the summer. Two chipmunks made a streak of yellow and brown across the path and gave the dogs something to chase. Here and there fluttered a belated butterfly. Dorothy, Lucy, and Gay had been shy of asking Marcia what her plans were, but now she began to talk about herself. She was to be sent to a large girls' school in the country.

"I'm going to study hard," she said; "oh, so hard. Aunt Mary says that if I work my very best for two years, I shall have found out if I have any particular bent, — whether I had better go on studying, or take up music or art." She paused a moment, then added, with a deeper tone and more deliberate emphasis as the possibilities of the future crowded on her, "Somehow, some time, I mean to do something."

They all felt sure she would, but they felt it like a physical pain that she would be away from them; they shrank back dizzy before that vision of her.

They reached the bridge and looked down at the clear, running water. The willow-tree, which dipped into the river as the wind swayed it, had not lost all its leaves, but it looked dreary. They walked across the stubble to the spring-lot, and stood on the green, grassy banks and stared wistfully into the basin where the fountain gushed forth boiling out of the sand, and at the rivulet dancing down the hill.

" It seems to me," said Gay, " that everything in the world is running away."

They went back after sunset. Their eyes shone as they all bade Marcia good-by at the top of the lane.

Marcia forgot to take her flag in, and it was flying next day after she had gone. The children cried when they saw it more than they had cried that afternoon in parting with her. It reminded them of a lost and happy time.

Mrs. Deane was to be married from Mrs. Bickerdyke's on the sixteenth of November, and the remaining days before·that great event ran away very quickly now. Grandmamma Bicker-dyke used to hold out her arms to Dorothy every time she saw her, and Dorothy would go up and nestle close against her white necker-chief.

" I don't know who will do up your face-

cloths this year, grandmamma," Dorothy would
say. Sometimes the old lady answered, —
" I 'm sure I don't know. I think you ought
to stay and help me." Then again her head
would shake a little, and she answered not a
word.

Miss Hester, too, was not afraid to show Dorothy now that she loved her dearly. Indeed,
the little girl had fixed a place for herself deep
in everybody's heart, and she was not to pass
away and leave no trace. As for Jerusha and
John Pearson, they felt it was more than they
could bear to lose her.

Mr. Clare had already come twice to Swallowfield. When he came for the third time, Dorothy and her mother were to go away with him,
so it was now time for Dorothy to begin to pack
up her things.

Just a little while before, the children had all
three helped Marcia to pack ; now Lucy and Gay
were looking on as Dorothy was getting her
possessions together. Such heaps of things,
such droll things, such dear, worn-out, shabby
old things ! Nobody but Jerusha could have
folded and squeezed and tucked them all into one
trunk. Full as the trunk was, it could n't begin
to hold the things which had belonged to Dorothy's life in Swallowfield : the first beam of the

sun in the morning, which from season to season
gilded everything in her room; then the glimpse
of the valley and the river and the woods beyond; the sight of Sirius and Orion in the sky
as she went to bed. Her mother told her she
would find these beautiful things again; but
how could she?

Then came the final morning.

The sun shone, — still there was something like
a mist in the air; a faint haze like an impalpa-
ble frost; and the effect of it was to make the
last yellow and red leaves drop silently.

They all went quietly to church to see the
marriage, and finally Mrs. Deane came in with
Mr. Clare and Dorothy. Dorothy stood by her
mother all through the service, and then held
her hand as they came down the aisle. In the
vestibule she stopped and kissed Lucy and Gay,
who were waiting. Then they ran through the
churchyard and saw her once more as the carriage drove off.

Dorothy saw the twins standing hand in hand,
and she raised her own hand and nodded and
smiled. But she seemed to Lucy and Gay
already very far away. They had shared many
bitter things of late, but this was bitterest of
all, and they were exceeding sorrowful.

"Sh—sh—she says sh—sh—she'll c—c—
c—come b—b—back," whimpered Gay.

"Count three, Gay," said Lucy.

"I d—d—don't c—c—care," cried Gay. "I d—d—don't c—care.  I d—d—don't feel as if I c—c—could c—c—care for anything, now Dorothy and Marcia have g—g—gone."

"Oh, they'll come back," said Lucy. "They're sure to come back some time."

The Riverside Press

CAMBRIDGE, MASSACHUSETTS, U. S. A.
ELECTROTYPED AND PRINTED BY
H. O. HOUGHTON AND CO.